THE BABY SITTER LIVES

THE BABY SITTER LIVES

STEPHEN GRAHAM JONES

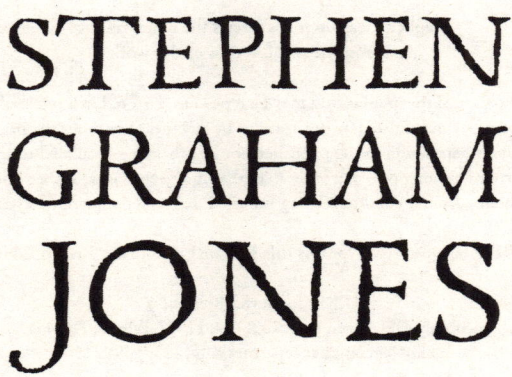

TITAN BOOKS

The Babysitter Lives
Print edition ISBN: 9781835410301
Black Crow Edition ISBN: 9781835417195
E-book edition ISBN: 9781835410318

Published by Titan Books
A division of Titan Publishing Group Ltd
144 Southwark Street, London SE1 0UP
www.titanbooks.com

First Titan edition: July 2025
10 9 8 7 6 5 4 3 2 1

A CIP catalogue record for this title is available from the British Library.

EU RP (for authorities only)
eucomply OÜ, Pärnu mnt. 139b-14, 11317 Tallinn, Estonia
hello@eucompliancepartner.com, +3375690241

Set in Adobe Caslon Pro by Richard Mason.

Printed and bound by CPI (UK) Ltd, Croydon, CR0 4YY.

For Josephine "Tiny" Calflooking Jones, my grandmom.
You were born in 1929 and you made it all the way to 2021.

A mother carries her six-year-old daughter into the tiled bathroom where the bathtub is already running, is still running, is overflowing, and for a moment the girl calms, seeing her little brother floating facedown in the water, his hair a golden halo around him, but then this mother is guiding her face-first down *into* that water, that, as it turns out, isn't just water but scalding water, and eleven years later her scream is the drawer screeching out of the counter by the sink.

Charlotte turns away from the sound and Mrs. Wilbanks does too, even sucks some air in about it.

"Sorry," Mrs. Wilbanks says, tilting her head to the side to guide her earring in. "I need to get Rog to call somebody about that."

"I can—" Charlotte starts, but Mrs. Wilbanks is already moving away from the toothbrush drawer to her daughter's pink and turquoise bedroom, to explain how the inhaler works. Like every other inhaler in the history of inhalers, surprise. The daughter, Desi, six, cute as a button, is sitting up in the middle of the huge pink beanbag in the corner, watching the stranger Charlotte is, her eyes big with wonder.

Charlotte sneaks a wave to her, and Desi's dimples appear right when she's shying away.

"Mom, Mom!" Desi says to Mrs. Wilbanks in a whisper that's louder than her real voice can possibly be. "Your dress is—"

"I know, I know," Mrs. Wilbanks says about the zipper up her back that's flapping open. "I've written everything down in the kitchen," she goes on, walking and talking again, leading Charlotte down the hall into the master bedroom, neatly stepping around the lamp table, which is pretty much asking to be tipped over. "But you'll be fine, they're good kids, never steal cookies or draw on the walls or play hide-and-seek in the freezer, any of that. We don't even let them in the garage. They do think they're funny, so expect some big joke, I guess, wearing each other's clothes or saying they only drink milk with ice or who knows. At worst they might try to fudge when lights-out eyes-closed usually is, but—"

"One hour from now," Charlotte fills in.

"Is it eight *already*?" Mrs. Wilbanks says, her eyebrows coming up in panic. "Shit. Shit-shit-shit. Okay, um, if we're not back by midnight, Roger says we'll add twenty dollars, does that work?"

Charlotte nods yes, yes, that will most definitely work, thank you, her brain defaulting to the test mode it's been locked in for the past month: *If babysitter X earns thirteen dollars an hour for four hours and gets a twenty-dollar bonus, then that babysitter's smile will increase by a factor of Y plus what?*

She rubs her forehead with the pad of her finger, trying to smush that kind of thinking away for just five minutes, please.

"I just want the two of you to have a good time," she says,

stepping in to work that zipper up. Mrs. Wilbanks stills at the touch and draws her breath in, holds it, is suddenly this tall perfect porcelain doll, ready to shatter.

"Thank you," she says, her eyes clocking the depths of the mirror, Charlotte's pretty sure. Clocking it to see if her husband happened to have stepped in, seen this unasked-for intimacy, this dark girl lightly touching his milky-white wife.

"Full-service babysitter," Charlotte says, taking a long step back into her own space like the help she is.

"And if the doorbell rings—" Mrs. Wilbanks starts, leaving the blank for Charlotte to fill.

"There shouldn't be any trick 'r treaters until tomorrow night," Charlotte says.

"But if someone's got their calendar flipped to the wrong day . . ." Mrs. Wilbanks says, leaning in to unsmudge her eyeliner.

"Then nobody's home," Charlotte says with the right amount of perk, straight out of the handbook she's always imagining. Specifically, the chapter on dealing with paranoid parents who haven't been out on a date since their kids were born.

"And if that homeless man comes back?" Mrs. Wilbanks prompts, widening her eyes to get her line straight.

"Homeless who?" Charlotte asks.

"His calendar is flipped to the wrong *decade*," Mrs. Wilbanks says. "Neighborhood Watch will call the police on him if he comes back, don't worry."

"Is he . . . hungry, you think?" Charlotte asks.

Mrs. Wilbanks refocuses her eyes about this, no longer looking at her makeup in the reflection but at Charlotte.

"Don't engage," Charlotte says, on cue—what Mrs. Wilbanks wants to hear. "Nobody's home."

"And you know the security code," Mrs. Wilbanks prompts, her tone leading Charlotte to the proper answer.

"The *temporary* code," Mr. Wilbanks says from the doorway of the master bedroom, then—for his wife—"I thought some rooms were going to be off-limits, dear?"

His hands are pulling on the hanging ends of the plaid scarf looped around the back of his neck, and there's a diagonal red crease pressed into his forehead, like he's been leaning in the doorway for a little bit, just watching, and listening.

"Yes, yes," Mrs. Wilbanks says, sketching a fleck of black onto the white of her eyeball and, instead of flinching away from it, Charlotte can clearly see that she's making herself feel that burn. "Our room's out of bounds, of course"—now she's dabbing the eyeliner away ever so gently with the very corner of a tissue—"no reason to be in here. And Roger's office, naturally."

"It's already locked," Mr. Wilbanks says from his station in the doorway, and shrugs his office at the end of the long upstairs hall into the non-issue he most definitely wants it to be for Charlotte.

"All I need is Desi's and Ronald's bedrooms to tuck them in nice and tight, the bathroom to make sure they brush their teeth—"

"Bathrooms," Mr. Wilbanks corrects, since each kid has their own.

"Bath*rooms*," Charlotte repeats, no insult in her voice at all, thank you, "the kitchen, where the lasagne should just about be done, and the kitchen table, so I can study for my SATs after lights-out eyes-shut."

She shrugs one shoulder at the end of this and practically kinks one knee up enough to twirl her toes into the hardwood floor, her hands clasped at her lower back like she's in some pervy anime.

"Lights-out eyes-*closed*," Mrs. Wilbanks says into the mirror.

"I know we probably sound . . ." Mr. Wilbanks starts in with a self-deprecating smile, "it's just, the off-limits rooms—we've heard, and they're probably the urban legends of our, our age group, but you hear things like—"

"Sex parties, drugs, rifling through personal belongings, absconding with passwords," Mrs. Wilbanks says, ticking through them. "Unmentionable things done to silverware. Intimate photography that, well, compromises home values and probably leaves emotional damage besides."

Charlotte blinks once, trying to gauge whether this is an accusation or not.

"You checked up on me, of course?" she says to each of them, not in a challenging way but a reassuring way—no, a *reminding* way. Because of course they did: 3.96 GPA, Honor Society, Mathlete, president and pioneer of the high school's Premed Club, on the volleyball team that went to State last year, certified in both adult and infant CPR, and no brushes with the law. In short, babysitter extraordinaire, and then some. Like she was grown in a vat to watch their kids, or ordered up from a menu. Plucked from a daydream.

"The Lopezes were very confident in your performance, yes," Mr. Wilbanks says—which is an odd word, right? "Actually, we considered whether or not you might be blackmailing them into being so positive."

For a moment after delivering this he doesn't smile, but when he does, Charlotte can too.

"I love their little Arthur," she says. "My main regret about going off to college is not getting to see him grow up. The next few years will be so formative for him."

"But surely you'll miss your—your parents?" Mrs. Wilbanks asks, her eyeliner pencil held in suspension until Charlotte delivers the next correct answer. "When you go off to college?"

"My mom's working overtime to pay for the applications," Charlotte says, a hint of challenge rising in her voice in spite of her trying to play it so neutral here.

"Speaking of sons," Mr. Wilbanks says, leaning back to look down the hall then speaking to his wife again, as if Charlotte isn't there at all: "Has she met Ronbo?"

Charlotte tucks this nickname away for later.

"I'd love to," she says, skipping forward without waiting for permission from Mrs. Wilbanks.

Mr. Wilbanks backs out of the doorway, presents the hallway to her, and all Charlotte can think for the two doors down to the far bedroom is that her ass is probably going to catch fire here, with all this laser-focused attention she can feel it's getting. But that's part of it too, she knows: the husbands— that's how she thinks of them, not "fathers," because yuck—they want and need her to be a good girl for this babysitting gig, but at the same time they'd trade anything to be the boyfriend they know is hiding in the bushes, waiting for a romp on the dining room table, the curtains not even drawn.

Charlotte stops by the closed door and raises her hand to knock but holds it, looking back to him for confirmation. He gets his eyes up just in time and brushes past her, his top-heavy bulk somehow sinuous, his hand finding the knob perfectly. "Kids don't have privacy at this age," he says, and swings the door in.

Like Desi, Ronald is six—twins—but unlike Desi, he's not in pajamas yet, just tighty-whities that are pretty much a match for what Charlotte is guessing must be the signature Wilbanks pallor.

His back is to them. He's hunched over something, is skinny enough that his individual vertebra are pushing up through his skin in a knobby ridge.

"Ronald?" Charlotte says, an inviting smile to her tone, a safe look prepped and ready on her face.

Ronald doesn't turn around to the new voice. His right arm moves the littlest bit.

"*Ronnie*," Mr. Wilbanks says.

Neither he nor Charlotte exist for this six-year-old. Only whatever he's working on.

"Maybe we should just let him—" Charlotte tries, making peace before it's even all the way broken, but Mr. Wilbanks is already crossing the room to his son.

Charlotte presses her lips together for the arm-grab and sudden haul-up she knows she's about to have to witness and, against all her training, not report, but at the last moment— maybe *because* she's there?—Mr. Wilbanks steps around Ronald, brings his laser eyes to bear on what's got all his son's attention.

"He's usually not this rude," he says. "I apologize, Charley."

"No, no," Charlotte says, stepping in but keeping to the side, to see what's got Ronald so fascinated. She's not a Charley, is a "Charl" at best, but this forced familiarity hardly even registers.

Instead, she's focused on what Ronald's working on so intently.

A . . . an antique *jack-in-the-box*?

He's turning the red metal crank a fraction at a time, like trying to draw out the moment before release. Like trying to make it last—no, Charlotte decides: like a safecracker in a movie, right? Like he's unlocking something he's not supposed to be getting into.

"It's a playground story," Mr. Wilbanks says, dismissing it even as he says it, his hands still gripping the ends of his scarf like a gym towel. "When the cafeteria flooded, all the grades ended up taking recess together, I don't know. The older kids pulled some of the younger ones under the equipment where the teachers couldn't see, and they—I guess they tried to scare them, you know how it is."

"Ronald?" Charlotte says, taking a knee to be on his level, which she knows might be giving a certain husband a leery angle down the too-big flannel shirt she's got tied at her waist, but screw it. It's not a preview if he's never getting to the main attraction.

"Shh," Ronald says, not looking over to Charlotte even a little.

He's still turning the crank one single plastic tooth at a time.

"This sixth grader evidently told the first graders that everybody stops when the clown pops up because they think that's the end," Mr. Wilbanks explains. "But there's supposed to be a certain spot *later* in the turn that—"

"Where did he find that again?" Mrs. Wilbanks says from the doorway, already bustling in, snatching the jack-in-the-box up. It jostles it enough that the clown pops up all at once, its black diamond eyes and painted-red smile startling Charlotte back into some rattly action-figure case, then the wall. A huge press-on vinyl poster or banner of the night sky billows down around her—the oversize kind of thing you have made for your kid when your company's got an account with the printer. Instinctively she fights out of it back to the light. Instinctively and a little more desperately than she would have liked, since she's supposed to be the one in control, the one they can trust *not* to panic.

Ronald draws his breath in in the most satisfied way about the jack-in-the-box, his eyes tracking the little clown up and away.

"*Clothes*," Mr. Wilbanks tells him—orders him—then, to Charlotte: "This isn't in any of the parenting manuals, but having to teach them shame? That's the part I never expected."

"Shame is societal, not biological," Charlotte hears herself saying, trying to stand up from the poster without ruining it, then padding her hand into the rug for the tacks that must have been holding it up.

"You really are an honor student, aren't you?" Mr. Wilbanks says, the words themselves harmless, but there's something behind them that's pretty much the opposite.

"1460 on the PSATs," Charlotte says. "But tomorrow I ace it."

"They do tests on Halloween?" he asks.

"Scarier that way," Charlotte says with a shrug.

"I think I hear the lasagne," Mrs. Wilbanks cuts in with all due impatience, the jack-in-the-box tucked behind her back as if Ronald isn't staring straight through her at it, waiting for that crank to turn one delicious click more.

"What time is the reservation for?" Mr. Wilbanks says in a fake and formal way to Mrs. Wilbanks, which is their cue to flutter down the stairs, start the goodbye process.

"He'll be okay with his pajamas?" Charlotte asks on the landing, about Ronald.

"He's a big boy," Mr. Wilbanks says, and, before hauling his own overcoat out of the closet by the front door he flourishes Mrs. Wilbanks's red one out, holds it open for her. It's cute; they haven't been out on the town since that overcoat was in style, Charlotte would bet.

"The numbers are all on the fridge," Mrs. Wilbanks says, straightening her husband's collar, which is really just her nerves keeping her hands busy.

"Our thing's over at eleven, eleven thirty," Mr. Wilbanks says for maybe the third time so far. "We're here by quarter til. Not even that."

"They'll be fine," Charlotte says, making a show of ferreting the key from its high basket in the closet, using it to twist the deadbolt back, punching the *temporary* code into the alarm pad—pure chipper performance, but that's part of it. She opens the door, presents the outer world to these two nervous fledglings.

"Of course they will," Mrs. Wilbanks says, and leans forward to give Charlotte a quick, awkward hug, her right hand, the one closest to her husband, to Charlotte's shoulder, her left to Charlotte's opposite hip, the fingers of that hand tucking something into the waistband of Charlotte's mom jeans, like repaying Charlotte in kind for zipping her dress up—intimacy for intimacy.

Charlotte stiffens, wonders if she's just been tipped or

propositioned or what, and nods a courteous bye to Mr. Wilbanks, who, instead of some suggestive goodbye, calls out that Ronald needs to pee like a big boy before bedtime.

"Like a big boy," Charlotte confirms, which is maybe the first time she's ever said this out loud, or at all, and the moment the door's shut she's sliding the key in and turning that deadbolt over so they can clearly hear the *click*.

Standing with her back to the door, the alarm's green light blinking steady, she can finally breathe. Let the muscles of her face go normal and slack. She pulls the scrunchy from her hair, shakes it loose, luxuriates in this small but so-necessary freedom. Next she palms her phone, sends the text she's been working on in her head all day: *sory, do over?* Autocorrect doesn't want to let her misspell like that, but the misspelling's the whole thing. Will Murphy be able to resist texting back to correct?

Fifty-fifty, Charlotte figures, and makes herself pocket her phone instead of staring into it, waiting for Murphy's typing ellipses to burble back. Now to just get the twins fed and asleep, which, if they're anything else like every other six-year-old Charlotte's worked with, should be cake. That should be her next book, even, for new moms: *How to Reclaim Your Life by 9 p.m.* But that's all later, after food and games and brushed teeth.

Now . . . she curls her right side in, extracts the scratchy paper from the waistband of her jeans.

It's not a ten or a twenty but a Post-it folded over twice, the adhesive keeping it shut enough that she has to apply some serious fingernail. Written inside in hasty blue ink, probably upstairs at Mrs. Wilbanks's vanity while Charlotte was getting the Ronald intro, is . . . a *book title*?

Charlotte looks upstairs for any small faces watching her through the jail bars of the wooden railing. When there aren't any she crosses the living room, finds the dark bookshelves built into the wall behind the television. The book Mrs. Wilbanks wrote down is *Plutarch's Lives*, which Charlotte suspects will be about zero-point-zero help on tomorrow morning's SATs.

She starts to haul the heavy volume down, not sure what Mrs. Wilbanks intends here—will there be a quiz? another note folded into the pages?—but then she sees: on the book *beside* the Plutarch is an eight-inch rubber lizard, blue on top, paler blue on bottom. The kind you find tucked in every place in any house with kids, even places as moneyed-up as this.

Only, instead of a hollow throat, this lizard has the iridescent eye of a nanny cam. Motion-activated, surely. Meaning it's recording now. If its rubber tail could switch back and forth like a predator watching its prey, then that's exactly what it would be doing, Charlotte knows.

She holds her face normal, unfocused, and keeps moving as if just scanning this library for something to read for the night, book-girl that she is, and knows now not to change her shirt on the couch this lizard is so interested in. Good to know. Also good to know: Mrs. Wilbanks didn't tell her about this lizard because she wanted to keep Charlotte in line, she told her about it to keep her safe. From *Mr.* Wilbanks.

Great. Wonderful. Just the kind of stress Charlotte needs before the biggest most life-deciding test of her whole life. Checking the Native American/Alaskan Native box on all the forms doesn't mean jack if you choke on test day.

But at least there won't be more cameras, Charlotte tells herself. If there were, Mrs. Wilbanks would have polite-hugged her longer—long enough to tuck Post-it notes all over Charlotte, effectively going ahead and doing the sexual assault she was trying to warn her about.

"You can do this, you can do this," Charlotte tells herself, licking her lips for resolve, then nodding to herself when that doesn't quite take.

Not only *can* she do this, but she's been doing it every Friday night for the past two years, pretty much, all over town—she's the dependable girl, the one sure not to have weekend plans, the one who gets *paid* to hit the books for an hour or two after her charges are safely tucked in. Take that, everybody else from senior class who has to flip fryer baskets until end of shift and then pay taxes to the Great White Stepfather. If she's lucky tonight, the Wilbankses' big important "second first date" will even cross into Halloween by a few minutes, for an easy twenty dollars. Just, she reminds herself, be careful when Mr. Wilbanks offers that lift home. And remember that his eyes are cameras too.

On the way upstairs, already trying to twitch her lips into the smile the twins need, Charlotte caches the jack-in-the-box in the top of the closet by the front door and angles her head over so her face can be at the same jaunty angle as the clown's.

"Yeah . . . I don't think so," she says, and closes that door, rattles the knob to be sure it caught. Behind her the key to the deadbolt is still *in* the deadbolt, exactly as she was warned not to do. But it's their house, she reminds herself. Their paranoid rules. She reaches down for the key but stops at the last moment, narrows her eyes at the closet door.

Was there just a click in there?

Surely not.

After turning the oven off per handwritten instructions and sliding the lasagne onto the kitchen island to set, peeking under the foil tent to make sure things turned out all right, Charlotte leans against the counter and checks for the text she already knows isn't there.

She shakes her phone like that might help, then checks the signal—strong enough—but, just to be sure, she tries to tap into the Wi-Fi. When she needs a password she peels up the night's instructions, turns the sheet over for some cryptic string of numbers and letters.

This was one of their concerns, though, right? That she would snake access then sit outside their house for all the nights to come, using their network to upload terrorist plans and traffic kiddie porn and read all their secret emails?

More like she'd be submitting college applications.

Screw it.

She's got some kids to tire out for bed.

"Fee-fi-fo-fum," she calls up the staircase, less pulling herself up with the handrail than *bouncing* up the steps, "here I come . . ."

There's no giggling in response, no hurried footsteps.

Don't kids know this game from birth? When the teenager goes into monster mode, spreads her fingers wide like claws, you giggle and look around, hide if you can, shriek when the jig's up and there's nowhere to go.

Charlotte crests up onto the second-floor landing and

considers which kid to fake-attack first. Desi, she decides. Because she'll need the fun one on her side if she's going to pull the serious one into some make-believe run-and-chase game.

Charlotte galumphs into the doorway of Desi's room, throws an arm up onto the jamb like she's been running for miles, but . . . no Desi?

"Dez?" Charlotte tries in her own voice.

She checks the bathroom, the shallow closet, the hot-pink beanbag, then, smiling, she pulls the frilly pink bed skirt up all at once, her face right there for the little girl who's got to be hiding.

She's not.

"What the hell?" Charlotte mutters.

Instead of flouncing dramatically into Ronald's room, she walks right in, casing every nook that could hide a skinny six-year-old, her hands opening and closing by her thighs.

"Ronald?" she tries, then, getting desperate, "Ronbo?"

Charlotte ties her hair into a sloppy bun—playtime's over—mentally backs off this situation to see what she could be missing.

Twin one: missing.

Twin the other one: just as gone.

She flashes on the key she left in the deadbolt, has a sudden vision of what she's already warned herself never to think of again, ever: two weekends ago, the last time she babysat Arthur for the Lopezes. Arthur, who had never until that night sleepwalked. Charlotte with Murphy in the dining room, perhaps in a somewhat compromising position, hadn't heard him slip out the front door, hadn't even known he was gone until her mom—her ride, not supposed to be there for twenty more minutes—rang the doorbell, a bleary-eyed five-year-old on her hip.

Where she'd found him: in her headlights.

Instead of what he should have been: a lump in the rearview mirror.

Charlotte had fallen to her knees, had made such an empty sound that Murphy had come out of hiding to see what was wrong, and Charlotte's mom had just shaken her head, wordlessly exiled Murphy to her car, then carried Arthur upstairs herself, stayed to talk with the Lopezes about their date, her every utterance about to be the one that told on Charlotte, that revealed what had almost, almost happened there that night.

But she never did say it. And Arthur must not have been checked-in enough to remember. So they drove home in complete silence that night, Murphy in the backseat to be dropped off on the way.

The one question Charlotte's mom finally asked was, "You learned your lesson?"

It had made Charlotte burst into tears.

It's what's about to happen now, too.

"Be serious," she tells herself.

This isn't a repeat of that. It can't be. First, twins might share a birthday, but that doesn't mean they sleepwalk together. Second, she was only in the kitchen long enough to pull a lasagne from the oven, not nearly long enough for a couple of *awake* six-year-olds to have manipulated the stiff deadbolt, slipped out into the night. Anyway, their mom said they don't do that kind of stuff, right? No, there's no way they could have gotten downstairs without passing her. They're not ninjas, and invisibility cloaks aren't real, and they can't—they can't crawl on walls and ceilings, or tunnel under the carpet. There's no carpet anyway, just rugs everywhere on this pricey hardwood.

Charlotte makes herself go Sherlock then, and looks all the way down the hall, to the only possibility now that everything else is pretty much eliminated: Mr. Wilbanks's office. Mr. Wilbanks's *locked* office.

"No way," she says, and shakes her head, balls her hands into fists, makes herself go down there. Just on the chance.

It's just as locked as Mr. Wilbanks said it was. She bangs her open hand on it all the same, calls for the kids, and . . . *are* they in there? Is this the game? The big joke Mrs. Wilbanks warned about?

Charlotte stills, listens harder, closer, eyes closed, more trying to feel the space on the other side of the door than actually hear it.

Is that breathing?

"Desi?" Charlotte says, more alarmed now, and, if asked why she thought it was Desi more than Ronald, there's nothing she can put her finger on, exactly. Just, for some reason, she got *girl* from what she was or wasn't hearing more than *boy*.

She claps on the door again, listens again, then, mouth a thin line, she turns, goes full-on Terminator, gridding her visual field into sections and processing them each with scrolling text: door one, the hall entrance to Ronald's bathroom, locked; door two, Ronald's bedroom; after that, Desi's bedroom door; and, at the far end around the corner, right past where the stairs spit her up here, the master bedroom. The *off-limits* master bedroom, but screw it, that's the only place left, right?

On the way to it Charlotte realizes there's another door,

on the left: a linen closet flush with the wall and not going all the way to the floor. Making it actually a cabinet, she guesses? She grips her hands into the inset handle groove and pulls it open, fully expecting two giggling kids to spill out.

What comes down at her instead is tall and fast and . . . an electric dust broom thing. The upstairs vacuum cleaner, "Featherweight" model, bright red with grey accents. She guides it back, eyes the space behind it. Linens and board games, every shelf stuffed to spilling.

"I'm going to kill them," she says, shutting the door fast to keep the vacuum from tipping out again.

It feels transgressive, twisting the knob on the master bedroom door that Mr. Wilbanks was sure to pull shut behind them, but there's no other choice.

She walks in, can't find the light at first. When she does it brings the ceiling fan on as well, rustles some papers on Mrs. Wilbanks's antique vanity.

"Desi?" Charlotte says tentatively. "Ronald? Don't make me call your parents . . ."

If there's a camera in here, then the Lopezes are hearing about this, she knows. And everybody else as well. But forget all that. She's really getting nervous about the kids. For all she knows they're hiding in the closet right now, playing scuba diver with dry-cleaning bags. Which would be exactly what she deserves, would just be the world calling in its markers after she pulled the lucky card of it being her own *mom* who found Arthur toddling down the road.

Charlotte rushes across the room, pulls the closet door open, rattling the louvres, some sensor glowing the light on automatically—the *lights*: not just a single overhead, but an

LED strip tracing the cubbies of shoes, the racks of dresses and blouses and slacks.

"Shit," Charlotte says, legit impressed, and kind of humbled. She's heard of other babysitters playing dress-up while the parents are away, but playing dress-up here would take all night.

No kids, either.

And they're not huddled together in the shower stall, or under the California king bed, or tucked into the leg space of Mrs. Wilbanks's vanity. Charlotte pushes the heavy stool back under, ruffles the edge of the Post-it note pad like there's going to be some secret written on one of the hidden pages.

"Don't cry," she tells herself, trying to get the pad back exactly where it was. "That's not who you are."

All the same, she can feel it building.

She slumps back out into the hall, knows she's about to have to do the Thing she's never done—make the dreaded call, ruin a couple's first date in years, burn them on going out altogether—but then she hears something . . . downstairs?

She gives one last look to the office door at the other end of the hall then, committing to this, she steps out of her shoes, picks her way down the stairs two and three timid steps at a time, hand tight to the rail.

"Desi?" she says. "Ronald?"

The living room is just as she left it. She checks the deadbolt—still locked—pockets the key for safety. Almost into the nanny cam's field of view, she backpedals to the closet, has to look in.

The jack-in-the-box clown is still there, same jaunty angle. Not even moving on its spring or anything.

Charlotte presses that door shut, turns around, and doesn't even have time to gasp, really: she's not alone.

Standing side by side in the middle of the living room, one in My Little Pony pajamas, one still in tighty-whities, are Desi and Ronald. They each have a saucer with lasagne on it. Ronald's mouth is sloppy with tomato sauce.

When Charlotte flinches back like she has to—her body does it with or without her say-so—her heels catch on the step up to the entryway and, like that, she goes down, the back of her head catching the closet doorknob hard enough to rattle her teeth, rush the taste of blood into her mouth.

She pulls her knees up in pain and rocks forward, holding her head with both hands.

"Charlotte?" Desi says, from the distant end of some long dark tunnel.

Charlotte holds her right hand up, keeping them back, back, just until she can get this pain to stop.

Don't pass out, don't pass out, she says inside.

Good babysitters stay awake. Good babysitters don't let the world grey at the edges. They hold on to the light. They, they—

"I'm okay," she says, wincing from her own voice.

When she can open her eyes again, the twins are spooning lasagne in and studying her.

"You're supposed to . . . to use *forks*," Charlotte says, pressing her back against the closet door and sliding up to stand again, still cupping the back of her head with her palm. "And, do your parents let you eat in the living room? Really?" When they don't answer—which *is* an answer—she collects their dripping saucers of lasagne, leads them back into the kitchen, walking confidently for the lizard with the hungry eye.

Instead of eating the lasagne ("Indians didn't come up milking buffalo" is her mom's embarrassing go-to for lactose intolerance), Charlotte asks the kids where their snacks are, goes elbow-deep into that big plastic bin in the pantry, and makes herself a dinner from two boxes of animal crackers, some gummy worms that somehow aren't sugar but protein, and a green apple that's small enough to probably be organic.

"So," she says, standing by the island in the kitchen, surveying the damage two kids can do to a perfectly good lasagne. Instead of cutting it into squares, they've . . . she's not sure: either clumped hunks out with their tiny hands or maybe stuck their faces directly in, used their mouths like crane buckets to deliver bites across to the saucers Mrs. Wilbanks had left out. Though Charlotte shouldn't disallow the possibility of using the saucers themselves as scoops, she supposes. Whatever the case, this lasagne looks like it had a firecracker planted right in its center. One that left a ragged crater.

Without meaning to—unable *not* to—Charlotte imagines Mrs. Wilbanks at midnight, alone in her kitchen, trying to imagine what kind of babysitter lets this kind of damage happen on her thirteen-dollars-per-hour watch. The idea of a lasagne this big has to be leftovers, right? As in, her and her husband each having a piece for lunch tomorrow, while congratulating themselves on having selected the right girl to watch the twins last night.

"Are you really from Thanksgiving?" Desi asks, pulling

Charlotte from her deliberations. Charlotte turns, her face pleasant—they're just kids, raised in a pasty-white dream—and focuses in on Desi, then Ronald.

"Is that how your parents explained me?" she asks back.

Desi looks to Ronald and Ronald looks to Desi, and Charlotte's pretty sure they've each been coached that it's not "Indian," it's "Native American."

"We like cranberry sauce," Ronald finally says for both of them.

"Who doesn't?" Charlotte says, opening cabinets now to salvage this lasagne situation. "Have you two figured out what you're being for trick 'r treating tomorrow night?"

"I'm going to be from Thanksgiving too!" Desi says, her excitement bubbling over.

Charlotte selects the right spatula for the job, manages a wooden "Oh, wow," the pleasant look on her face more a mask now. Not for Halloween so much as for life. But college will be different, she knows. Nobody on campus will assume she's the designated expert on *One Flew Over the Cuckoo's Nest*. Nobody will ask if her relatives live in tipis. No one will be elected to ask her if this or that spirit ribbon is offensive or not. The worst thing about being Indian, it's being the only Indian.

She balances a neat square of lasagne across to the first container, leaving room for two more.

"*All* Native American, though," Desi adds, using her whisper-voice again. "Not half-and-half."

Ronald leans into her like shutting her up but she rolls with it, her eyes transfixed on Charlotte.

"Half-and-half?" Charlotte asks, trying to get the lid to seal.

"Like for coffee," Ronald says, saving Desi from having to.

The scene builds itself in Charlotte's head: Mrs. Wilbanks explaining the new babysitter over breakfast and using what she has at hand: her morning coffee. *Your new babysitter, kids? Come here, come here now, listen*, at which point she swirls her cup and explains how a walnut-colored mother and a creamy-white father can have a daughter who looks just like . . . *this*. Except of course Charlotte's father's not really white. More like invisible since the night-of, as her mom refers to it, pretty uncryptically.

"Come here, I'll let you in on a secret," Charlotte says, kneeling down and pulling the twins in. "You either are or you aren't Indian, did you know that?"

"Like this," Desi says, and holds her pudgy cute little hands up like a field goal, like butterfly wings, like moose antlers, having to concentrate to get it just perfect. She leans forward, waggles the tip of her tongue over where her thumbs touch, says—*recites*, Charlotte can tell—"In the middle."

It's good that Charlotte's mom isn't here for this.

"Sure," Charlotte says, swallowing the rest down, and then Ronald's pulling on her hand.

"I'm a nurse!" he says around the bite he's trying to get down.

Part of the babysitter certification process is choking hazards and how to clear airways. The big choking hazards are supposed to be peanuts and cut-up wieners, grapes and hard candy. But lasagne isn't exactly porous.

"Smaller bites, Ronald?" Charlotte says, standing but not losing his hand.

He moves his body back and forth like he's embarrassed.

"Veronica," Desi primly corrects.

This brings Charlotte around, first to Desi again, then Ronald—*Veronica*.

Hmm.

"A nurse, you say?" she asks, starting on the second container, carefully carving around the center of the lasagne, which looks more like Hamburger Helper now. Which is something they probably don't even know about in this house.

"I'll show!" Ronald says, and drops from his stool, scurries the other direction. Not to the living room but . . . Charlotte thinks he's headed for the garage at first, which is supposed to be off-limits, but then he veers around the island and into the utility room, not stopping to turn the light on.

"He didn't even say excuse me," Desi says, trying to make her spoon work in the curvy folds of cheese and big flat noodles.

"Here," Charlotte says, and passes across one of the forks Mrs. Wilbanks had left out.

Desi pokes into the heart of the flat noodles, opens wide to balance this sloppiness in.

"I guess I am from Thanksgiving, yeah," Charlotte says, the three containers stacked on the island now, the tin lasagne pan beside them, still with what probably amounts to two pieces of ragged mess in it. Which will be how much Mrs. Wilbanks will assume their new babysitter ate, once it's crumpled into the trash can.

"So do I call him Veronica?" Charlotte says to Desi—not in a serious, defenses-up way. Just normal voice, for this everyday thing.

"It's Halloween," Desi says with a thrill, and Charlotte

hears . . . but it can't be. Was that a footstep *upstairs*? Like a kid, running.

"*Almost* Halloween," Charlotte corrects, not one hundred percent involved with this anymore, then turns to Ronald/Veronica bustling back in, holding his nurse outfit proudly in front of him like a shield.

He wasn't lying: it's nurse whites, the old-fashioned polyester skirt-uniform kind, white hose and Florence Nightingale tiara cap and all. There's even, according to the label on the packaging, a collapsible medical bag that can be used for candy. The tiara cap and the bag both have a big red plus sign on them, and there's a name sewn on the chest in black thread: VERONICA.

"Beautiful," Charlotte says, and means it.

"Mom says he has to wear sensible shoes with it," Desi says with adult eyes, which mostly means leaning her face forward, leading with her forehead.

"What about you?" Charlotte asks. "Where is *your* costume?"

Ronald looks up to them like *oops*, then he's off to the utility again, is opening . . . is that the dryer door? Is that the secret hiding place for Halloween outfits?

Charlotte starts to step over, make sure Ronald isn't endangering himself in any way, but then Desi drips her next bite onto the floor, which needs immediate attending to.

"Moccasins," Desi says out of nowhere, swishing her feet back and forth.

Charlotte looks up at her like to ask about this, but then Ronald's bursting back in all out of breath. He's got the Authentic Squaw costume Charlotte's dreading. Beaded headband, fake buckskin full-body dress. Shoe covers that have the necessary fringe, and of course, the jet-black wig, braids and all.

"Nice, nice," Charlotte says, inspecting the packaging, the model, the price.

"Like your hair!" Ronald says.

Charlotte looks across the island to the utility.

"Are there stairs back there?" she asks.

Both kids try to suppress their laughter, fail pretty miserably.

"Show me?" Charlotte says, standing, holding her hands out for each of them to take one.

"We're not supposed to," Desi says.

Charlotte considers this.

"If there's a fire," she says, "it's important I know every exit, to keep you safe."

"Will you get us out if there's a fire?" Ronald asks, his eyes widening with concern.

"There won't be a fire," Charlotte assures him. "Is it a secret stairway?"

They both nod eagerly, seriously.

"Those are the *best*," Charlotte says, taking both their hands in hers.

"We're not supposed to show you," Ronald says sadly.

Why would the Wilbankses care? And how was it not part of the tour anyway? Charlotte mentally rushes back through that tour: first floor, second floor, one central stairway connecting them. No basement, no loft or attic. Just the garage.

"Maybe . . . what if it wasn't you showing me?" Charlotte

says to the twins. "What if it was a nurse and a . . . an . . ."
—she can't seem to physically say "squaw," but neither can
she call that costume Indian, quite—"a Native *princess*?"

The twins' eyes go as round as the saucers they were eating
from.

"Not until tomorrow night," Desi scare-whispers.

"We can fold them back in perfect," Charlotte tells her,
eyebrows raised, allowing room for this one wonderful possibility to sneak through.

The twins look over at each other, hardly able to contain
themselves, and when Ronald bursts ahead for his costume and
tries to follow through to the living room to change, Charlotte
snags him by the arm, pulls him around, says, thinking lizard--
with-the-glass-throat thoughts, "In here, 'kay?"

Charlotte stacks the three lasagne containers alongside
the milk on the main shelf of the refrigerator so the
Wilbanks will have to see them, and by the time she gets back
to the twins, Ronald has both legs in one side of the white
stockings like some nightmare mermaid and Desi's wearing
the headband like a choker.

Charlotte wrestles Ronald into shape first, since he can
actually ruin the hose if left to himself, and then, instead of
the wig, Charlotte works Desi's own hair into two careful
braids, her hair finger-parted in the middle.

"But I'm a *Native American*," Desi says, her eyes filling.

"It's not about hair," Charlotte says, tying the second braid

STEPHEN GRAHAM JONES

off, "it's about here," and she touches her own chest with her palm.

"But that's not how—" Desi says.

"We wear our hair *all* kinds of ways," Charlotte says, "but like that too," and tilts her head over to separate her hair, get three strands ducking under each other on the right side, pulling them tight as she goes. By the left braid, Desi's got a reluctant smile.

"How are we doing, Nurse Veronica?" Charlotte says over to Ronald.

"Ronnie," Ronald says. "Mom says both names work like that."

"They do, they do," Charlotte says, letting the second braid flop down.

Ronald's nurse costume has a toy stethoscope, as it turns out. He's trying to listen to his own heart with it. Charlotte takes the end, says into it, thumping her voice down into *beat-beat*, "You're so cute, you're so cute."

He laughs and pushes her in that way kids have where it's really a hug.

"This all of us?" Charlotte asks, playing the teacher on the field trip.

"Yes!" Desi says back, thrilled with it all, her beaded headband actually not that bad, at least with real braids.

"Well then," Charlotte says, holding their hands to take the first step of this big adventure. Except . . . at the door to the dark utility room, Desi lowers her chin into her chest for six-year-old seriousness, stops them.

"What is it?" Charlotte asks, barely clipping the *now* off the end of that in time.

"He has to go first," she says, nodding across to Ronald.

Ronald nods solemnly, lets his hand slip from Charlotte's.

"This isn't . . . *dangerous*, is it?" Charlotte asks, a nervous smile ghosting the corners of her mouth up.

This time the twins don't volunteer anything.

Ronald looks up to Charlotte and steps into the darkness. Charlotte reaches in to feel for the light but Desi pulls her back, says, "That's not how it works."

"It?" Charlotte says.

"Shh," Desi says. "Native Americans are quiet."

"I mean, some are," Charlotte says as gently as she can, trying to see into the utility but the room's stupid—you walk in and there's an immediate right turn to get to the washer and dryer and everything.

Still, "What is that?" she says louder than she means to— fear is infectious.

"Shh," Desi says again.

Is Ronald talking to someone in there? Whispering?

"Ronald?" Charlotte calls, tentatively.

"Veronica," Desi corrects, her voice defensive.

"We're going in," Charlotte decides out loud for both of them, and, not letting Desi's forty-odd pounds stop her, she steps right in, finds the light immediately.

Ronald's just standing there, almost facing them.

"There," he says to Desi, about the bifold closet doors on the wall right of the dryer—what she must have thought was the sound of the dryer opening, right? The louvres in the doors mean it's probably the water heater closet.

"The stairs are there?" Charlotte says, looking around at all the—the nothing. Just a normal everyday utility room: washer, dryer, both top-dollar, up on pedestals or something, and a wide laundry cart on wheels that's probably nice even if the hanging part's tall enough that it had to be assembled in here. Cabinets up high all around, probably built to order, another cabinet that's probably got a foldout ironing board in it, and two industrial-looking storage containers sturdy enough for the garage. The only thing different from when Mrs. Wilbanks swept through here on the big tour is that now there's kid clothes trailing out of the open dryer, meaning she heard *right*, earlier. That doesn't make it make sense, though.

"I don't like that one," Desi says to Ronald, toeing the floor with her fake moccasin.

Ronald holds his hand out to her just the same.

"You have to keep your eyes closed," he says to Charlotte, his mouth serious so Charlotte can get how important this is.

"Excuse me?" Charlotte asks.

"You can't look," Desi says, just a fact.

"O-*kay* . . ." Charlotte says, waiting for the punch line that has to be coming.

Ronald picks through the clothes on the floor in front of the dryer, comes up with a pair of black tights, probably Desi's. He hands them to Charlotte, says, "They're clean."

"For your eyes," Desi explains.

"What kind of game is this?" Charlotte asks.

"*You* promised to show her," Desi says to Ronald.

"I didn't promise," he says back.

"Show me," Charlotte says.

At best she was expecting secret stairs for, she doesn't know, a maid? Never mind that this McMansion can't be more than twenty years old. At worst there was supposed to be a dumbwaiter back here, probably with an electric motor because kid arms aren't that strong.

What she's getting is a blindfold and no answers.

"Does your mom know about this?" Charlotte asks, working the upside-down tights onto her head like a stocking cap but not pulling the too-tight waistband over her eyes yet.

"Which one?" Ronald asks back, which is when Desi, at the light switch somehow, darkens the room all at once.

"It works better like this," she says, serious now.

Charlotte's heart is beating in her throat. Even Ronald's toy stethoscope could pick it up, she bets.

Desi's strong little hand finds Charlotte's. Ronald folds one of the doors open.

"How can we all—?" Charlotte starts, but Desi's already pulling her in.

The water heater is dusty, and Ronald, skinny as he is, has already pushed in past it, to the corner Charlotte would never willingly lean into, not in a thousand years. Desi turns sideways, slips through as well, right behind him.

"Your eyes," Ronald calls back from the darkness ahead, and Charlotte shakes her head no but pulls the waistband over her eyes, hooks it under her nose. It unbalances her for a moment and she reaches out, finds the cold side of the water heater, jerks back not because it's hot, not because it's coursing with electricity, but because she doesn't know exactly how water heaters work, tucked away in the musty dark places all the time, so it *could* have been boiling hot or coursing with raw electricity or worse.

"The door," Desi says to her, as if the world's upside down all of the sudden and she and Ronald are the adults. Charlotte feels back for the knob that isn't there—bifold doors don't work like that—but she's able to grab the edge, close the three of them in. She isn't sure exactly what changes the moment that door flattens out—not temperature, and the concrete floor under her feet stays solid—but she . . . there's the sense of *space* around her. Like, were she to say anything, it wouldn't echo back to her for seconds and seconds, if ever. The air around her would slurp it up, digest it for centuries. But at the same time, there's a pressure, like . . . like the *opposite* of going up over twelve or fourteen thousand feet. Like going down *deep* deep, where gravity pulls harder, where the air's pushing on you from every side, where your chest feels the kind of tight like you might not be able to breathe so easy, next breath.

Charlotte gasps, reaches forward for the anchor the water heater can be—anything, please, even that—but the water heater's not there. She sucks a mouthful of this thick air in, screams it back out, sure she's falling, sure she's drowning, sure there's nothing real to breathe here, and, reaching up for the tights covering her eyes, she realizes she's not holding Desi's hand anymore.

S pider eggs.

That's what Charlotte thinks before she even realizes she's thinking.

The waistband of the tights is chocked on her forehead now, she can definitely feel that, but it's . . . not dark, exactly.

It's *white*, but a fabric-y, light, nothing kind of white. Like spider eggs.

Charlotte opens her mouth and the eggs find their way in, are dry on her tongue, on the roof of her mouth, and she's immediately coughing and retching, pushing her arm all around to find her way up, out, through.

Is she thinking spider eggs because this is a water heater closet? Yes, but there's more. Spider eggs are pretty much web spun powdery and gossamer, she doesn't know exactly what's up with them really, just knows one hundred percent what they feel like when her fingers find them under furniture, or high up in corners.

And when they burst, there's thousands of tiny desperate legs there.

She fights harder, pushing, feeling, trying—

There's something there, something almost solid. Not hard like the water heater . . . it resists her fingers but it gives some too, shifting all the spider eggs around her so they cascade with a hiss, chitter into the empty spaces under her back and legs.

Charlotte slows, makes herself process, her head dialing down to SAT mode: *If a thousand spider eggs hatch at once, and all those newborn spiders are both healthy and hungry, then, never mind how many sharp little legs that will be crawling across babysitter X's face and lips and eyeballs, but how long will it be before babysitter X retreats so deep into herself that nobody ever finds her again?*

Not much longer, she answers.

She feels with her hand for that resistance again, follows it around, around, making herself go slow and rational, and what she finally finds is a seam, a cold, notched line her fingers can trace. It leads her to a metal tab.

She pulls it—*zipper!* zipper zipper zipper!—stands up from the big pink beanbag in Desi's room, the white beans or puffy beads or whatever the hell they are raining down all around her, and static-clinging to everything they can. She spits the ones in her mouth away, looks around the My Little Pony bedroom.

The twins are on their knees on the bed, laughing and laughing, their eyes hopeful that this is as funny to Charlotte as it is to them.

"What the—?" Charlotte says, cutting herself off just in time and stepping fast away from this impossibility, looking back to it just to be sure it maybe really actually might have happened. Because, really, there's no fucking way. Did she hit her head on a pipe in that closet downstairs, and they somehow dragged her up here? But . . . not that they could have . . . but why hide her in—

"The beanbag, the beanbag!" Desi's saying, like this is the best most exciting thing ever in the whole world. "It's never the *beanbag* anymore!"

Ronald is more contrite, it seems, his eyebrows up, waiting to see if he's in trouble. It was his trick, after all. His game. His joke.

Charlotte flips the beanbag over for the trapdoor that has to be under it. That *isn't* under it.

"What just happened?" she says to the twins, trying to keep her voice from rising into a shriek.

"She only shows Ronald," Desi says, stepping down from the bed, her tone all about the essential unfairness of Ronald being the only who knows whatever *this* is. "Ask him."

"Ronald?" Charlotte says, trying to get across that he's not in trouble, that nothing he says here will get him in trouble. "Who shows you what? And why?"

He's bouncing up and down on his knees now.

"Because he's a miracle," Desi says, proudly.

Charlotte translates this, rewinds back to the walking and talking tour of the house, the out-loud biographies of the twins: Desi was born first, showed up with asthma before she was one, will probably outgrow it, and Ronald was born minutes later, not breathing at all. Not until the doctors got him to, minutes after other doctors would've given up: a legit miracle.

"That's . . . that's why *what*?" Charlotte says, not following.

"Why she tells me where they are," Ronald says, his chin pruning up, face tilting down. "Because I'm the only one who can see her sometimes."

"Where what are?" Charlotte says in her kindest, gentlest voice.

"The funny places," he says, obviously, like that's the most boring part of all this.

"She's not our real mom," Desi adds in, then, quieter, in secret, her eyes widening to deliver it, "*She's better*."

"She's not," Ronald says, as if afraid.

"Is she here now?" Charlotte says, playacting a look around the room, which, it turns out, is exactly like a real look around the room. "Can I—can I meet her?" Charlotte asks, brushing fuzzy white beads from her peripheral vision.

Ronald shakes his head no, no.

"Was she in the closet?" Charlotte asks.

Both twins shake their head vigorously no, definitely no. No way no way.

"She can't go," Ronald says. "She can only use normal doors."

"Or the stairs," Desi adds.

"Does your mom know about her?" Charlotte asks.

"She says she's not real," Desi says with a shrug of one shoulder, dancing from foot to foot on her rug in some game only she's playing.

"We've got to—" Charlotte says, not at all sure how she's going to finish, "I've got to call—"

"*You can't tell*," Ronald says, delivering fully half of that with his eyes and eyebrows.

"It would make her mad," Desi says. "She would probably cry again."

"Again?"

"She doesn't like to do bad things," Ronald says.

"Like bubbles," Desi adds quietly.

Charlotte nods, writing this down in her head, milking it for every iota of possibility.

"This can't—" she finally says, or tries to. "What just happened. It's not right. It's wrong. I don't understand how it can even—"

Ronald's lower lip thrusts out and his eyes get shiny.

Charlotte plunks down beside him, pulls him to her.

"I'll come back, sage the living hell out of this place," she says.

"Is that Native Indian?" Desi says, blinking large and innocent.

Charlotte straightens her arm out to her, opens and closes her hand, telling Desi to come up here too.

"You can help," she says, pulling her to her other side. "I'll teach you. But I've got to tell your mom and dad. I wouldn't be a good babysitter if I didn't."

Now Ronald's full-on quiet-crying. Then Desi is too, just because.

"I'm sorry," Charlotte says to them both. "My job is to keep you safe. Make sure you grow up to be an amazing nurse and the best—the best Native Indian ever. A lot better than me."

Ronald nods *okay, okay okay okay*, and the way he's doing it, Charlotte can tell he's scared too, that he knows this is wrong, even if it's fun and secret.

She pulls him tighter, kisses the top of his head.

"How do your parents not know about this?" she asks.

"She won't talk to him when they're here," Desi says, sobbing.

"But she will when I am?" Charlotte says, just out loud, which is when the doorbell rings.

Charlotte's first reaction is terror: Mrs. Wilbanks told her about the one camera *she* knew about, but maybe the whole house has been keeping tabs on her. Cameras in every room. Meaning Mr. Wilbanks has been watching his phone in his lap all through dinner, keeping track of her . . . oh shit: of her letting the kids dress up in and possibly ruin their Halloween costumes; of her losing the kids long enough that they could trash the lasagne. And now, when the babysitter has for some reason decided to bury herself in the beanbag—he can't watch every moment, there has to be some jumps in time—now the adults have had to cut their fancy dinner short, come home with thin lips and grim eyes.

Good, Charlotte wants to say. There's impossible wrong shit happening here, shit that was not in the initial job description, shit not in any of the babysitter manuals, shit none of the other girls posting fliers up ever even whisper. Either that or she hit her head on that doorknob harder than she thought, in which case she doesn't need to be in charge of little ones, probably needs some medical care, never mind if her mom makes a federal case out of it at the ER.

Right on the heels of that, though, she realizes that there's zero reason for the Wilbankses to ring their own doorbell. Not just because they'll probably park in the garage when they come back for the night, but because parents are duty bound to never give you that kind of warning. Exhibit one: Mr. Wilbanks walking right into Ronald's room. Kids don't have privacy. Neither do the babysitters in charge of those kids.

It's not them, then.

Who, then? That homeless guy Mrs. Wilbanks was all stranger-danger about? Or was that a setup—has Mr. Wilbanks dressed up in layers of castoff jeans and jackets to test her? But nobody's that paranoid, are they? They wanted a date, not a game of catch-the-babysitter.

It's not them, Charlotte tells herself. Don't be stupid.

But it is somebody.

Most other jobs, most other normal Friday nights, a ringing doorbell means already-paid-for pizza. But you don't order pizza when there's perfectly good lasagne. And packages don't come this late. And Charlotte's car isn't parked in some wrong place. She knows that for sure because she doesn't *have* a car.

"Go, go!" Desi says, kneeling to pull the edge of her Pinkie Pie rug up, wriggle under like it's . . . a blanket?

Ronald slides off the bed, runs to the hall fast enough that he has to catch himself on the railing, bounce off the other way, toward his room.

"What are you—?" Charlotte says, following him but keeping a hand up, like for spiderwebs. She reaches the hall just as Ronald is stepping up into the linen closet, having to hold the door open and the little vacuum cleaner back.

"You've got to go in the *beanbag*," he tells her, which isn't even close to being on the list of Things She Never Thought She'd Have Told to Her, but that's only because it's so left field that it wouldn't have been in the running.

Still standing in front of Desi's bedroom, Charlotte looks back to the exploded beanbag, to the lump Desi is under the rug, then to Ronald, still holding the door of that high linen closet open exactly like it's the top hatch of a submarine, one about to dive.

"Why?" Charlotte asks.

"*Because that's the way it works*," he says, heating his eyes up to show her how important this is. "You have to go back the way you came through. And don't open your eyes. That's the only two rules."

"And don't tell Mom or Dad!" Desi calls from somewhere behind.

"Okay, three rules!" Ronald says, exasperated in his six-years-old way.

"I'm not doing that again," Charlotte says, looking back

to—not to Desi, to the lump she is under the rug, but to that lump flattening *out*.

She rushes across the room, jerks the rug away and there's not a secret tunnel there, there's not a hole, not a slide, not a stairway, not a pole. There's just hardwood. She touches it to be sure then slams her hand on it, shuts her eyes against all of this.

"You have to go *now*," Ronald says from the doorway.

Charlotte looks up to him, is trying hard to process all this but keeps hitting snag after snag, all of which are some version of *No, this is crazy, stop.*

She stands on unsteady legs, braces herself on the side of the bed, then nods that she can do this, that she's the closest thing to a grown-up here, that—that reason and rationality have to push everything else down. They do, don't they? The rules have to hold. They have to.

She walks past Ronald to the railing in the hall that balconies down over the living room for about as far as she can reach with both arms.

"Desiree!" she calls.

Desi laughs from what's got to be the utility room, and now the doorbell's ringing *again*. Because sometimes, Charlotte knows from experience—why wasn't this the first thing she considered?—sometimes the parents will be nervous enough that all the neighbors will be tasked with stepping over to check on things throughout the night. Never mind that this babysitter's already been told not to answer the door. Shit. Shit shit *shit*.

"I can't handle this," she tells Ronald, her only confessor here. "I've—I've got the SATs in the morning, this was just supposed to be a chance to brush up on some of the practice questions and get paid for it, nobody said anything about, about . . ."

About whatever this is.

"What happens if I don't, if I just—" she says to Ronald, not even able to form the thought into proper words.

"You get stuck?" he says, shrugging his shoulders and his eyebrows both.

"I get—" Charlotte says, looking around, none of this tracking. So then. Focus on what you *know*, she tells herself. On your training, your duties, your responsibilities here. Because they can't be wrong. "Your sister can't be down there alone," she says, less for Ronald, more just to hear it out loud, like reminding herself. Like faking rationality but making herself accountable to it. She makes for the stairs but now Ronald has her by the wrist with both hands, is leaning back with all of his weight, his feet set as hard as he can get them, his face more serious than any kid's should be.

"You've got to go in *there*," he says, tilting his head at Desi's room. "It'll shut!"

"The beanbag, you mean?" Charlotte says, about to collapse into laughter. "The magic beanbag will shut?"

In response, Ronald's eyes well up.

"I don't—" Charlotte says, and stops because . . . the hallway light is dimming? No, *all* the lights in the house are dimming.

"That's the warning," he says, pulling her harder. "You've got to go back the way you came!"

Charlotte can see the intensity on his face, the plea in his whole desperate little body.

"You mean," she says, "you mean you and your sister didn't

come up through the beanbag like I did?"

It was zipped, some other part of her remembers, minutes too late. It was zipped and the kids didn't have those spider eggs stuck all over them. And—and he was climbing into the linen closet, and Desi slipped under the rug.

Meaning . . . the water heater closet, it must have spit them all out in different places. One way in, at least three ways out. And if this woman the twins call their other mother has to tell them where the funny places are each time—each time no adults are around—then, then that must mean it's not the water heater closet every time, is it? Of course it isn't. When Ronald went into the utility room by himself the first time, to get his costume from upstairs, he must have gone into the dryer, just like it sounded. Meaning he also came *out* of the dryer, dragging those clothes out along with him.

Is the rule that it has to be a dark, tight place?

To keep it secret, Charlotte tells herself. Rule three: don't tell the parents. If Ronald or Desi ever get caught, then they were just playing hide-and-seek, shh.

It's kind of perfect.

"*Now, now!*" Ronald is saying, the lights dialing down even lower, and then he can't wait any longer, he's racing back to the linen closet, the tiniest nurse on the most urgent mission.

He climbs in and that stupid useless little vacuum tilts out so he can't get the door shut, and he can't figure out how to pull it *and* the door in at the same time, and he's crying and breathing too fast, is almost having a panic attack.

Charlotte steps in, guides the tall handle of the vacuum in, pushes the door shut, holding his big eyes until the last moment, and she wants worse than anything right now to rip that door back open, see him treading back through some great blackness, or fizzling into static, or sucking down to a pinprick of himself, but what if it works layer by layer, taking the skin first, then the fascia, then the muscle, then—

If babysitter X has to see the boy she's in charge of stripped of his skin, then it's going to be like it wasn't her mom who found Arthur in the street, but the front bumper of some sophomore's new car, one that drags Arthur for Y feet, which makes the question: how long does Arthur get dragged on the asphalt before he's mercifully dead, and is this what he looks like?

The lights dip even lower and the doorbell rings again and this is all too much, this is all so wrong. Charlotte retreats into herself, clings to the only thing she for sure knows: how to think like a babysitter.

Desi is alone downstairs, isn't she? And now Ronald should be too.

That cinches it, then. She's supposed to be watching them, and she can't do that from up here. No taking the beanbag express down, either, only stairs, normal-normal stairs.

Right when Charlotte is three steps down, the lights flicker down to absolute black for a blink and there's a distinct *click* in the hall behind her.

She shakes her head, knows that ridiculous antique fucking haunted jack-in-the-box is going to be sitting there, ready to give her the heart attack to end all heart attacks. But it's probably just that linen closet door swinging back open, she tells herself. From that vacuum cleaner leaning drunkenly against it, now that Ronald isn't there to hold it.

Except . . . it's not the linen closet, is it? And it's not that jack-in-the-box either.

It's Mr. Wilbanks's office door, creaking back.

Charlotte swallows, shakes her head no, *please please no*, and then the doorbell rings *again*, more insistent if that's possible, like there's a depth a finger can press that makes the chime louder, that makes it hang at the top of its sound for too long.

"Okay, okay," Charlotte says, keeping her eyes on that open office door until it's gone from view, her hand gripped hard to the handrail like that can save her. By the time she steps down onto the slick white tile of the entryway, the lights are back to normal, are bright enough that nothing could have really been wrong, right?

"We're not supposed to answer the door," Ronald says from right behind her, and the first and maybe most wrong thing about him is that there's dried tomato sauce all down the front of his nurse whites, sending Charlotte immediately into a vision of her running all over town tomorrow to find this exact "Veronica" Halloween costume, and then faking like she left a book here, so she can sneak around, smuggle the stained one out in her purse, replace it with the one that doesn't make her the worst babysitter.

That's hours and hours away, though. This is now. And . . . it's not making sense, is it?

"How did you—did you eat the rest of the lasagne?" Charlotte says to him incredulously.

"I told him you would come back," Desi says, her beaded headband a choker again, her braids both let go, just hanging pigtails now.

"Come back?" Charlotte says, "I was just—" but then it registers: where they're standing. Right in the lizard's eye.

The doorbell chimes again.

"Just . . . stay, stay," Charlotte tells them, keeping her hand up and out while she steps across to the peephole. As if whoever's out there didn't hear her coming down the stairs, yes. As if whoever it is can't see the lights in the windows going up and down. But just because they know you're in there doesn't mean you have to answer. Really, this many dings in, the polite thing to do would be to back off, come back another time.

Charlotte leans in to see who could be this rude.

At first there's no shape through the thick little fisheye lens, just the porch and the lawn and the street and the night, but then, right as Charlotte's about to give up, a fool's cap jumps up into the fisheye lens like it's on a spring. The cap is a happy mass of three red and black tentacles going every which way, but then, in the image Charlotte takes with her when she jerks back, they taper into stubby-funny arms that end with . . . not bells, like she's pretty sure she's seen on harlequins and jester costumes, but pom-poms, red on the black arms, black on the red one, the skullcap black too, all of it stretched and wrong in the peephole.

"What?" Ronald says.

"Trick 'r treater," Charlotte says, trying to get her breath, trying to push the jack-in-the-box from her mind. The one she was just thinking about. The one she was just expecting upstairs.

That can't be connected to this, though. That was just in her head.

"But it's not even Halloween," Desi says, loving this, coming up onto her toes like that'll get her a glimpse.

The doorbell rings again and Charlotte leans back into the peephole, this jester stepping back enough so she can see the bone-white, kind-of-peeling face, the stretched-out black diamonds painted over the eyes, the lips bright red and sharp at the corners. The . . . pale yellow contact lenses?

The eyes are the worst part, easy.

The jester rocks back on its heels, hands behind its back so innocently, and then it tries on what looks to be a practice smile. One that shows its dull yellow fangs.

"We don't have any candy," Desi says.

Charlotte smiles, says, "We *are* the candy," and digs for the key in her pocket, guides it into the deadbolt.

"No," Ronald says, eyes wide, but Charlotte hauls the door open grandly all the same, exposing this visitor all at once, because you have to take charge. Most bullies run when they see that you're not going to cringe and cry.

The jester looks from face to face, finally settling its pale eyes on Charlotte.

"Premature, um . . ." Charlotte says, little ears behind her funneling in every word, "costumification?"

The jester does a quick soft-shoe that ends with her right leg curtsying forward, her face down, arms out like thrown-back wings.

"I'm . . . sorry?" Charlotte says, to the jaunty top of this fool's cap.

The peeling white face comes up. And the eyes soft behind those yellowy lenses.

"No," Murphy says, standing into her usual slack posture, her left hand bringing her phone up, screen out, "I think you were *so–ry*."

"You fall for that every time," Charlotte says. "I didn't tell you where I was, though. You didn't—did you locate me with your phone? We promised never to check up on each other like that, didn't we? Did you get your dad to use some cop trick to find me?"

Murphy rubs her gloved fingertip uselessly across her phone screen, says, "Swung by the ER, told your mom you'd left a study book at my place, that you would probably flame out at the SATs tomorrow if you didn't have it right now, *stat*!"

One of Murphy's favorite things is saying *stat* all emergency like that.

"You could have asked *me*," Charlotte says.

"And you would have put me off until tomorrow," Murphy says with a shrug, because this is so obviously true. "You've got work tonight."

"I do have work tonight."

"Anyway," Murphy goes on, "these gloves are too much trouble to peel out of, they go all the way to the elbow." She holds her billowy costumed arms up like that proves her case. "They're from when I was the Grimy Reaper last year, remember? Dirty fingernails and a rusty scythe?"

"Nice eyes," Charlotte tells her.

"The better to drink you up with," Murphy says back, and angles her whole body over to see the nurse and the Indian princess.

"We're not supposed to let anybody in," Ronald says.

"What *are* you?" Desi asks, her face flush with wonder.

"She's my . . . friend," Charlotte answers, and holds both hands out for Murphy's. Murphy takes them, their fingertips catching together, pulling into each other, and at the last moment Murphy whispers, "On the cheek, you don't want this lipstick on you."

Charlotte kisses her on the lips anyway, lingering a smidge longer than would be acceptable on Murphy's front porch.

"Ronald, Desi, this is Murph," Charlotte says, wiping her lips with the back of her arm. "The . . . vampire jester?"

"Dracula harlequin," Murphy says, with full-on mock disappointment. "But vampire jester, I like that. That's like the generic version of Dracula harlequin."

"She's not coming in, don't worry," Charlotte says to the twins but *for* Murphy. "She's just wishing me luck. That test I've got in the morning? Murphy took it last year. She's here to make sure I do great in the morning."

"She's your boyfriend!" Desi says, loving it.

"Yeah, *boy*friend . . ." Murphy says, asking the question to Charlotte with her eyes. "Not coming in, you say?" she adds, using more than just one question mark.

"It's my first night here," Charlotte hisses back, keeping her face pleasant but her eyes insistent. "What use are the SATs if I don't get enough repeat work to pay for tuition?"

Murphy looks away, down the long porch, and Charlotte winces: that's what the fight was about—Charlotte leaving for good, forever, for always.

"What's wrong with your eyes?" Desi asks Murphy, coming closer by a timid step or two.

"Drank too much lemonade," Murphy says with what sounds to Charlotte like forced cheer, then she gets into it, mimes the pee-pee dance, which her jester costume amplifies by a factor of at least ten. "Speaking of?" she says to Charlotte.

"She needs to use the bathroom!" Desi says at celebration volume. Because: six years old.

Charlotte looks over at Ronald, his face cupping his worried eyes.

"Just for a quick squa—" she says, and bites it off, comes out with "Just for a minute" instead. "Okay?"

"Thank you thank you," Murphy says, and makes to squeeze through the doorway past them but stops, her lead foot comically held up. "Can I enter these premises, ladies of the house?" she asks both the Indian princess and the skirted nurse.

"Because you're a vampire . . ." Charlotte drolls, her shoulders slumping with how little this surprises her.

"Hey, my kind needs permission," Murphy says, like the good girl she most definitely isn't. "I don't make the rules, do I?"

"*Yes* you can come in!" Desi says.

"Thank you, thank you, says my bladder," Murphy says, and takes an overexaggerated step across the threshold.

"We're not supposed to let anybody in," Ronald repeats.

"You're not supposed to be wearing your costumes either, are you?" Charlotte says, hating herself for blackmailing a first grader like that. But she *does* need this job.

"Thing One, Thing Two," Murphy enumerates, pointing to Desi and Ronald in turn, like activating them.

"Why are you already . . . this," Charlotte says, waggling her fingers over Murphy's whole getup.

"Test run for tomorrow night," Murphy says, primping the arms of her cap, luxuriating a bit too pornographically on the plush resistance of one of the pom-poms. "Your mom's big Halloween blowout after you jam on those wimpy SATs?"

"If this house doesn't eat me first," Charlotte mutters back.

Murphy gives Charlotte a look about this, reaches out to tug on one leg of the tights Charlotte is still wearing on her head.

"Thought you had to pee," Charlotte tells her flatly.

"Vampire bladders are surprisingly—"

"Just past the shelves," Charlotte says, but then, before Murphy can actually *go* there, Charlotte has her by the wrist.

Murphy looks down at this, tracks up Charlotte's arm to her face.

"Um, emergency situation?" she says, shifting her weight from foot to foot. "This is a one-piece, you know?"

"Just, here," Charlotte says, doing her eyes big and words packed to bursting with code, so Murphy will fall in without asking questions in front of the kids, "*let—me—reshelve—this—book—over—here.*"

Murphy digests this, looks to the kids, says, "Your parents bought you a robot babysitter? How do you like her so far?"

"She doesn't always talk like that!" Desi nearly screams, loving it.

"She should have gone in the beanbag," Ronald says, his dejection pretty much palpable.

"Like, gone *pee-pee* in the beanbag, you mean?" Murphy asks back, which explodes Desi into laughter.

Ronald just watches Charlotte, his eyes about to cry again.

"Don't worry," Charlotte says, passing him, threading his bangs out of his eyes. "She's not a stranger, it's okay. We'll keep her secret, and we also won't tell about any stains on any nurse costumes, cool?"

Ronald looks away from this.

Charlotte, to *Plutarch's Lives* now, reaches up to pull a random book out from a higher shelf, saying "Now" back to Murphy in a loud whisper, and, while taking a solid ten seconds to get that book down, the lizard's mouth open against her flannel shirt, she hears Murphy and the two six-year-olds tiptoe across the living room behind her, then realizes she can see them in the television's dead screen as well, like ghosts of themselves.

Before joining them in the kitchen, she goes back to that closet door one more time, counts to three, and pulls it open all at once.

The jack-in-the-box is still there. Not in the downstairs bathroom.

"Thank you," Charlotte says, just to the world, and shuts that door again, crossing the living room without looking upstairs even once.

"Let me guess," Murphy says, squatted down in front of Desi and Ronald, "twinsies?"

Ronald flicks his eyes up to Charlotte, somehow making that eye contact into a plea.

"You didn't even bring any books," Charlotte says to Murphy. "What if my mom shows up?"

"Books have boring answers and boring knowledge in them," Murphy says, adjusting Ronald's nurse cap for him, getting it just so. "The SAT isn't that kind of test. You know this, C. It's about how well you can *think*. It's testing your mind, not your data banks."

"It's testing how well I *test*," Charlotte corrects.

"Which is an intelligence thing," Murphy says, standing, taking this posh kitchen in appliance by appliance. "Eliminate multiple choices by assuming that no test with any self-respect, or with a decent randomizer engine, is going to have C be the right answer three times in a row. So, if you have four to choose from, now you've got three. And the first answer, nine times out of ten, is the one they want you to pick, which can poison your read of the rest of the options, just like they want. So, now you're down to two. At which point it's just a matter of—"

"Plugging one of them in, seeing if it works, blah blah blah," Charlotte says. "We've covered all this, haven't we?"

Murphy fixes Charlotte right in her stare.

"Is this pre-test jitters I'm sensing?" she says. "Is this a defeatist attitude from the girl who's going to score so well that she escapes this town, and"—melodramatic blinking—"everyone in it?"

"Your eyes do look weird," Charlotte tells her.

"Classic non-answer with a side helping of deflection," Murphy says, and takes a long step back to clap ponderously with her gloved hands.

"I don't want to leave you," Charlotte says. "I'm not doing this because I'm trying to get away from you."

"And I won't let you hold yourself back *because* of me. See? We're on the same side."

"Are we really doing this again?" Charlotte says, then, about the twins, gulping all of this in, "have we practiced this argument enough that we're finally ready for an audience?"

"I'm sure Mommy and Daddy have adult discussions from

time to time," Murphy says, studying Desi and Ronald as well.

"But Mommy and *Mommy* don't," Charlotte says.

"They're not old enough to . . . have those prejudices," Murphy says. "Are they?"

"They're perfect and wonderful," Charlotte says, kneeling to redo Ronald's nurse cap the way *she* likes it. "And in thirty minutes they need to be tucked in and sleeping."

"Wow," Murphy says. "We never got to stay up that late, did we?"

Charlotte doesn't follow, casts around for a digital clock— clocks, *plural*: they're blinking green on every appliance, even the refrigerator.

10:15?

She starts to lodge an objection about this but can't even form the words. She pulls her phone out. 10:16, now.

"No," she says, looking around for an anchor, for anything that can tie her back to half past eight. "The lasagne," she eurekas, biting her lower lip in about this victory.

She brushes past Murphy, yanks the refrigerator door open, and pulls out the top container, sets it importantly on the island, exhibit one.

"Okay . . ." Murphy says.

"It's still warm," Charlotte says, nodding for Murphy to prove her wrong. "I pulled it out of the top oven almost right at eight. Not even thirty minutes ago. No refrigerator works that fast, not even rich people's."

Murphy looks from Charlotte to Ronald and Desi.

"It's okay," she says to them. "The adults are just having a breakdown the night before the big test."

"Touch it," Charlotte says, nodding to the container again.

Murphy shrugs, pinches a plastic corner up, holds the body of the container with her other hand, and pulls, slips, grabs again, pulls harder, and—the lid comes off all at once, flies behind all of them.

"It's warm, isn't it?" Charlotte says, about the lasagne.

"I've kind of got gloves on . . ." Murphy says.

"Here," Charlotte says, and rips the container away, jams her index finger down, undoing one of her neat spatula cuts.

Instead of smushing all the way through into a dark Italian heart, her finger stops at the top layer of cheesy pasta.

It's cold.

Charlotte rushes to the refrigerator, grabs the next container, has no choice but to register that it's the *last* container. Of what was three.

"Ronald?" she says about this.

He looks away, right to the sink, where the other container, what was the top container, is balanced. Where he was standing, eating.

"He *likes* it cold," Desi says. "Dad says that makes him a weirdo."

"If it's anything like cold pizza . . ." Murphy says, and holds a fist out for Ronald to bump. He doesn't.

Charlotte touches the top of the last container.

It's not just cold, it's fogged.

She covers her face with her right hand, leans back against the counter shaking her head no, no.

"How long did it take me to get downstairs?" she asks, weakly.

"I was considering using the bushes, if that's any indication," Murphy says.

Charlotte doesn't want to cry but can't help it either.

It changes the tone of the room. She's supposed to be the one in charge, she knows. But Murphy's here, Murphy's here. Charlotte hears her asking the kids if any of their favorite shows are recorded, maybe? Do they know how to work the remote?

Two minutes later, after a toilet flush that sounds like a jet engine, Murphy jesters back from the living room alone, takes Charlotte's wrists and guides her hands down from her face.

"You were going to tell me something," she says.

"It's not—this can't be happening," Charlotte says.

"Of course it can't," Murphy says, picking a spider egg from Charlotte's hair and inspecting it on the end of her red finger. "But, what? *What* is it that can't be happening?"

After the painful tedious apologetic blow-by-blow of the night so far, which Murphy dutifully soaks in, missing time and all, her painted-white eyebrows V'ing higher and higher with concern, Charlotte pulls the bifold door open in the utility to prove it.

They stand there hand in hand.

"So it's an enchanted water heater?" Murphy finally has to say, unable not to grin about it.

Charlotte hip-checks her softly.

"You said you wouldn't laugh," she says.

"That's just the face paint," Murphy says, leaning in to inspect the walls. "There's probably just a hollow wall they can shimmy up, think? They're skinny little rats."

"*I* didn't shimmy," Charlotte tells her.

"So sayeth Concussion Girl."

"Try it, then."

Murphy looks at her with her black-diamond, yellow-iris eyes.

"You've noticed I wore my *good* Dracula vampire outfit?" she says, straightening her arms out to show it off.

"Thought it was Dracula harlequin?" Charlotte says.

"It is," Murphy says, turning back to the darkness of the closet. "I was testing your recall. That was practice for tomorrow morning."

"Then I'll go again," Charlotte decides out loud.

"Is there even a light in there?"

"You can't have lights on for it to work."

"These are rules the *kids* told you?" Murphy asks, to show the obvious flaw in Charlotte's thinking.

"I'm figuring them out," Charlotte says.

"The kids?"

"The rules."

Murphy steps back, giving this demonstration over to Charlotte. Charlotte shakes her head no, starts to step in but then goes to Murphy instead, holds her face in her hands and kisses her long on the red-red lips.

When Charlotte draws back, the insides of all her fingers are pale with white paint, and she's sure her mouth looks bloody.

"That wasn't goodbye," she says.

"Where I'm from, we call that kind of action foreplay . . ." Murphy says back, holding tight onto both of Charlotte's wrists.

"We're kind of from the same street," Charlotte tells her, stepping in, her fingers trailing out of Murphy's hands.

"Then it *was* a promise of things to come," Murphy says.

"Just count to, I don't know, count to ten," Charlotte says, her hand set to pull the door shut.

Murphy holds Charlotte's eyes in hers, says, "If you start screaming—"

"Get your clown ass in here," Charlotte finishes.

"Dracula harlequin, thank you very much," Murphy says, and gently pushes the door from her side, using both hands.

The blackness is sudden.

Charlotte sucks her breath in sharp, nearly throws up from inhaling what she's ninety percent sure is a cobweb. That is, something that came from a spider's ass. Something that has sucked-dry gnats and flies gummed up in it.

She bats her arms around her face, manages to clang her left elbow into the water heater tank, and that must trip something in there because it whooshes on, a blue glow casting out at knee level.

Charlotte pushes back into the corner, knows there has to be all manner of unspeakable detritus and husks there, but she can't help it.

And: there *is* a corner. Not a whole world of empty space pressing in around her. She grunts a sound out, testing the closet, and the darkness doesn't drink those sound waves up.

It's not working. This isn't a funny place anymore. She waited too long.

The door cracks open and Murphy's jester face is tilting in, a floating white visage with pale eyes.

Charlotte edges out past the heating-up water heater.

"That's not how it works," Ronald says, suddenly there, Desi tagging along.

"She has to point where to go," Desi says, her voice small like she thinks she's going to get in trouble.

"She *who?*" Murphy says to Charlotte.

Charlotte shakes her head no but Murphy seems to hear through that.

"*She* . . ." Murphy repeats all the same, tasting it with her clown mouth as if she almost has it identified.

"What are you—?" Charlotte starts to ask.

"*No,*" Murphy is saying now, backing off Charlotte, and away from the twins as well, her black-diamond eyes looking at the ceiling of this utility, at the walls, at all of it in a new and not-good way, like she doesn't trust it anymore. "This isn't *that* house, is it?" she asks. "The . . . what was their name?"

"What house? Who?" Charlotte says, cutting her eyes to the twins in an attempt to censor whatever Murphy, the retired homicide detective's daughter, is about to say.

"It was Halloween . . ." Murphy's saying, her face somehow even paler now. "Oh shit, C. It was Halloween then too, wasn't it? Don't you remember? Second grade? First for you?"

It was the year they didn't get to go trick 'r treating, the year the church started its "*trunk* 'r treating" blasphemy: the whole parking lot lined with cars, trunks and hatches and tailgates open, bags of candy mounded in, a parent stationed there to hand it out, assembly-line fashion.

The take was good—the parents were all trying to buy their kids' lives with taffy and chocolate—but Charlotte and Murphy, just best friends then, came to realize that Halloween wasn't just about the candy, was it? It was about running through the darkness from house to house, your costume falling apart all around you, skeletons and ghouls and ghosts on every sidewalk, coffins and zombies stationed on the lawns, spring-loaded to stop their hearts for a moment, so they could restart them with shrieks and laughter.

Halloween in the church parking lot Charlotte's first-grade year pretty much sucked. But they didn't die, their parents reminded them, so there was that, right?

It wasn't until probably third and fourth grade that they even learned *why* their Halloween had been ruined, and even then, what they got was the legend, whispered behind the open doors of lockers, smuggled from stall to stall in the bathrooms.

The homeschool kids, Tad and . . . and something like "Tad." *Tia.* Tad and Tia *Spinell.* A brother and sister Charlotte and Murphy had never seen, names they only learned when they slipped into school legend. Not because their parents were homeschooling them, but because they'd been killed. And not just that, but killed *by* their mother, and the night before Halloween, which pretty much canceled Halloween.

There were a lot of different versions of it in circulation. The facts were that this Spinell mother . . . was it "Nia," to go with Tia? No: *Nora.* She had, for her own reasons, no note left behind or anything, drowned her six-year-old and her four-year-old in the bathtub, and then tied a rope to the railing of the upstairs hallway and stepped off into the open space of the living room. Her husband, busy with all the other dads building the haunted house in the park, had found her.

Those were the facts.

But the story got a lot juicier than that in the retelling.

The part that thrilled all the kids in elementary was that Nora Spinell had hung herself naked, and that her head had popped off, and also that—kind of a combo deal—she'd jumped off that balcony in her nightgown, actually, but her head had still popped off, letting her body slip down out of it to the floor, the nightgown up there for the husband when he got home late that night, the head rolling around everywhere.

The embellishments didn't stop there, either.

Tad and Tia got involved, of course.

The part that finally started giving some of the third graders nightmares, which is when the principal had to step in, was that the water in that bathtub had been boiling, and that Tad and Tia had risen from it after they were dead and run barefoot all through the house playing hide-and-seek, their skin peeling off. The proof that they'd done this was that when the cops got there to carry the husband into the white van that would take him away, there were little footprints all over the house, still with white tufts of bubble popping in them.

Of course the husband, this dad, had gone crazy, never got a name, just got carted off into a white van.

How this killed Halloween was that the murders happened the night *before* Halloween, meaning, by Halloween morning, it still wasn't clear if Nora Spinell had done this, if the dad had done this, or if somebody still out there had done it.

So, last-minute trunk 'r treating in the church parking lot, maybe because hallowed ground was less prone to horror.

Each costumed kid carrying two or three bags of candy to sell back to the dentist next week.

Charlotte was a hippie that year—round glasses, home-made bell-bottoms, her fingers always saying *Peace, man*—and Murphy was her favorite animal, a chipmunk, which was mostly face paint and the way she acted, always sniffing everything.

Yes, Charlotte remembers.

"That was *this* house?" she says to Murphy, being vague because the twins are still right there.

Murphy keeps her Dracula harlequin face pleasant, as if they're just talking about nothing.

"We drove by here once a few years ago for the community garage sale," Murphy says, "and my dad wouldn't come to this driveway, even though we'd been looking for a canoe and there was a canoe right here."

"Canoe?" Desi asks.

Charlotte blinks the heat from her eyes.

Murphy's dad, the homicide detective. The one, they found out later, who had been first on-scene that night. Which maybe had something to do with the sea of vodka he was swimming through these last few years?

"So you're not sure," Charlotte says, trying to find a ray of maybe.

Murphy steps neatly to the twins and then behind them, cups her hands over Ronald's ears.

Charlotte steps in, covers Desi's ears from the front.

"Who is this 'she' they're talking about, then?" Murphy asks, boring her eyes right into Charlotte's.

"That mom was, she was disturbed or something," Charlotte says, insists, "not—not evil. Not still *here*."

"Then why are they seeing a woman, not a man?" Murphy asks. "If they're just trying to scare themselves, don't they conjure up a tall scary *man* to do that? And if they wanted a playmate, it'd be a kid, wouldn't it? Or a—a *dinosaur*?"

Charlotte looks past them, to the part of the kitchen she can see.

"I can't do this," she says, Desi's little hands wrapped around her wrists, her big eyes turned up, waiting for the babysitter to make everything right.

"This?" Murphy says.

"Here," Charlotte says. "I'm going to—I'm going to call them. The parents."

"Smart," Murphy says, releasing Ronald's ears. Instead of letting him go, though, she hikes him up onto her hip, which gets Desi reaching up. Charlotte pulls her up as well.

"It's nothing, nothing," Charlotte coos to her, and to Ronald too. "Just, I'm going to call your mommy and daddy, okay? I have to ask them a question."

Ronald nods yes to this. *Yes yes yes, thank you.*

"They're going to say you're scaring yourself," Murphy says. "That it's the season, that it's a big house."

"I don't care," Charlotte tells her. "Long as they come right the fuck home," then, to the twins, "Excuse my bad mouth."

The four of them trail back into the kitchen and Charlotte dials the number on the notepad into her cell. No answer. Then the next number. It rings and rings, and finally the line opens.

"Mr. Wilbanks?" Charlotte says.

He's not the one she wanted to have to explain this all to, but he's who she's got.

Or not.

"Is this a good time?" she asks when he doesn't say hello.

But there is something.

"Shh, shh," she says to Murphy and Ronald, rattling and crackling through the contents of the pantry. Murphy looks up and Charlotte steps over, switches Desi across to Murphy's free arm. Murphy, a trouper, takes the weight.

Charlotte steps into the living room and squats down, covering her other ear, because there *is* something coming through the cell, isn't there?

It's . . . it's other kids?

But they're far from that receiver. They're laughing and—and *splashing*.

Charlotte stands, shaking her head no, looking all around for Murphy, just so she doesn't have to be hearing all of this alone.

There's just the lizard, watching her.

She's hearing back into the past. Into . . . into eleven years ago. Tad and Tia, bath time. Eleven years ago a mom, on her way upstairs to check on the kids—to *drown* the kids—has stopped to pick up the phone ringing on the wall.

The reason she's not saying anything is that she's listening. To Charlotte.

Charlotte drops her cell, backs fast enough away from it that she catches the couch with the bends of her knees and falls down into it, then jerks forward when she's sure a shadowy form is about to rise up *behind* the couch, catch her in its wet arms.

Murphy's right: she's let herself get spooked. Also—of course—Murphy's standing in the doorway for this performance, Desi still on her hip, Ronald beside her, trying to open a mini candy bar.

"We broke into the Halloween candy," Murphy confesses, shrugging one shoulder like she does.

"What does she look like?" Charlotte says to Ronald. "This—the woman who tells you where the funny places are?"

"The Grey Mommy?" Ronald asks back.

Charlotte's stomach drops.

"You can't go again," Desi says, and Charlotte tracks up to her.

"Why not, love?" Charlotte says.

"Go where?" Murphy asks.

"Because you're already there," Ronald says, and bites into the candy bar.

"So they didn't answer?" Murphy says maybe thirty seconds later, about the Wilbankses.

The twins are parked in front of the medieval episode of *SpongeBob*, which Desi volunteered was off-limits because of name-calling but Murphy said was a special treat for the night before Halloween, like the candy.

Charlotte and Murphy are in the kitchen, the water in the sink running to hide their voices.

"*She* answered," Charlotte says.

"'She' as in—" Murphy says, throttling an imaginary kid in her hands.

"I'm serious, Murph," Charlotte says, licking her dry lips.

"And, the boy, Ronald, he said I was 'already there,' whatever that means."

Murphy reaches across, touches Charlotte's shoulder like confirming she's not anywhere else.

"I don't know what he meant," Charlotte says. "It creeps me the hell out, though."

"Okay," Murphy says, messing with the faucet's handle, going from hot to cold and back again. "But, but this . . . this whatever-she-is, she only talks to the boy, right? And when nobody's around?"

"He was born dead," Charlotte whispers. "I think that's the connection."

Murphy holds Charlotte's eyes about this, leans back to reconsider Ronald on the couch. "But he's all right now?" she asks.

"It's not his fault, obviously."

"So we just, what?" Murphy says. "Stay in the same room with him until the parental units are back, right? Problem solved? If he's the only one she talks to, and if she only talks to him when he's alone . . . ?"

"She's getting them to, to take *shortcuts* through the house," Charlotte says. "I think she wants to trap them between places or something. That's got to be what it's building towards."

"You know how out there this sounds."

"I wouldn't believe me either."

"I believe *you* believe it," Murphy volunteers.

"That really helps," Charlotte says back. "Thanks. Humor the crazy girlfriend."

"If it's real to you, then it's real to me," Murphy continues. "So, evil killer mom-lady—the, the Grey Mother or whatever."

"Nora. Nora Spinell."

"So, Lady Spinell is coming for the little angels busy getting brainwashed by Sir SpongeBob in there. But . . ." Murphy draws it out until Charlotte has to look up for her big delivery: "But not on *our* watch, right?"

"It's my watch," Charlotte says. "I just—I can't leave knowing she's still here."

"Because you're that good of a babysitter."

"Because I can't let her do it again."

She looks to the water steaming in the sink.

"She can't hold them under though, right?" Murphy finally says. "Ghosts can't do that, can they?"

"She can lock them in the dryer, or a cabinet nobody ever opens, or a cardboard box under a car in the garage, I don't know."

Murphy considers this, gauges Charlotte, then nods, finally says, "So, what's plan B, then?"

"We leave."

"That's really next in line for solving this, SAT girl?" Murphy asks.

"We can't call the cops," Charlotte says. "I mean, we can, but it'll be a shitshow."

"A shitshow with authorities here," Murphy says. "With guns."

"Would your dad help?" Charlotte eurekas, ramping off Murphy's "guns."

Murphy eyeballs around for a clock—10:38—says, "For this place, yeah. He might call in a favor or two."

"But?"

"But it's after three o'clock in the afternoon," Murphy

says, crossing the kitchen for the landline on the wall. "I'll try, cool?"

She stops with her hand to the phone, Charlotte's eyes boring into the back of that hand.

"What are you—what are you *doing*?" Charlotte asks.

Murphy comes around, her face blank, her eyes moving from Charlotte's to the twins, watching her from the couch as well, everybody sort of holding their breath.

"Oh yeah," Murphy says, her face cracking into a guilty smile, her other hand palming her cell up, "my cell's almost dead, yeah?"

She pulls it back to her, thumbs into it, and reads the number aloud as she punches it into the landline's clunky buttons.

She turns around, holds the phone sideways from her ear so Charlotte can hear. It rings and rings, and when it shunts to voice mail she hangs up softly, shrugs apology to Charlotte.

In reply, Charlotte recites Murphy's home number. The same one they've had since forever. The one Murphy just had to look up.

"That's because you just heard me say it," Murphy says, fundamentally offended. "Nobody knows phone numbers anymore, doll. Here"—she swipes higher through her contacts, stops at one only she can see—"tell me yours."

She lays her phone facedown on the island like hiding Charlotte's own number from her.

"This is stupid," Charlotte says. "Did your dad ever say anything about that night?"

"Because he wanted me to become a raging alcoholic too?" Murphy says. "He probably told my mom, I guess. They used to be all hunky-dory and share-bear like that. Not good to keep stuff inside. Unless, you know, your big secret is that you like girls, gasp!"

Charlotte squeezes the side of Murphy's gloved hand, says, "I know I ruined your life."

Murphy squeezes back, says, "You saved my life."

"Don't blame your mom," Charlotte says. "She just—she wants grandkids."

"So do I," Murphy says. "I mean, someday. But kids first. That's the right order, isn't it? You can't just jump to the good part, can you?"

"Can't have your pudding if you don't eat your meat," Charlotte recites, their joke since elementary, when they found that record in her mom's closet.

"I wish my mom was cool like your mom, though," Murphy adds. "They could have coffee, talk about their carpet-muncher daughters."

"*Shh*," Charlotte says, tilting her head to the idea of the twins. "Anyway, you think it's easy being the family's official two-spirit, whatever the hell that even is? You should see the way she trots me out at pow-wows. I mean, no, you shouldn't."

"*She'd* come get us, wouldn't she?" Murphy asks. "Your mom? No questions asked, isn't that her policy?"

It is, yes.

"I told her this was an easy night, though," Charlotte says, "a nothing night. That it wouldn't interfere with the SATs tomorrow morning." She shrugs, adds, "And . . . she's at work, too."

"You can always put it in the scales," Murphy says. "Let them decide for you."

"Scales?"

"How mad she'll be about messing her shift up weighed against how happy she'll be that you're not freaked out, which—"

"Messes up my SATs," Charlotte finishes, not able to resist this logic. "But," she says, feeling it out as she goes, "she'd see Desi's costume, wouldn't she? And then she'd park on the couch, wait to give her big lecture to the Wilbankses when they get back. Cultural appropriation, misrepresentation, training the next generation of colonizers, Manifest Destiny never really stopped, blah blah whatever, you know how she can be."

"Oh, yeah," Murphy deadpans. "*That* old speech. I tell you about the crime-scene photos my dad tried to scare me back into the closet with?"

"I'm sorry," Charlotte says.

Murphy waves it off, says, "So, my dad's zero help, as usual, your mom's *too* much help—"

"As usual."

"And we still have one hour before the parents get back," Murphy says. "Where's that leave us?"

"Not here," Charlotte says. "That's the main part. I'll figure out the rest later. Along with my new job."

"Your what?"

"Nobody's going to hire the spooky babysitter. The one who doesn't have any proof. The one who freaked out for no reason. The one who took two six-year-olds out into the cold until midnight and fed them sugar to keep them awake."

"Good point," Murphy says. "Where do we go when we leave?" she asks then. "I mean, where isn't going to freak the kids out, make them think we're kidnappers? Do we just sit on the lawn until the parents get back, say the house smelled like it had a gas leak or something?"

"I want to be all the way off the property."

"You bussed here?"

Charlotte nods, says, "You?"

Murphy presents her velvet shoes, curled up at the toe, one red, one black.

"So we're hoofing it," she says.

"The park?" Charlotte tries. "We can sit in the rocket, right? That's safe. Like a jail cell."

"Kind of cold," Murphy says.

"We'll make it fun," Charlotte says. "I'll bundle them up, you'll make hot chocolate. I'm sure there's a thermos in here somewhere."

"Marshmallows?"

"Bring the whole bag," Charlotte tells her, and lets Murphy's hand slip out of hers.

When the kids are still zoned out on *SpongeBob*, jaws slack, legs not even swinging, Charlotte ducks into the bathroom, since the one at the park is probably locked, this late. The toilet is still a jet engine, one you don't want to be sitting anywhere near. Washing her hands, she looks up, draws her breath in sharp: she's still got Desi's tights on her head somehow, the two black legs almost matching up with Murphy's fool's cap. Raising her hand to touch one of the hanging-down, empty legs, she remembers Murphy running her hand down along that slackness as well, only—she pauses the sensation as well as she can—only: feeling the oh-so-seductive texture of a pair of tights while wearing *gloves*?

Charlotte dials back in her head to be sure Murphy actually *did* have those stupid gloves on, and: yes, for certain, for sure, one hundred percent, zero doubt. In this slice of a memory, too, Murphy's mouth is right to Charlotte's left ear, the lips moving in what should be the most secret secret, but there's no whisper, there's just her lips, moving, like, like—

Charlotte peels the tights off all at once, hangs them on the towel rack and pets them smooth with her *bare* hands, watches them until the feet stop swinging.

"You're losing it," she says to herself, her voice creaky, and finds herself getting lost again, this time in the tights' *stillness*. Because, because if she just stays right here, stays right in this moment, then nothing bad can happen, right? Or, nothing she has to know about. Everything bad, that's the stuff that's going on outside this bathroom door. Not in here with her.

But she's the babysitter, isn't she? She says it out loud, to make it true: "I'm the babysitter." It's an hourly job, sure, but it's a responsibility, too. And if she can save Desi and Ronald from whatever's going on here, that'll prove that Arthur sleep-walking into the street was a fluke, just a one-in-a-million spot of bad luck, of the almost-worst luck. If she can save Desi and Ronald, though, it'll be like Arthur never sleepwalked out into the street at all, and then she can go off to college because she *wants* to, not because she's running away from a scene she shouldn't have been able to walk away from.

She does her best to wipe all the tension from her face, blinks her eyes twice fast, holds her chin high, and opens the door, steps back out into the living room, SpongeBob's machine-gun laughter going off right beside her, and . . . and—

The twins are gone?

No, they're hiding.

Under the couch cushions.

She just catches Desi's faux moccasin sliding under a couch cushion, and for a slipping-away moment she can make out Ronald's face sideways under that same cushion, like this is the big trick their mom warned about, like the couch is the one hiding place nobody ever finds them, because nobody but a skinny six-year-old could ever fit there.

Charlotte shakes her head no to Ronald, that this isn't funny, and steps ahead to stop this game before it starts, but then Ronald pulls the couch cushion down over his face, is gone, and it's less like he's having to scrunch under, more like he's . . . stepping down *into* a different space. A hidden stairway, a tunnel, the top of a slide.

Charlotte's running now, sliding to her knees on the thick rug, banging her hip on the coffee table, shoving her arm as deep into the couch as she can.

All she comes back with is a nurse's cap.

She peels the cushion back. There's only the box-spring part—the bottom of the couch, a thin silver bracelet with a single charm on it about to slip down into the crack. The charm is a megaphone, for the cheerleader Mrs. Wilbanks must have been once upon a time.

"No!" Charlotte screams. "No no no fucking *no!*"

She stands, her fingers hooked under the front of the couch, and tips it onto its back. Maybe she can catch the kids sliding down or up whatever tunnel they're in.

It doesn't work like that, though.

The couch tumps back halfway, catching on an end table or decorative footstool or whatever, and there's just dust bunnies and hardwood underneath, and one lone Cheerio.

"*Ronald!*" Charlotte yells, aiming her voice upstairs, her hands balled into fists. "*Desiree!*"

They don't answer, but she's pretty sure there's a rattle up there, metal on metal, a loose sound . . . yes: that night-sky shower curtain that matches the vinyl poster in Ronald's bedroom. Meaning they're in his shower. Or, one of them got spit up there, anyway.

Charlotte steps over the coffee table to run up there but stops, turns slowly to the kitchen.

Shouldn't Murphy have burst out to see what's wrong?

Charlotte counts to three, trying to make this make sense.

"Murph?" she finally says.

No answer.

Charlotte tries to watch the kitchen doorway while at the same time checking every shadow and corner of the living room, not sure if seeing a Dracula harlequin standing alongside the curtains is what she wants or the last thing she needs.

The bathroom, then? Already. No. Okay. The utility, then? The garage? The—the walk-in pantry? Yes. Murphy's looking for marshmallows, of course. And the sink's still running anyway, because that's how Murphy makes hot chocolate: from the tap, not from water heated up on the stove or in the microwave. Maybe she didn't even hear Charlotte calling for the kids. Maybe all the canned goods and bags of noodles in that pantry are muffling the rest of the house. And she's got that stupid cap on anyway.

"Murph?" Charlotte says again, crossing the living room now, giving the television and the coffee table wide berth. When she draws even with the swung-back bathroom door she nearly dies right there, but that's only her own reflection in the mirror.

The doorway into the kitchen, though, there's no way to both step through *and* watch behind her. Not without walking into who knows what. She does it anyway, latching onto the doorframe and pivoting in less like a soldier, more like a fraidy cat.

The water is still running, billowing up steam that's fogging the glass-fronted cabinets.

"Murphy?" Charlotte says with less confidence, stepping into the heat to quiet the water, the heat from the sink instantly clinging to her wrist.

The pantry light isn't even on. Because the marshmallows were right there, just past the doorway, on a high enough rack to keep them away from grubby six-year-old fingers. But now they're hanging half off the rack, the bag torn open, spilling white down onto the tile floor, the quietest, sweetest avalanche.

"*Murphy?*" Charlotte says again, with all the control she has left.

She can see that the utility doorway is dark, that the window in the door to the garage isn't lit up, and—and where else can Murphy even be?

Back in the box, some part of her says before she can stop it.

The jack-in-the-box.

In the same instant, Charlotte asks herself how long *did* it take to make her way down the stairs when the lights blinked?

The question makes her slap at her left ear like Murphy's lips are still there. Not whispering but gulping. And— Charlotte can feel this now too, can remember that her left hand was wrapped around to Murphy's right shoulder blade—Murphy was shorter than her for this, wasn't she? Just like she most definitely *isn't*?

It doesn't make sense. Not even a little.

Charlotte turns, runs across the living room, swaying her back in because she knows there's going to be something behind her, that it's been shadowing her all night. She slams into the closet door by the entry, holds onto the doorknob like something's about to drag her away.

In this new quiet she hears it as distinct as her own slamming heart: *click*.

In one motion she turns, flings that closet door open, not remotely ready for anything but having to face it anyway.

It's still just the same jackets and overcoats as before. The jack-in-the-box on the high shelf.

"Fuck you!" Charlotte screams up at it, and hauls it down, shoves the stupid clown back in as deep as she can and jams the flap down over it. Then she collapses to her knees, hugging that box, muttering apologies to it. Her chest and breath are crying but her eyes are dry, her mind blank.

"Charlotte?" a small voice asks, bringing her back.

She cranks her head up, looks through her hair.

It's Desi and Ronald, holding hands at the top of the stairs. Both of them are crying, scared, the high schooler in charge of them losing all control.

Charlotte opens her arms, meets them halfway, goes to her knees to hug them to her.

"Don't be scared, don't be scared," she tells them, her left hand finding a right shoulder blade again in a way that slows her thinking down. "We're—we've got to go down to the park. Or next door, okay? Can you do that for me?"

"What about Murph?" Ronald asks.

"She'll be okay," Charlotte says, looking around at where they are on the stairs. If it did take her two hours or whatever to get down here when the lights blinked, then this is where she would have been, right?

"We have to put on our warmies," Desi says, standing like a brave little adventurer, ready to do this.

"Just," Charlotte says, letting Ronald go as well when he stands. "Do you have sleeping bags? Just bring those, I can wrap you in those. Or blankets. We don't have time, I'm sorry."

"Is something wrong with the house?" Desi says, looking around.

"Nothing," Charlotte lies, checking all around for a flicker of motion.

"My sleeping bag's in his room," Desi says, afraid of messing up.

"I was building a fort," Ronald adds, standing up for her like a brother should.

"Go, go," Charlotte says, ushering them the rest of the way up the stairs. "I've just got to—to write your mom a note, okay? Fast, I'm counting to ten, *go*."

They scurry down to Ronald's room, the nurse and the Indian princess, and right when they duck in, Charlotte steps into the off-limits master bedroom for the second time, beelines to Mrs. Wilbanks's vanity.

@ the park, just call! she writes in loopy blue ink, then tags

a jaunty happy face on the end of it like code, like whispering that everything's fine, it's all all right, don't worry that I've taken your two young children out to a dark place late at night without permission.

"Five . . . six!" she calls out, and steps back into the hall holding the Post-it, ready to stick it to the front door—the *outside* of the front door. "Eight . . . nine . . . nine and a half!" she says around the corner, not quite as loud, and on what would have been *ten*, Desi and Ronald burst out trailing blankets and sleeping bags, two perfect little kids.

Two perfect kids framed by an open office door at the other end of the hall.

"Here, here," Charlotte says, spreading her arms for them to come to her, and their little legs and little arms and intense eyes are all focused on exactly that. Until Ronald steps on Desi's trailing sleeping bag and they go down in a pile.

Charlotte smiles—this is a live-action *Saturday Evening Post* cover, pretty much—but then, just when they're untangling, banging into this wall then that one, one of those walls turns out to be the linen closet door. It swings open, just needed a touch, the red Featherweight vacuum cleaner's long handle tipping out against the opposite wall like a crossbar in front of them.

"Charlotte!" either Ronald or Desi screams.

"It's okay!" Charlotte yells back, already wrestling with the stupid little vacuum, but when she lifts it, the business end hooks under one of the shelves and all the board games and sheets avalanche down.

Charlotte kicks and pushes, can fucking *do* this, but: "You came in through the bathtub, didn't you?" she says, awareness washing down her face.

Ronald's eyes go big.

"I was under his bed," Desi says.

"Go back that way," Charlotte tells them. "You've got to anyway, right?"

The silence from the other side of the linen closet door means . . . it means that this stupid vacuum cleaner, it just saved them from—from whatever hell Charlotte's already in, from only coming through one way, not taking the return trip.

"I'll meet you down there!" she says under the linen closet door, and the twins scamper away, either with or without their sleeping bags, who cares anymore. Getting out is more important than hypothermia.

Charlotte stands, slams the linen closet door, and then checks it hard with her hip, telling it she's had about enough from it tonight. It stays shut.

She runs to the railing, sees the twins crawling up from the half-overturned couch, their hair even more mussed and cute, somehow.

"Stay there!" she says to them, and they look up to her.

"Where are you going?" Ronald asks.

"The way I should have before," Charlotte says, and is already turning, already walking into the inky darkness of Desi's My Little Pony room.

Instead of turning the light on, she just stands over the burst-open oversize pink beanbag.

She knows what has to have happened to Murphy: there

was what Ronald and Desi call a funny place in the kitchen, probably right in the pantry doorway—it's dark, secret enough—and Murphy stepped right into it, only had that bag of marshmallows to hold on to. Meaning she's still in there, is falling through the hidden spaces of this wrong house. And she didn't have anybody to hold her hand, tell her not to open her eyes.

"This will work," Charlotte tells herself, about the beanbag.

It has to. It can't have shut yet. Please.

She drops to her knees, scoops as many of the spider eggs back into the beanbag as she can, because maybe they're part of it, maybe they're fuel pellets for the door to open under her.

"I'll be right down!" she calls to the twins, her voice not faltering. Then, to herself, adds *with Murphy*. She'll tumble out of the water heater closet or the dryer or the couch cushions holding Murphy's gloved hand, and then the four of them will run and run and run.

She steps in, works her feet down through the spider eggs to the solid ground, the floor of Desi's bedroom, and then she sees herself doubled in the dresser mirror—just a silhouette flecked with white dots. She nods to her reflection and sits down, working herself in until she has to lie back in it like a body bag.

This is stupid, the traitorous, sane part of her mind is telling her.

But this is the only way, she says back with all necessary curtness, and reaches down for the zipper, pulls it up all at once. She covers her lips with her hand before drawing a breath in, and then, because this is part of it, she makes herself close her eyes.

The darkness is a crawling darkness.

In it, she again feels Murphy's lips brushing her ear, Murphy not even having to lean over or bend down to do this, the lights around them dialed down to almost nothing, Charlotte's left hand nosing through the white interior of the beanbag on instinct, like wrapping around Murphy's back to pull her in, hold her there—

Charlotte stiffens, bucks, the memory of Murphy's mouth being forced away, but . . . but pushing Murphy away wrenches Charlotte's jaw up. The whole side of her head. Because Murphy isn't whispering or kissing, these aren't sweet nothings at intimate range. Her mouth is going up and down because she's *suckling*. She's drinking Charlotte in, taking her out through the ear, or the porous bone right behind the ear, and the reason she's not having to lean over to do this is she's standing a step lower on the stairs, and *not* in a fool's cap, Charlotte would have fabric tentacles in her face if Murphy had that on, meaning, meaning this had to have happened during that hour or whatever when the lights blinked—Charlotte sucks air in and the spun dryness of beanbag beads lodges in her throat. She gags, coughs, sits up on reflex against the backside of her soft pink coffin but can only writhe against it.

And then, moving slowly like it wants her to feel this, one of those beads, beans, whatever, one of them still on her lip, it crackles open. Sharp tiny legs feel out, and all around her, her arms, her stomach, her neck, her ankles—the spider eggs are hatching all over her, all around her, the inside of the beanbag skittering into a thousand-thousand desperate legs.

Charlotte rolls hard to the right in a complete panic, thunks into the dresser, and then she shoulders and kicks back the other way, screaming, hitting, convulsing, gagging, spitting—dying, she knows it.

The tiny spiders crawl into her ears, across her eyeballs, are in her hair right by her scalp, are between her fingers, are up her pants leg, are, are—

She forces her hands up to her face, covers it like that matters, and makes herself breathe, breathe.

At the end she's sobbing. At the end she's lying in a beanbag she zipped shut over herself in a dark room in a house she doesn't really know, with two scared kids listening downstairs.

"Charlotte?" Desi's saying from the living room, her voice so far away.

Charlotte latches onto it, uses it to pull herself back, her fingers finally pinching the zipper tab up from the darkness.

She stands, the unhatched and weightless spider eggs raining down off her.

For a bad moment she's sure her reflection isn't waiting for her in the mirror, but her vision settles. She's really here.

"I'm okay!" she calls to the twins. "Turn *SpongeBob* back on!"

Dutifully, Bikini Bottom washes up the stairs.

Charlotte steps free of the beanbag, looks back to it for the baby spiders she knows aren't going to be there.

But they were. It wasn't just in her head.

That's a dead entrance now, or for the moment, but that doesn't mean a little of the other side doesn't leak through all the same.

Okay, she tells herself.

Murphy's in here somewhere, in the house, but so are the twins. She can do this in stages: kids out the door first, then come back, dig into every dark corner for her girlfriend.

"I'm coming!" she calls down from the top of the stairs, and—no: when she latches onto the handrail, it's slick with . . . bubbles?

Charlotte pulls her hand back, crashes down three steps at a time, holding her arms close.

Desi is on the couch, hypnotized by Sir SpongeBob, and Ronald, he's doing what he's been wanting to do all night: sitting hunched over that jack-in-the-box again, his head turned to hear every click he's cranking up.

"No!" Charlotte says, sweeping him up, away from that, then holding her hand out for Desi too. "We're going down to the park," she tells them, trying to sound more confident than she is. Less shaken.

"What about—?" Ronald says.

"*We're going!*" Charlotte says, hauling their light little selves across the living room to the front door.

Which is, of course, deadbolted.

"Shit!" Charlotte says, about to collapse. She sets Ronald down gently, parks him by Desi, and she digs in her pockets for the key, the key, the key, knows it's going to be upstairs in the spider nest beanbag.

She comes up with it. It's the single most glorious key in the whole history of keys.

And it fits, and it turns.

Before she hauls the door open, though, she enters the temporary code on the security keypad thing. It swallows those four numbers, blinks green twice.

"We're, we're going to the—" she says, taking Desi's hand, already holding Ronald's, and she steps them over the threshold feeling . . . not heroic, but like a survivor. Like they're the lucky ones, getting out when they shouldn't have. Maybe because of that, because it doesn't feel like she earned this, the sky looks phony somehow, like there's no depth.

Or?

Is it phony?

There's not usually a ringed planet hanging up there so close, is there? And now there's more . . . not texture, but *contour*, like empty space itself has ripples.

Charlotte, still pulling Desi and Ronald ahead, brushes her face into that ringed planet.

It's painted on. It's painted on some, some layer or—

Charlotte holds tight to Desi's hand, even tighter than she was, and brings her other hand up to this sky her forehead is most definitely pushing against.

Plastic? Vinyl?

What?

This isn't the sky, it isn't space, it's the nighttime sky printed *on* something. On an oversized wall poster, on a shower curtain hung all around the house, hemming it in.

Charlotte grabs it to pull it away, but, while it will wrinkle and fold, it won't pinch up quite enough for her to *grab*. She pushes against it and it gives, but only so far.

"What is happening?" she says.

Ronald reaches his hand out like to touch it, but Charlotte guides his hand back down.

"I don't, this doesn't—" she says, looking back into the living room, which, bubbles on the handrail aside, and not taking into account all the secret passageways and the beanbag filled with spiders, is still a functional *house*. Unlike everything outside the house, evidently.

"Are you still in it?" Ronald says up to her, and Charlotte looks down at him, trying to let his words make sense.

"I want to watch *SpongeBob*," Desi says, her lower lip trembling.

Charlotte steps back, closes the door gently, twists the key in the deadbolt and leaves it there, then uses her temporary code to tell the alarm not to worry, they're fine. It's a lie, of course. Maybe the worst she's ever told.

Desi scampers back to the couch they must have rolled back forward—twins working together—and Ronald is already looking around for the jack-in-the-box.

Charlotte lifts him up, settles him down on the couch with Desi.

"Count to twenty," she tells them. "It's a slow race. Whoever can do it the slowest gets a marshmallow, okay?"

"Are you playing?" Ronald asks.

"I've got to check something in the kitchen," Charlotte says, standing, the television casting her shadow down over the couch.

"Onnnne . . . two-woo . . ." she starts, stretching the numbers out to show how slow they're supposed to go.

"*Three*-eee . . ." Desi says, picking this game up instantly.

Ronald is looking around her to the television in that blank, hungry way kids have. Good enough.

Charlotte gathers her hair, ties it into a one-minute bun at the back of her head, and steps into the kitchen. Not for the marshmallows, but the garage door.

She steps out into that concrete coolness, flicks the light on and makes sure the chest freezer's just the chest freezer, the Audi just another rich-people second car. Maybe all the dangerous tools are on their pegboard, maybe not, but she can't get caught up thinking about that.

She feels the wall beside her for the big button and the door grinds up on its loose chain, the whole garage shuddering. When it's done Charlotte steps down into the empty space.

Through the two-car-wide garage door space is . . . either the nighttime sky or a print of it. She steps gingerly around the kitty-littered oil stain, walks purposefully into the garage door's sensor, making the light above and behind her blink with danger, strobing her shadow onto the slick concrete at her feet.

"Please," she says, and pushes her hand out into what she wants to be coolness, emptiness, nothingness.

It's slick, taut vinyl.

The whole nightscape wavers and stretches, would look good as the backdrop of a high school play, probably. But it sucks as the outside she wants to blast into.

"Are they home?" Ronald says from the doorway behind her. "I heard the garage."

Charlotte shakes her head no and looks around the garage, around the garage . . . *yes*: the high window on the other side of the Audi.

"She said this is what can happen," Ronald says, quietly.

"She?" Charlotte asks, trying not to scare him.

"The Grey Mommy. If you don't go back through before it—before it shuts again, then you're stuck between the houses."

"I don't—" Charlotte says, her plea to a six-year-old. "If, if this is happening," she says, "how did she say you get out?"

Ronald's lower lip comes out a bit and he blinks fast.

"It's okay, it's okay," she tells him. "I'm figuring it out. Just—just stay right there, 'kay?"

She hauls a blue and white cooler down from its wire shelf, plunks it down against the wall as a stepping stool and comes up to the window's level in one shaky step. The window opens easy, wasn't even locked. Dried wasp bodies hiss down and she flinches back, looks up to the nest she just crunched the top of the window into.

"I'm just seeing if it's cold," she calls back to Ronald—it's the worst explanation ever—and forces her hand through fast, punching right through the screen.

More vinyl.

"*No!*" she screams, and scrambles down, goes straight to the pegboard, comes down with a pruning saw with a bowed-up back like a witch's index finger. She looks back to Ronald, who has Desi beside and kind of behind him, now that the babysitter's suddenly got weapons in play.

"I got to twenty," Desi says.

"Good," Charlotte says, "you're amazing, both of you are. Now I've just got to—"

She runs at the vinyl print hanging over the garage doorway and slashes down with the saw, tearing a gash open.

"Yes!" she says, and drops the saw, finds the flap she tore, pulls at it with all her weight, ripping the sky open all the way down to the concrete.

Behind it is the same thing. More vinyl. More ringed planets and cartoon stars.

She falls to her knees, her hands in her hair, her bun already falling out.

"Do you want me to close it?" Ronald asks.

Charlotte nods and the door grinds down, burps to a stop when she's still in the sensor. She scooches back and Ronald presses the button again, then one more time. The door comes down right in front of her, like severing her from anything outside the house. Like being sure she knows that.

Breathe in, breathe out.

"You *both* get marshmallows," she says to the twins, and walks purposefully back to them, taking them both by the hand. When Ronald isn't fast enough she hauls him up onto her hip. She deposits him by the pantry, reaches up for the bag.

Desi squats to pinch up one of the spilled marshmallows but it strings out. She yelps, tries to shake it off.

"Yeah, we only want the good ones," Charlotte says, and steps over for a paper towel, cleans Desi's fingers one by one.

"I'm sorry," Desi says.

"You're not going to cut us with the saw, are you?" Ronald asks, his chin pruning up again.

Charlotte's lips tighten the same as his. She shakes her head *no, never*, pulls them both to her, says, "Your babysitter's not being a very good babysitter, is she?"

Neither of them know what to answer but they both flinch in Charlotte's arms when the phone on the counter rings. It's Murphy's guitar-carnival ringtone. Murphy's left-behind cell.

"It's for you," Ronald says.

Charlotte shakes her head no but picks it up all the same, thumbing the line open, drawing the screen up to her ear and then shaking her bun loose over it like that can keep this private.

At first there's nothing, then . . . muttering. Clinking. Silverware? No. Glasses.

"What did you say she was?" a man is asking, his voice breathy. "Was it dots, or, you know, bows and arrows?"

"They don't do dots *plural*," a woman says back. "Just one, right here."

"Like a bullseye for an arrow," the man says with a chuckle.

"You're not supposed to ask that anyway," the woman says back to him, and now Charlotte makes that voice: Mrs. Wilbanks. This is them at . . . at some bar, maybe? They're getting drinks after whatever their date was. They're discussing their new babysitter's skin color.

"I'm not supposed to ask *her*," Mr. Wilbanks says. "I'm asking you. She's not Mexican, is she?"

"Because Alfred and Maria are?" Mrs. Wilbanks says back—the Lopezes, Arthur's parents.

"I mean, maybe that's why they gave her such a good recommendation."

"*Seventeen* is what she is," Mrs. Wilbanks says.

"Should we check on her?"

"It would probably wake the kids," Mrs. Wilbanks says, stopping to take a drink it sounds like. "And if we call we'll just sound paranoid."

"Because we are paranoid," Mr. Wilbanks says. "We can be paranoid. It's our kids. We can be anything we want."

"*I'm right here!*" Charlotte screams into the phone, startling the twins. Charlotte turns away from them, says into Murphy's phone, "Come home now! We need you! There's something going on!"

"I told her about your little lizard," Mrs. Wilbanks says, oblivious.

"Little?" Mr. Wilbanks purrs back, his lips probably close to his wife's neck.

"*Come home!*" Charlotte screams louder into the phone, one of the kids actively blubbering now, but this is more important.

"Is that Mommy?" Desi asks, reaching up, her arm straightening out she's so short.

"Bad connection," Charlotte says, then, one last try: "Mrs. Wilbanks! Mr. Wilbanks! This is Charlotte, the babysitter!"

"How about we find a place to pull over on the way home," Mr. Wilbanks is saying. "It'll only cost us twenty dollars. I'd pay a lot more than that to . . ."

"*No!*" Charlotte screams to them. "Come straight home! Please! I don't want the money, just get here fast!"

"Second stall at the car wash?" Mrs. Wilbanks says back, her voice dialed down just for her husband, not the whole bar. "Is that lightbulb still out, you think?"

"It can be," Mr. Wilbanks says, and then the phone's dead.

Charlotte holds it out in front of her to make sense of this and there's a thin line of bubbles coming up through the mic, the speaker.

She drops it in the sink, which Murphy must have had the plug in when the water was on. The phone plunks in, swims sharply to the side, comes to a rest faceup, the screen flickering once then shorting out.

"Murph isn't going to like that," Ronald says, wiping his right eye—*he* was the one crying.

"Murphy," Charlotte corrects before she can stop herself. "I'm the only one who calls her Murph."

She looks down, hates herself a little more, even: Ronald's eyes are about to spill over again, even more.

"Is that Squidward I hear?" she says in her most cheery voice, and pushes on her nose, drooping it down, making her eyes all hangdog. It gets Desi to smile a bashful smile, Ronald to look away like maybe he *wants* to smile. She'll take it.

She leads them back into the living room, parks them on the couch, deposits the marshmallow bag between them.

"Now don't go crazy on these," she says, eyebrows serious.

They both nod, little liars.

"And, and," she says, kneeling down in front of them for all their attention, "this is going to be a *new* game, now."

Desi's dull eyes and Ronald's suspicious ones lock on hers.

"*The floor is lava*," Charlotte tells them in hushed confidence, reaching down to the rug with her palm, making the hissing sound herself and drawing her hand back up fast. "This means stay on the couch, right? Do you know how to play this one?"

"You're already burning!" Desi screams with delight, standing, pointing.

"Ah, you're right!" Charlotte squeals, and comes up fast, steps up onto the very edge of the coffee table, looks around for what's next: the overstuffed chair.

From there, with both kids watching, she's just able to jump across to the entryway. She hops on one socked foot while holding the other, like she got a bit singed.

"This is water," she calls back to them about the tile, lowering her fake-burned foot to it. "It feels so good."

Desi laughs and laughs. Ronald is still considering this.

"Now, I don't want your parents to get back in thirty minutes and ask me how did the kids' clothes get all black and ashy, okay? We don't want it to smell like a barbecue in here, do we?"

"Barbecue!" Desi says.

In spite of himself, Ronald smiles.

"And no going in any funny places anymore, okay? Promise? No listening to any—anyone who tells you where they are?"

"It wasn't the Grey Mommy this time," Desi says, and Ronald claps his hand across her mouth.

"You . . . just *knew*?" Charlotte says.

Desi, after checking with Ronald, nods contritely.

"No more funny places at all, cool?" Charlotte says.

Ronald finally nods as well.

"Can we roast the marshmallows on the lava?" Desi asks half in secret, already giggling.

"Just don't burn your fingernails," Charlotte says, and takes a mental picture of the two of them there, then reaches out for the jack-in-the-box, floating in the lava.

It goes back into the top of the closet, and she closes the door on it again.

"Where are you going?" Ronald asks her, his voice ramping up into the scared register.

"Nowhere," Charlotte assures him. "Just—just upstairs. I lost that note I wrote your mom, need to write another one, don't want her to be scared when she gets back and we're not here."

When Ronald can't poke any logic holes in this, he nods *sure.*

Charlotte pastes a smile on her face and turns, makes herself go up these stairs one last time.

She can't get them out of the house, no, but she *can* go deeper into it. There's still one place Murphy could be. One room left.

Charlotte doesn't expect the hallway light upstairs to work, but it does. She even flips it on and off to be sure. She leaves it on, pulls the red Featherweight vacuum from the linen closet, holds it in both hands in front of her like a rifle, like she's a soldier going to war.

Backing up to be sure, or because she doesn't want to do this, she sights down through the balcony railing, gets a line on the twins' feet dangling off the couch. One of them, probably Desi, is holding her marshmallow out over the heat she's imagining.

"Everything good down there?" Charlotte calls through the railing.

Ronald leans forward, peers up at her, says, "What are you doing?"

"Cleaning," Charlotte says, and steps ahead, out of his view.

A small black spider darts up from the doorframe of the master bedroom then must see her in its cluster of eyes. It freezes, waiting for her to make the next move, and she can practically hear its sharp feet gripping the wall, ready to go any which way, including straight out at her. Maybe it's just a normal spider, she tells herself, but knows it could also be that the—the membrane between the house and whatever's under the house is thinning, is punctured, is leaking across.

Through the master bedroom doorway Charlotte can see the monstrous closet's accent lights are on, for no reason she can come up with. She's not up here to investigate lights, though. She pulls that door shut, doesn't need to think about a shadowy figure stepping out when her back's turned.

What she's thinking is that when she stepped into the water heater closet and took the back way upstairs, then didn't shut that door by going back through the beanbag, something else was able to come through, after her. Some*one*.

It's a babysitter's worst nightmare: a stranger in the house. Not just any rando, either, but the one person she knows has killed before and died here. The mother who has a history of drowning young children in the bathtub. The mother who wants the rest of the children as well. The mother who's been earning the trust of Desi and Ronald by playing harmless fun games with them.

But she only comes out for them. Meaning she must be going back somewhere else the rest of the time, right? And Ronald said she can't use the funny places, didn't he? At this point in the night, Charlotte's been in every room of the house, she's pretty sure. Except the room that's locked. Except the room whose locked door she *saw* opening.

That's got to be when Nora Spinell came out. It has to be. Meaning—meaning there's something *about* that room. If that's where things start, then that's where they can end. Maybe all Charlotte needs to do, even, is shut that door again, right?

Or maybe Murphy will be in there taped to a chair, stuck to the ceiling, tied in the closet, bleeding out on the floor, trapped behind a mirror, suffocated in a shopping bag, trapped in a giant jack-in-the-box—*Don't think about it*, Charlotte tells herself, and rolls her grip tighter on the vacuum, which is *not* "featherweight."

"Murph?" she calls down the hall.

She's not even sure if she wants a voice to answer back. Even Murphy's, since what she'll see, she knows, is Nora Spinell standing dead center in the office, speaking with Murphy's voice, her arms dripping bubbles down onto the rug. She might even have Murphy's pale eyes, her sharp teeth. Just, they'll be real.

Charlotte's heart is battering at the walls of her chest, trying to get away.

At the doorway to Desi's room she reaches in without looking deeper, pulls the door shut. She does the same at Ronald's room, and his bathroom door is already shut. She looks behind her for any straggle-haired dead women slithering up the stairs or crawling along the wall—movies have poisoned her—but it's only her, and all the shadows are hers too.

She places her palm to Ronald's bathroom door just for the solid feeling, for something to push off, and right when she pulls her hand away a bathtub faucet roars on behind her. From Desi's room—Desi's *bath*room.

So that's where it happened. That's where Tad and Tia Spinell died. That's where they were held under the water, that's where they probably looked up *through* that scummy surface at their mom, holding them there.

Charlotte doesn't want to have to know this.

The head of the vacuum cleaner scrapes the wall and she jumps to the other side of the hall, swinging down at the noise her head knows she just made. Tell that to her body, though. To her hands, her arms.

Desi erupts in giggles that straighten Charlotte's spine even more.

Do I even have to be doing this? Charlotte asks herself. Can't she just plant herself on the couch with the kids, wait for the garage door to groan up, pretend not to notice the Wilbankses' wrong-buttoned shirt and mussed hair from their car-wash rendezvous, accept the twenty they slide her then slope out into the *non*-vinyl night, wait for the last bus home?

Yes, she could, she should.

Except for Murphy.

Murphy's trapped somewhere in this house.

"Hello in there?" Charlotte calls ahead of her, through the office's open door.

She edges closer, can see that the light is off in there, but there's a blue glow all the same.

Charlotte shakes her head no but does it anyway: switches the vacuum to her other hand, having to balance its awkward weight while her right hand feels around inside the office for the light switch, her wrist turned the wrong way, her hand blind.

Which is when the worst sucking noise she's ever heard reels up right by her head.

The vacuum. Her left hand's blundered into the power switch, and evidently this model is battery-charged.

Charlotte screams and jerks and drops it, but, but—

It's pulled her hair in.

Her head goes down with the vacuum, both hands pawing for the stupid power switch, that spinning roller whirring closer and closer to her face.

The vacuum finally winds down, its open mouth right up to her forehead, half her hair deep in its dusty guts. She's sobbing, not breathing right, the office sideways to her eyes. But there's no feet standing there, thank you. No bubbles.

Charlotte extracts her hair as well as she can. But there's tearing, for sure. And the smell of burnt keratin. Finally, when there's just a few tens of strands left, she pulls the vacuum steadily away, gritting her teeth against the sound, against all those years of growth ripping away.

She's free, though.

She drops the vacuum, stands from that wreckage, inspects the office from a normal angle.

It's just what she imagined it would be: three lateral file cabinets, degrees and family photos on the wall, bifold closet doors folded flat, a shuttered window, and, below that window, Mr. Wilbanks's desk and computer, the screensaver a digital clock batting around from side to side on the monitor, corner to corner.

11:36.

Charlotte turns the light on, scrunches her fingers through her hair on the left side, feeling out the damage. The office looks the same lit up, just more detail.

Just to be sure—no surprises—she crosses to the closet doors, rips them open, ready for whatever.

Legal-file boxes, stacked and leaning. A closet that hasn't been opened in a while.

"So?" she says to the office, to this last room she had to work up so much nerve for.

She steps over to the window, wonders if, past those shutters, it's the same vinyl nightscape. She wonders what if one of the funny places downstairs would have spit the twins up in here one time. The door, if it locks—and it does, it was, Mr. Wilbanks said it was—has to lock from the inside, doesn't it? They wouldn't be trapped. And surely they come in here anyway, when their dad's working.

She leans over on the desk to survey the office one more time, and her spread fingers nudge the mousepad, which moves the mouse, wakes the screen, lights the room up a different way.

Even in the new reflections in the glass over the multiple degrees, though, there's nothing. Just her own shadowy form, and the square of light Mr. Wilbanks's computer screen is now.

At least now she can lock the door back when she leaves, she thinks. Make it look like she followed *this* rule anyway, never mind the rest.

She feels through her hair again—it's ratted out on one side—crosses back to the door, turns the light off, looks back one time, and . . .

The computer screen?

It's just Mr. Wilbanks's desktop background, some pale office building he probably either designed or works in, but down at the right corner there's something darker, something moving, or playing.

Charlotte looks behind her, then to both sides of the office, and steps hesitantly over, settles herself into his tall chair with arms higher than she needs.

What's moving in the lower right corner of the screen is the feed from the living room. The nanny cam.

That's why he didn't want her in here, the perv.

Charlotte maximizes that little window, fills the screen with it.

The kids are sitting there, their high-stakes life-or-death game mostly over, the lava floor cooled down to imaginary black. Desi is tranced out, staring right into the lizard's mouth—into *SpongeBob*—and Ronald is at the other end of the couch, hanging over the arm to reach onto the end table, turn the crank on the jack-in-the-box he can't stay away from, the jack-in-the-box that has a shimmer or something to it through the lizard's mouth, probably because of its antique paint.

Charlotte touches the screen lightly with her fingertips, shocking herself enough that she jerks back, has to laugh at how stupid she's being.

This is just another Friday night gig. Murphy's probably just playing a joke. Charlotte's spooking herself. It's the curse of any babysitter around Halloween, isn't it? In the morning she'll take her SATs, and in the fall she'll blast off for somewhere else, Murphy right there with her. They'll live together, and Murphy will be her secret study weapon, quizzing her deep into the morning hours, rigging up flashcards on all the biology and chemistry Charlotte will be loading up on, to get ready for med school proper. Charlotte smiles, minimizes the window again just like Mr. Wilbanks had it, and is standing to go downstairs, open the front door, tear through however many layers of vinyl she has to in order to climb back to the real world, when—

What?

Something in the nanny-cam window.

Instead of enlarging it again, Charlotte leans right down to it.

It's . . . *Murphy?*

She's—she's climbing up over the back of the couch. Like . . . like she was there all along?

Charlotte turns to the open office door as if she can look

downstairs, into a few minutes ago, when the kids had disappeared under the couch cushion and she'd flipped the couch back, looking for them.

It hadn't tipped all the way over, had it?

It had caught on something. Charlotte had assumed there was a footstool or ottoman or some decorative doodad back there for the couch to kickstand back on. But it had been *Murphy*? Murphy who hadn't said anything? And she'd stayed there until the twins rolled the couch back forward? She listened in on Charlotte starting the lava game? She hadn't answered when Charlotte had been desperate for her to?

Charlotte maximizes the screen, sits back fast from how close the living room is now.

Desi looks over to Murphy, settling between the twins, and Ronald turns to her as well, his lips a thin line.

Murphy's eyes are still pale.

She smiles wide, her vampire teeth lapping over her bottom lip.

Desi pushes away, her eyes widening, but then Murphy's shoulders move in silent chuckle and she reaches her gloved fingers into her mouth, pulls the fangs out, sets them down on the coffee table.

The twins watch those teeth in wonder, then come back to Murphy.

She takes one of their marshmallows, pops it in, says something the lizard can't hear. The twins smile, even Ronald, and she peels out of her gloves, gives one to each of them. Desi immediately runs her arm into the black one she has, pulls it all the way up to her shoulder. Ronald just holds his, watching Murphy.

Next, moving carefully, Murphy leans her head back, applies her bare right fingertip to her right eyeball, and pulls the contact up.

"What the hell?" Charlotte says, standing to go downstairs, stop this . . . this whatever-it-is. But—but she has to know how it ends without her interfering, too, doesn't she? She sits back down, has to watch.

Murphy leans to the side to dig inside her jester costume for her contact lens case. She deposits the right contact into its side, then extracts the left, puts it in as well. She blinks fast and big, shakes her head like trying to unblur her eyes.

Ronald and Desi step down onto the crust of lava, come around to see her face. She looks from one to the other, pops another marshmallow in, says something that makes the kids laugh again.

Now she's . . . she giving Desi instructions? Yes. Desi scampers off, is back a few shakes later with the hand towel from the bathroom, wet.

Murphy runs her finger up into it, dabs at her white makeup.

It comes off agonizingly slow, in deliberate circles, and—and it's *not Murphy*?

"You did come back," Charlotte says to the screen. To the dead mother she knows is going to be under that makeup. Because—because the Grey Mother killed Murphy, stripped her down, took her fangs, her contacts, her costume, and, and . . .

It's worse.

Charlotte stands again, shaking her head no.

The resolution on Mr. Wilbanks's camera isn't high-def, but—

"No," Charlotte says, shaking her head. She's not insisting. It's a plea.

It's—but it can't be—it's *Charlotte*. Her face is still pale from the face paint, and the black diamonds are dull shadows bisecting her eyes, but . . .

Charlotte feels her own face. It's partially to be sure of the contours and planes and angles she's seeing through the nanny cam—like watching security footage of herself—but it's also to be sure that she's still *her*, that she's just been . . . been *copied*, not replaced. Like that makes anything even close to sense.

It does to the twins, anyway.

They're jumping up and down from this wonderful excellent joke. From Murphy disappearing long enough that Charlotte could go upstairs, dress like her, then sneak down for a Halloween trick. The best one ever.

The Charlotte downstairs points to the Charlotte upstairs —no, no, to the television—and pushes her nose down and downer with her right finger, miming Squidward just like Charlotte had done for them in the kitchen.

"That's not me!" Charlotte screams, pushing away from this, the chair clattering over behind her.

She bangs on the desk like that can do anything, and is about to turn away, race downstairs, when . . . when the recording changes?

The webcam is too slow to keep up with whatever's happing. Walls and rugs, darkness and light.

"What?" Charlotte says.

When the recording settles again, it's her, from the side, and she's giant. No, the camera is *low*.

She turns to the doorway, one hundred percent expects Murphy to be there, ready to laugh about whatever impossible joke this is, but the doorway's empty. No, *not* empty.

She tracks down to the blue lizard looking up at her, its mouth open.

She falls back against the desk and tries to climb up on it, tipping the monitor over and down. The lizard turns, zips away, leaves Charlotte breathing deep, her knees up to her chest, her breath fast and shallow, her head shaking *no, no, this can't be happening, this isn't real.*

"Call me Charley," the Charlotte downstairs says clearly to the twins, and louder than she needs to, like she wants to be sure her voice makes its way upstairs.

It brings Charlotte back to herself. She feels her eyebrows come down, her lips set.

She steps down onto the plastic mat Mr. Wilbanks's chair rolls on.

It accepts her weight, lets her cross slowly to the door. She grabs onto the doorframe, finally convinces herself to pull through.

She stops when there's a nightgowned woman walking away from her. Nora Spinell. Her arms are wet and bubbly, and she's crying so hard she can barely stay upright, her whole body shuddering with each sob.

She's just done it, Charlotte knows. She's just killed her children. And, and there's a yellow nylon rope trailing from her hand, probably from the closet of this office when it was a different room.

Nora Spinell doubles it, loops it over the balcony railing and then has to stop, collapse into even worse sobs. She shakes her head no, though, *no*, and stands, raises her chin to tie the other end of the rope around her neck. She pulls it tight-tight, then looks back to Desi's room, and . . . does she see Charlotte?

She sort of does. Charlotte shrinks back, her hands over her mouth, and this child-killing mother doesn't look away, keeps Charlotte in her eyes the whole time she's stepping up onto the balcony, having to duck and hunch to keep her head from scraping the ceiling.

And then, both too fast and in the slowest possible motion, she plummets down, her arms out to the side.

The railing creaks and shudders and splinters, looks like it's going over as well, but it holds her.

An instant later the rope pops back up, slack, the body it was holding gone.

There's no sound of it hitting downstairs.

The twins don't scream.

Charlotte tries to process this, their nonreaction, and then—no.

She hears Ronald again, telling her she has to go back through the beanbag. Ronald asking her if she's still there. It hadn't made sense when he said it, but . . . he was right, wasn't he?

She's on the wrong side of the house. She's *in* the wrong house. And she somehow left enough of herself behind that Nora Spinell was able to step into it, occupy her, *be* her, as far as the twins can tell.

Now *Charlotte's* the shadow who can tell Ronald and Desi where the funny places are. Except she also told them not to listen to that woman anymore.

And, and Murphy, she was never even really here, was she? When the lights went down earlier, what Charlotte thought was a blink but had to be more like an hour, that was long enough for . . . for Nora Spinell to body up to Charlotte on the stairs, put her lips up to Charlotte's ear, and drink enough of her memories out to sneak away, dress up as Murphy, wait out the transition that was already happening to them, between them, whatever.

All so she can take a couple more kids.

Charlotte closes her eyes, shakes her head no, and steps forward, knows that at any instant a headless nightgowned body is going to be trudging up the stairs, her hand to the rail because she doesn't have eyes to gauge the next step.

But a good babysitter doesn't hide upstairs, either.

Charlotte steps forward, forward, her hand to the wall like that can prove she's still real, that she's at least still *connected* to something real, and when she passes Desi's room, her fingertips skating across the door, the water shuts off in there. And now, bubbling under that door—the laughter of kids at bath time? Not the twins, right? It can't be.

Charlotte twists the knob and steps in, feels for the light but . . . she has to look to be sure: the light switch is just a blank slate.

Because she's where she is—on the wrong side of the house.

She makes herself breathe in, breathe out, and steps to the side, just far enough to see through the open door of the bathroom—which is how you leave it when kids are bathing: open, so they don't get up to anything dangerous; open, so everybody in there stays alive, including them if they're splashing water out onto the floor one more time.

The tub is empty. No twins, and no other kids either. Because Tad and Tia Spinell died forever ago.

Charlotte turns to leave this place, just catches that laughter of bath time again. The tub is still empty when she turns around, though.

"Stop, *please*," she says, and then she *sees* that bath time. In the mirror.

Both Spinell kids are alive. She assumes that's who the blond girl and her little brother are. The bubbles are mounded everywhere, are floating up in tufts like a unicorn daydream.

Charlotte steps forward, keeping the angle of the reflection right, and touches the mirror.

It's just glass, isn't wet or anything.

"She's coming," she warns the kids in that reflection.

They can't hear her.

Charlotte looks behind her all at once, for the headless mom in the doorway, too close all at once, but she's not there. Yet.

Back to the kids. Back to this movie still running all these years later.

Tad slips under and Tia reaches in instantly for him, guides him back up, clears the bubbles from his face, taking care like big sisters do. He starts to cry but she covers his mouth, her scared eyes looking around for their mom, probably. Because she doesn't want to get in trouble.

Tad calms, laughs through his sister's fingers, and comes up with a bright green turtle he can squeeze to shoot a jet at Tia.

She sputters the water away, her lips thin with surprise and anger, but then, still playing, she piles bubbles into her hand and sculpts it into hair for him, scolding him to sit still for this. When she's done he stands to try to see this in the bathroom mirror, which is out of Charlotte's view, and then Tia stands by him, both of them slathered in bubbles, trying to see their reflections.

Which is when Tia turns her head just enough to see Charlotte in the bedroom mirror. Charlotte's chest hollows out and she staggers back from this, loses her angle into the bathroom for a moment. By the time she comes back, the corners of Tia's mouth are twitching up into an almost smile, and then she turns to her brother to sculpt his hair again, fix the left side, which is calving off in the slow way of bubbles. He stands still for it, and at the end Tia calmly guides the turtle down from his hands, away, then brings her own hands to his cheeks to fix his dripping beard. Right after she's got it perfect, she rotates her hands on his cheeks and jams her sharp little thumbs through his eyeballs, having to change the angle of her arms to get all the way in, and through. The fluid in his eyes spatters her face, and then the red comes, slathers down Tad's cheeks and Tia's hands, and still she pushes deeper, moving her sharp little thumbs around in his head, making his shoulders and arms puppet helplessly.

Tad starts to scream so she falls forward, driving him into the water, holding him there and holding him there until a line of drool comes down from her mouth, disappears into the white bubbles. Tad's not shaking anymore. The water sloshes over the edge of the bathtub once and then finds its level, and by the end of it Charlotte's face is cold, her hands over her open mouth.

If—if Nora Spinell had come in and found Tad just *drowned*, then it could have been an accident. Even with just one eye pushed in, still, that could have been the plastic tail of a toy dinosaur. But with *both* his eyes punched in like this, then, then: a mother knows, doesn't she? She knew it was her daughter. And . . . that was why she was being homeschooled probably, wasn't it? Because she was displaying violent tendencies? Because she did something to the class guinea pig in kindergarten? Because naptime always ended in disaster when she was lying there on her mat, her lips moving with whatever she was dreaming, whatever she was muttering into the heads of all the other sleeping kids? Because she had this in her and her parents knew it, Charlotte knows. They knew it but thought they could love her enough to fix it. Like you do. Like anybody *would*.

But they couldn't get her to stop being her.

Charlotte turns to the doorway again for this mom who killed herself not out of guilt but a grief so massive she couldn't contain it, but she's still not there, and when Charlotte comes back to the mirror, the reflection of the bathtub looks the same as it does straight on: just dark, empty, nobody there.

But now she knows.

"Tia," she says, intones.

It's not Nora Spinell downstairs in Charlotte's left-behind body, is it? It's her dead daughter Tia, grown up in this dark house, in this house under the real house.

She's been waiting for years for someone her age to show up, so she could crawl across, sneak out for the night. It wasn't some sixth grader who told Ronald about that jack-in-the-box, either, Charlotte knows. It was the shadowy woman only he can see. The one who smuggled that antique jack-in-the-box across somehow, to use like an anchor, like a grappling hook set in the real world, one she could pull herself through with, if some kid would just put enough heart into cranking it, each slow turn pulling her closer. But now that the Wilbankses finally got brave enough to call a babysitter in, Tia doesn't need that anymore, can just step into that babysitter's body, if only that babysitter can be stupid enough to leave her body behind, empty.

Tia's been waiting for this perfect . . . not storm, but winning lotto number.

Charlotte shakes her head no, walks out to the railing to scream to the kids that that's not her, to run, but they're . . . not on the couch anymore?

Charlotte slides her hands wide on the railing to lean over the stairs, see more of the living room, and the railing, splintered from Nora Spinell's suicide, snags her right palm, tears it open.

She draws her hand up without looking, brings it to the side of her mouth, and then, finally, has to look down to her cut when her lips and tongue aren't finding the warmth of blood.

The cut's not red, it's not bleeding. It's just open, with dry, springy white inside, like . . . like *tofu*? Like the spackle her mom made her use to fill all the tack holes in her bedroom wall when she finally took her junior high posters down. Like . . . it's like she's nothing, now. Like what's under her skin isn't supposed to be seen, is just a form keeping her looking like herself. For . . . for as long as she remembers what she looks like?

She shakes her head no, pushes back, and turns to race down the stairs but now the headless mom *is* walking up them, following the handrail just like Charlotte knew she would.

Charlotte backs off, cringes down, her hand finding the floor to balance her and, just like all the stories in her elementary halls said, her palm finds a wet footprint, a wisp of bubbles.

And now the headless mom is to the top of the stairs, is about to walk right into Charlotte.

Charlotte does the only thing she can: she clamps her hands onto the railing and climbs up, is going to balance there or hang there as long as it takes. Except this railing can't take anymore.

It cracks over, falls with Charlotte to the first floor.

She lands in the Lopezes' kitchen two weeks ago, her mouth filled with taste: Murphy's new coconut lip gloss.

Murphy has her pressed up against the Lopezes' wide refrigerator, Charlotte's shirt hiking up from Murphy's hands.

It was supposed to be a study session, but, well. The kid's asleep, the house is empty, Mr. and Mrs. Lopez—"Call me *Maria*"—aren't due back for another hour, and if Charlotte has to run through one more practice question, the rest of everything she knows is going to start leaking out her head.

"When the brain is full, the body must play," Murphy told her about ninety seconds ago. It didn't track, exactly, and wasn't really a saying either, Charlotte doesn't think, but this isn't exactly the time for thinking.

Charlotte presses her body out, against Murphy's probing hands.

If this goes any further, as in all the way, Charlotte wonders if the world will look different from that new place. Her mom told her not really—it's just sex, not a brain swap—but all the same she thinks colors might be more vibrant, something like that.

Right here in the kitchen, though? It is a nice kitchen, Charlotte guesses. With granite-cold counters, yeah, but their bodies are radiating heat, are practically glowing.

There are other considerations too, of course, the first of which would be Arthur suddenly standing in the kitchen doorway clutching his blankie, trying to figure out which of these naked tangled bodies is his babysitter (hint, kid: the dark one), and can she read him the story about the choo-choo and the horse again.

"Wait, what if he—" Charlotte says, this visualization all too real, but Murphy's mouth is there again, hungry.

"He won't," she says, working the snap of Charlotte's jeans now.

"In here," Charlotte says anyway, and breaks away hand by hand, lip by lip, grabs Murphy's waistband to pull her through the kitchen and into the formal dining room, the one Mrs. Lopez vacuums so intentionally that all the carpet nap is facing the same way. It means Arthur's footprints show if he goes in there where he's not supposed to be.

If he knows not to go there *already*, Charlotte figures, then surely he won't go in there at night when it's dark and scary, right? Not unless he hears sounds.

"We've got to be shhh," Charlotte says, her hands finding

their way up along Murphy's sides, her thin shirt hiking up against Charlotte's wrists, the pads of Charlotte's fingertips somehow hungry.

"Shhh," Murphy says back.

"Do you, you know," Charlotte says right into Murphy's neck, "*have* something?"

It's their running joke, kind of from Charlotte's mom: when Charlotte came out to her (commercial break during a *Next Generation* rerun, no eye contact), her mom had gotten up from her wingback chair, gone to the pantry where the clear plastic jug of gimme condoms from the hospital were, that she'd already said were just going to be there, uncounted, and carried them to the trash can, poured them in with a shrug, and told Charlotte that being into women wasn't going to make Charlotte's life drama-free, it was just, now, going to be a different kind of drama. It wasn't until the internet and friends over the next couple of months that she decided Charlotte was all special and two-spirit. But Charlotte doesn't want to be thinking about all that at this precise moment. She isn't even sure if she's shimmying out of her jeans or if they're actually melting off.

This is good, she tells herself. This is what it's supposed to be like: someone you love, dimmed lights, exotic place, just enough danger.

She tries to slow her head down so she can take every last detail in, since this only happens once. There's the wavery depression glass set in the front of Mrs. Lopez's china hutch, which is the main reason Arthur can't play with his little cars in here anymore. Murphy's back is in each frame in a different way. There's the Etsy chandelier or hanging light fixture or whatever—salvaged wood, hand-worked metal—running nearly the length of the long dark dining room table, all its Edison bulbs showing off their glowing-hot filaments. There's Charlotte's own hand curled around the top of one of the high-backed chairs, all her veins standing at attention, like they have front-row seats for this big event. And—and there's more and more clothes on the directionally vacuumed carpet, the carpet Charlotte is going to have to rake back into place when this is all over, since the vacuum might wake Arthur, and would probably leave its exhaust smell in the air anyway.

But that's all later.

Right now it's Murphy's mouth, Murphy's hands, Murphy's breathing and her own with it, over it, under it, inside it.

"Like this?" she says to Murphy, a few minutes in.

Murphy's groan is answer enough.

Their next joke, when it's over and Charlotte is back in her shirt in case the front door opens, is Murphy saying she wishes one of them smoked.

"Here," Charlotte says, miming a cigarette to pass over. She blows fake smoke out, her eyes slit to watch it slip away.

Murphy takes the idea of this cigarette and draws deep, looks at it in her hand while holding the pretend smoke in, and Charlotte, not even on purpose, takes a mental picture of her doing that, knows that's what she's going to remember best about all this: the cigarette they didn't smoke, in this elegant dining room they're not even supposed to be in, the carpet going every which way.

It's when Murphy blows that smoke back out and Charlotte tracks it up, imagining the paisley patterns, that she sees the blue and red lights in the depression glass of the china hutch.

"Huh," she says, directing Murphy to the window, to the street out front, where the police car evidently is.

Murphy stands naked but for her retro socks and makes her way to the huge window in the dining room, scrunching her hair up in back, completely comfortable with herself.

"Something's going on," she says back to Charlotte, and Charlotte comes up on alert, the blood rushing to her head and unbalancing her so that she tips over, nearly falls *into* that delicate treasure of a china hutch, and this lurching feeling in her gut, this sense of falling . . .

"What is it?" Charlotte says.

Murphy turns back to her, but Charlotte was just saying it to herself, not actually asking.

"This already happened," Charlotte says. "But . . . not like this."

Murphy turns back to the window, maybe can't hear, or process, and Charlotte steps into her jeans, hops to get them snapped.

"I'm going—" she says needlessly, tilting her head at the front door.

The blue and red lights pull her out the front door, over the lawn, into the street.

It's not just one police car, like she guesses she was expecting. There's three of them, and a fire truck, and an ambulance, and other cars besides, all the porch lights up and down the street on, people in house robes and glasses standing in their open front doors like they're completely ready to be ordered back inside.

"No, no," Charlotte says, drifting to the center of the lights, "this isn't the way it happened . . ."

Still, in the center of the street, a stretcher alongside, there's a small form under a sheet. Charlotte tracks up from it to, to the bumper of—

She falls away, shaking her head no.

Her mom's blue Pontiac.

Someone puts a hand on her shoulder and Charlotte looks around, follows this arm up to a fireman.

"You knew him?" the fireman asks. "The Lopez boy?"

"Arthur," Charlotte sputters. "Where's the—who hit him?"

The fireman points with his chin to the second cop car, and, behind that glass, her shoulders forward like her hands are cuffed behind her, is Charlotte's mom in her scrubs. The ones with little birthday gifts floating all over them.

"Why is she—?" Charlotte starts, shaking her head like this doesn't track. "Is she arrested?"

"Refused to take the breathalyzer," the fireman says.

"That's—she says to never take those!" Charlotte tells him, getting light on the balls of her feet to fix this, to save this, to . . . she doesn't know.

The reason her mom says to never take them is that cops always stop you for Driving While Indian, which is where you weren't doing anything wrong, but maybe they can find something under the seat, or you've got a bench warrant, or your registration's expired, or it *looked* like you were about to pull a weapon. All because of that eagle feather hanging from the rearview mirror.

This isn't like that, though, Charlotte wants to tell her mom. Who would no way have stopped for a drink between the hospital and picking her daughter up. She hasn't even been in a bar for years, so far as Charlotte knows.

Take the breathalyzer, she wants to tell her mom. *Prove it's not your fault.*

But then she sees it like her mom has to be seeing it, her mom who probably recognized Arthur Lopez the moment before he went under the car: him being out there is her daughter's fault. But if she can make it her own fault, then her daughter can get out of this town, maybe. Have a life.

Charlotte shakes her head no, no, this isn't real, this isn't the way it happened, her mom *saw* Arthur in her headlights, she *stopped*, he's right now up in his bed asleep, where Charlotte tucked him in.

"I've got to—" she says to the fireman, who's not even listening, and like that she's gone, her bare feet barely touching the grass between the street and the Lopezes' front door, their stairs, the second floor. Arthur's room, his nightlight the only glow, giving all the toys tall shadows.

There's a small form under the covers, just like there's supposed to be.

"He's here!" Charlotte calls back down the stairs, out the open door, and she covers her mouth because it doesn't seem like the right time to giggle. But she can't help it.

She steps forward and then remembers, stops.

"Murph?" she says, loud enough that Murphy should hear if she's still here, and—and this is just like before, isn't it? Wasn't she calling for Murphy earlier? In some *other* "earlier," or a "later" that somehow happened before?

Murphy wouldn't be in Arthur's bedroom, though.

"Artie?" Charlotte says softly to the sleeping form under the covers, not wanting to jar him awake.

The covers don't stir, don't rustle.

Because he's a hard sleeper, a deep sleeper. Because she got him double tired, since she knew Murphy was coming over, because she knew tonight was The Night.

Still, "Arthur?" she says, louder.

She touches the covers and he's really there, is solid, not just wishful thinking or a memory.

"Art, listen, I'm sorry, I just need to—" Charlotte says, pulling the covers down.

At first she must be seeing wrong, it must be the night-light's weird angle. But then she's not seeing wrong.

His eyes are gone.

Charlotte jerks back, her hands steepled over her mouth.

It's not Arthur Lopez, either.

This is Tad Spinell.

The glow from the nightlight intensifies and Charlotte looks over to it like she has to, and it's not the nightlight. It's that big pink beanbag, incandescent, its shadow crawling with legs.

Desi's My Little Pony Room.

Did—did Nora Spinell, after drowning her daughter in the bathtub, carry her murdered son to bed and lay him to rest before stepping off the balcony? None of the stories in elementary ever said anything about that.

"I'm so sorry," Charlotte says, and reaches down to pull the covers back over him.

His little hand comes up, his fingers circling her wrist. Then his other hand.

He starts writhing and convulsing then, like trying to work something up from deep inside. Charlotte pulls but he's got her. He's . . . he's pulling her hand now, guiding it to his face?

Is he trying to show her that his eyes are gone?

"I can—" Charlotte starts, almost saying she can *see*. "I know, I'm so sorry, I don't know why your sister would—"

She doesn't finish because this is when her index finger slips into the wet cavity that was Tad Spinell's right eye.

She tries to pull back but he holds on tight, his head coming up with her hand, driving itself deeper onto her finger, deep enough that—

When she looks to the sound in the hall, she sees what Tad must have: his dad rushing past. Meaning . . . if Tad *saw* this, then this was when he still had eyes, wasn't it? It has to be. Charlotte, looking through Tad Spinell's *memory*, steps out into the hall after him, but all she sees of him is his behind-leg, stepping into the master bedroom.

The other direction down the hall, Tia is standing there in her pajamas, not drowned yet.

This is before all that, Charlotte can tell. No bubbles whatsoever.

"Shh," she says to Charlotte. To Charlotte in Tad's head.

Charlotte shakes her head no, is sniffle-crying.

Tia, the big sister, sterns her face down, stares her little brother into submission. Dutifully, Charlotte trudges down. Together they step into her bedroom—*Ronald's* bedroom, some part of Charlotte registers—pull up the bed skirt, reveal the plate of scrambled eggs that are congealed over.

Tia squats down, pulls the plate out. The eggs are writhing with maggots.

"Where?" she says to Tad.

"I don't want to," Charlotte hears herself saying in Tad's small voice.

"You promised," Tia says. "I'll scream if you don't do it."

Charlotte can feel Tad's slow tears on her cheek.

She closes her eyes and a, a *sense* opens in her, like hearing but deeper, somehow thrumming through the muscles under her jaw. She can feel what Tia wants. It's down the hall.

"Mommy and Daddy's closet," she-as-Tad says, still crying.

Tia nods, takes his hand in hers and stands, balances the writhing eggs before them.

"Shh," she says at the open doorway to the master bedroom. They cross hand in hand, their mom and dad just mounds of sleep.

"There?" Tia says.

The big closet's light is on. It's just clothes and shoes and belts and, up top, hats.

Charlotte-as-Tad nods to the outlet on the wall, nothing plugged into it.

Tia goes to her knees before it, looks up to be sure her little brother isn't crying too loud, and then, moving delicately, she pinches a maggot up, holds it before one of the upright slots of the outlet.

It falls in, is *sucked* in.

Charlotte steps back, falls into the clothes, two empty hangers rattling.

Tia looks back, her eyes slits, and then she looks back to the outlet.

From the mouth part of the outlet now, the hole under the two slits, there's . . . skinny black legs? A fly crawls out, buzzes into the air.

Tia smiles, nods, and says back to Charlotte, her voice a whisper, "Here?"

Charlotte nods *yes, yes yes yes*, and Tia's fingers find the seam of wallpaper, follow it down to a corner, and she peels it up and back.

Instead of wall behind there, it's a yawning blackness.

"Where does it go?" Charlotte hears and feels herself asking.

"Tia?" their mom says from the bed, her voice creaky with sleep. "Are you two in my closet again? Do you know what *time* it is?"

Tia smiles, her eyes wet with happiness, and holds her hand back for Charlotte, to pull her into this blackness with her.

Charlotte shakes her head no.

Footsteps are approaching across the bedroom now.

"*Thaddeus,*" Tia says, and Charlotte hears and feels herself calling for Mommy and Daddy, which is exactly like telling on Tia.

Tia peels her lips back, showing her teeth, then shrugs *so what*, turns back to the wall, ducks down and in just as their mom steps through into the closet doorway, her scream already starting.

Charlotte—Tad—pushes back deeper into the clothes and boots and hanging scarves, feels more than sees Mr. Spinell crashing into the closet, his voice a boom of desperation, his knees hitting the floor, his long arm stabbing into the wall for his daughter, and this father's son tries to hide deeper in the hanging clothes, is fighting for space in there, pulling away scarf after scarf, hangers rattling down over him, over her. Slowly, Charlotte realizes that there's muted, kind-of-golden accent lighting all around her now.

Mrs. Wilbanks's closet.

She surges through the open door, falls into the bedroom, looks immediately to the king bed. It's made, empty.

"Desi!" she yells. "Ronald!"

And—is that their voices in the living room? It is. It has to be.

Charlotte smiles, stands, is dizzy again but she can stagger anyway. To the bed, then pushing off the bed to the doorway but the headless body of Nora Spinell is *still* coming up the stairs, using the handrail.

Charlotte falls back against the railing, which creaks behind her, gives way, sending her falling.

Again.

Still.

She wakes to the soft chiming of midnight, the right side of her face pressed into the living room rug.

The broken railing is on her legs and hips. Charlotte pushes it off, sits up, her eyes finding the clock on the mantel striking the hour.

It's officially Halloween, then. Just thinking this makes her look to the stairway, for that headless body. Or for Tad Spinell, his face pressed between two posts of the balcony, his bloody eye sockets watching her.

Her fingers feel around to the sharp pain on the back of her head and dig in through the split or crack in her scalp, touch the springy whiteness in there, making her gag so fast the impulse doesn't really come up from her stomach. It's more like it's a tight, humming line between that spot in her head and the sudden bulge in her throat.

She draws her hand back fast, pulls her knees to her chest.

The railing is broken on the floor beside her but it's still up at the balcony as well, like she's both here and not here. Charlotte touches the railing there on the floor with her and it's solid, real. Still touching it, she focuses hard on the balcony—the other railing. It's definitely there as well, unbroken. Which doesn't make any sense. *You're still there, aren't you?* Ronald had said to her. She must be, yeah. When you come through a funny place but don't go back through, then you're stranded, a foot on each side. Sort of? Something like that? But you're losing ground with every step, too. You're slipping into oblivion. Into this. That's why she can see Nora Spinell walking around. It's why she can see the kids in the bathtub. It's why she's made of nothing.

"This is such bullshit," she says, pushing away from the broken railing.

At which point she remembers she's not the only one lost in this. "Desi?" she says, swinging around to the couch, which leaves her dizzy. "Ronbo?" Where has Tia taken them? No, not Tia. "Charley." Where has *Charley* taken Desi and Ronald?

Charlotte plants her hands to push herself up but draws her right back up. It's not bleeding, it can't bleed, there's nothing *to* bleed, but it definitely hurts. And now it's torn open even wider, more of the white showing.

She uses her other hand to stand and immediately balances wrong, is falling across the room, into the television screen. It crackles and blues where she touches it, would probably just be a bump in the signal for anyone watching.

And, what's wrong with her? Why can't she stand without tipping sideways?

Her head stings, reminds her: *that*, yeah.

She feels up and some of the white is protruding in its dry way. This is why she can't balance, isn't it? She needs to hold it in somehow, with something. And bandage her hand to keep it from splitting open any wider, peeling back like a glove.

She takes a step and finds herself falling across the room again, over the coffee table, into the couch.

She comes up with the fool's cap Charley left behind. Murphy's fool's cap.

Charlotte works it down over her head delicately but it's too big, won't hold anything in. She sloughs it off, lets it drop. Her hand, then. She pulls up the red glove—the only one left—works it over her right hand all the way up to the elbow. Perfect.

For her head, she wheels and finally crawls across to the bathroom, pulls the tights down from the rack, works the waist down as low as she can onto her forehead and feels the thin fabric stretched over where her head is trying to spill out at the back. It's still bulging. When she touches it she reels into the wall, leans forward to puke nothing into the sink. Which she's thankful for. If she were to throw up, it would be dry white paste, she knows—if a babysitter's nightmare is a stranger in the house, then an Indian's biggest fear is being white on the inside.

"One, two," she says, and on what would have been *three* she uses two fingers to shove that bulging white back into her skull.

Her world spins, tilts, goes grey then black then shiny

purple like videotape, her whole life in frames on it, blurring past, but thirty, forty seconds later it settles.

Still gripping onto the counter around the sink, she straightens her arms, looks at herself in the mirror, just sees the open doorway behind her—*through* where she should be. Because she's not really here. The tights on her head are even still hanging on the towel rack.

Charlotte huffs a sick laugh out, turns to find the kids.

Walking is the same as it's ever been, now. Or: *again*. Her feet don't sink down through the floorboards, and she can't step up onto some pad of magical air either. She wonders if every house is like this—if there are people always walking among and around, a shade away, a blink to the side.

She lifts Mrs. Wilbanks's note from the island just to see if she can. She reads the first two bullet points—lasagne, TV time—but can, at the same time, still see the note where it was on the island.

"So this is death," she says, and knows that just because she heard her own voice doesn't mean it actually went anywhere real.

Her reflection isn't smearing from shiny surface to shiny surface of the stainless-steel appliances, and she tries to imagine ten-plus years of this. If Tia Spinell hadn't already been whatever she was, then walking around like this, nobody to talk to, never seeing herself reflected back, that would have turned her into something else, wouldn't it have? Something worse. As it is, it probably just ratcheted whatever was inside her up higher and higher, to a permanent screech, an always-there hiss, a whisper that never goes away. Especially if her headless mom was always walking around blind, groping through the dark with her long wet fingers. And there would be Tad floating in the bathtub, or maybe running around without eyes.

But maybe Tia would like that, too. Maybe her mom and her brother were trophies to her, right?

Charlotte shakes her head, decides it's time to either choose the utility or the garage. Charley and the twins have to be in one or the other—but wait: they can be outside too, can't they? And that's where they already thought they were going.

"Shit," Charlotte says, and pulls around the island for the garage, but then . . . what is that?

In the utility.

She slows, leans in.

It's a—a bright shadow? That doesn't track, not really, but that's for sure what it is: a shadow that's not being cast, but that's *casting*, like from a source. Not from some dark bulb but shining through from someplace so much darker.

Charlotte steps all the way into the utility, her fingertips to the wall. The bright shadow is coming from the open door of the dryer.

"It's the funny place again," Charlotte says, getting it. Because there's only so many enclosed places downstairs, probably.

She looks all around the utility to make sure she's alone, then steps hesitantly across to the dryer, jumps back when her left leg brushes into the shadow leaking from its open mouth.

It's cold, burning cold.

She pulls her pants leg up and more pores than not are weeping white, like she's being boiled. She rolls her pants leg back down, and her next step—back from the dryer—she nearly falls *into* the shadow when her hurt leg gives under her.

"Wonderful," she says.

She backs carefully away from the dryer, her eye on it long enough that she catches the bright shadow flickering, then fading. In a few moments the inside of the dryer is just the inside of a dryer again.

"Desi?" she calls, knowing it's useless. "Ronald?"

She steps back out into the kitchen. There's only the garage left now. She nods to herself, crosses to that door, and on the way realizes that she's not thinking right, that her insistence that the kids have to be either in the utility or the garage or outside since they're not in the living room or kitchen is wrong, since it's not taking into account the ten or twenty minutes she was conked on the living room floor after falling over the railing, *with* the railing, whatever.

If Charley's really going to steal her life from here on out, then the thing to do would be to tuck the twins in and get them asleep, right? Collect her handful of cash and walk right out of this house at last, or maybe accept a certain ride from a certain husband, already ready for round two of the night.

Still: the garage. To be thorough.

Charlotte steps down into it gingerly, like she doesn't trust the smooth concrete to hold her new self.

It's the same as it was last time. Just a normal garage with an Audi in it, cabinets and a pegboard for tools and the freezer and coolers and camping chairs, a high window with a punched-through screen that nobody will probably even find until spring.

She taps the button to raise the door, see if the vinyl's still there, but the door stays put. She punches it again, watching her finger to be sure the click happens, but the door doesn't move.

She steps down to where one of the Wilbankses parks, stands under the garage door's hanging motor, and finally reaches up, takes the plastic handle on its barber shop rope— braided red and white—and pulls down, disengaging the heavy garage door from the chain. Then she goes to the door itself, finds the handle, sets her feet, pulls, and: nothing.

It doesn't even creak, doesn't even acknowledge that she's there, doing this to it.

The door shakes in a satisfying way when she kicks it, so she turns around to kick it with her heel, and again, only stops when she sees white seeping out through the weave of her sock.

It can't have been this way for Tia, can it have? Maybe since—since she came across dead, not alive, she got a different kind of body. Or a more durable one. One that keeps its white in better. If not, then there's no way she makes it through eleven years of damage, when even the slightest hurt is massive, and doesn't heal.

Charlotte limps to the doorway, washes up in the kitchen breathing hard, her heart pulsing in her shin, her other foot throbbing.

"You're falling apart," she tells herself, holding her left leg out to see if her pants leg is dark down there, from leakage. The whiteness she's made of isn't damp, though. It just crumbles from her cuff. And on her other foot, the white that was seeping up through her sock is dry powder now, like large confectioner's sugar. Especially small spider eggs.

"You're not going to cry," she insists out loud, for whatever it's worth.

She takes a painful step, using the island as a crutch, but she can't take the island with her.

No way can she make it across two days like this, she knows. She's not going to make it another thirty minutes, even.

But—but if she doesn't, then Charley's going to go home tonight as her, isn't she? She's going to be in Charlotte's house and Charlotte's life, is going to be living with her mom, is going to have Murphy showing up on her phone at all hours. And she's probably skipping the SATs in a few hours, because who would want to sit in a classroom after being locked in the same house for so long?

But what can Charlotte *do* about any of that? She's over here on the wrong side.

She pushes off from the island, staggers back into the empty living room, stops to try to locate the . . . plastic clattering? What?

And then she sees: there's a jester squatted down in front of the television, before the open cabinet doors of the built-in entertainment center.

Tia. Charley.

She's . . . she's tossing something into the avalanche of DVDs and videogames?

Beads, from Desi's beanbag? No, these are harder.

Charlotte zeroes in on the heavy little jug on the floor by Charley's left foot: BBs, for a BB gun. A solid little pound or two of copper-coated balls.

Charley's tossing them one by one into the cabinet and then turning her head to the side to listen.

One BB bounces, comes to a rest, and Charley nods,

stands, surveys the living room, decides on the couch. She steps up to it and pulls the end-seat cushion up like a lid, exposing the box-spring part that must not have been there when Desi and Ronald went through earlier. Or, it was there but also not there, Charlotte doesn't completely understand. It was there and not there the same way the back corner of the water heater closet was sometimes there, sometimes not.

Charley holds a single B B out, drops it.

It careens off, pings onto the glass part of the coffee table.

"You want to go through again," Charlotte says, nodding with realization. "But you can't see the funny places anymore, can you?"

Charley steps away from the couch, hissing disappointment.

"Babysitter?" she says to the room, the house.

Charlotte cringes back, exposed in the middle of the room. She's not really there, though. Not in a way people in the real house can see.

Charley looks anyway, then shrugs, studies the coffee table for that rogue B B, finally has to kneel down to pinch it up from the carpet.

"Mrs. Wilbanks," she says, testing it out, "you—you might find B B s around. The kids got into them, spilled them, tracked them all over the house."

She nods, likes that.

"And I'll see them again next Friday, and the Friday after that?" she adds, batting her—Charlotte's—eyelashes in a *poor* way, a *pity me* way. "If Mr. Wilbanks's car is, you know, *dirty*, I'm sure the two of you could go down to the car wash . . ."

By the end of it her laughter is spurting out.

"You don't ever see these kids again," Charlotte tells her, stepping in.

"I've got the rest of senior year left," Charley says aloud, looking around and rattling the jug of BBs.

"Why do you want to go back through?" Charlotte asks, squinting to try to make this make sense.

Charley doesn't answer, has the remote now, is studying it like seeing it for the first time.

She points it at the television, unpauses medieval *SpongeBob*.

On-screen—it's either still the medieval one, or the twins restarted it—Squidward is the jester.

Charley huffs a laugh out, falls back into the couch exactly like every babysitter ever, once the kids are down. Never letting her eyes leave the screen, she peels out of her jester costume, and Murphy—"Murphy"—was right: it's one-piece, a pain. Under it she has Charlotte's mom jeans, her same too-big flannel shirt tied at the belly.

Charley hangs the empty jester getup over the far arm of the couch, and on the way back to her chosen place she collects the buckskin dress and the stained nurse whites.

They make Charlotte take a step back.

The kids left the living room without their *clothes*?

"Where the fuck are they?" Charlotte says to Charley. "What have you done with them? Tia, Tia, can you hear me?"

The real name doesn't work, though.

"This is such bullshit," Charlotte says again.

Charley shakes her—*Charlotte's*—hair out behind her, leans forward to tie it into a high messy bun.

"I don't wear it like that," Charlotte tells her. "I haven't worn it like that since elementary."

At Charley's jaw on the right side, kind of under, there's still a crumbly streak of leftover white face paint. And there's some in both her eyebrows too.

"Why a jester?" Charlotte asks her, cocking her head over like trying to shake the good answer up. Was it because of that stupid jack-in-the-box? The one Ronald was supposed to . . . do *what* with, exactly?

Charley brings her eyes back up from the hair-tying operation and studies the living room, says, not in Charlotte's direction, and not that loud either, but kind of sly and knowing and almost playful, "Are you here yet, babysitter?"

Charlotte doesn't move.

"You know what I'm waiting for the most?" Charley goes on, just generally, out loud. "A *bath*." She has to chuckle about this. "Seriously. I know, right?"

Charley stands up between the couch and the coffee table, trying out the arms and legs of this new body.

"Look, Mom," she says all around, "I dressed up for Halloween this year! I'm an Indian, can you believe it!" She claps whoops from her mouth, brings her knees up in dance, spins around with it.

"That's not your body," Charlotte tells her. "That's not your life."

"Or maybe you're not here," Charley goes on, giving up the Indian act.

"Just tell me where the kids are," Charlotte steps in to say, standing right between Charley and *SpongeBob*.

"But no trick 'r treating until all messes are cleaned up," Charley tells herself, and steps into the kitchen, comes out humming to herself, carrying the rest of the twins' costumes in her arms. And the packaging.

She plunks down onto the couch with it all, loses herself in *SpongeBob* for a solid thirty seconds, long enough that Charlotte finally has to watch some as well, to see what's so interesting. It's just the same Bikini Bottom, dialed back a few hundred years.

Her eyes still glued to the screen, Charley starts picking at the tomato sauce dried on Ronald's nurse whites, then sneers when crumbling that dryness off doesn't make the red underneath go away. Instead of taking them to the sink, then—it's hopeless, but you have to try—she folds them this way and that, trying to hide the stain. When it's good enough, she works it back into the plastic sleeve—just what Charlotte would have done, if she were a crap babysitter.

What this means, though? Tomorrow night, when it's dress-up time, Mrs. Wilbanks is going to shake the folds from these nurse whites, see what's obviously lasagne dripped down the front, and then look over the top of that costume to her guilty son, who has some explaining to do.

Halloweens have been ruined by less, haven't they?

Charlotte looks up to the second floor, trying to see past the posts, hoping to see Ronald at the railing, sneaked up from bed, and then she thins her lips, pissed at herself: when she went up there, it wasn't to find the kids—the kids were right there on the couch already, didn't need to be found. She'd been all about the office, and when she came *out* of the office she'd . . . she'd walked right past Ronald's room, hadn't she? She had, yes. And she'd only stopped at Desi's because the water turned off, never falling back to that night at the Lopezes'. What's important to her now about it all is that she never once looked into *Ronald's* room, just, sort of, Desi's. These kids are twins, though, and six years old, aren't they? They probably still sleep in the same bed more often than not.

"Found you," Charlotte says.

That has to be where Charley put them: to bed. Not because she's a good babysitter, but just to get them out of the way, so she could find the funny places. Charlotte's been having a panic attack about them for nothing. And now it's time for that panic attack to wind down, thank you.

She lurches across the living room on her bad foot and worse leg, pulls herself upstairs with the handrail, and, halfway up, SpongeBob's machine-gun laughter straightens her back. She looks back to the couch and Charley is still just folding and refolding Halloween, isn't fiddling with the remote, isn't thumbing the volume higher just to screw with the babysitter.

"Don't go anywhere," Charlotte tells her, climbing up, up, each step torture.

The master bedroom closet is dark now, the office door at the end of the hall closed again. Because Charley, Tia, whatever, because she's getting the house back in order for the Wilbankses' return, right? Because she wants to be here Friday after Friday, tossing single BBs into all the dark places, waiting for one not to bounce back.

Charlotte pulls herself into Desi's doorway, looks in again just to cross this bed off the list, and sees the little lump of her under her covers. "Shit yeah," Charlotte says. At last, something good, something right.

Except, some evil part of her whispers, what if it's really Tad again, eyeless, wanting to pull her into the memory he can't stop living. What if it's a roiling pile of maggots, or—or what if it's Desi, but it's Desi with scissors shoved down her throat deep enough to pin her to the mattress?

Charlotte hates her mind sometimes. All the time.

"Des?" she says timidly, not quite letting go of the door-frame yet.

The pink beanbag isn't glowing from the inside, at least. But all the My Little Ponies are most definitely watching.

Charlotte lowers her head, staggers forward, comes down on the edge of the bed. Enough to wake a sleeper, but she's not shaking the real mattress, probably.

"Desi?" she says again, and touches Desi's hip lightly.

Nothing.

Not Tad, not Tad, she says to herself, trying to make it true, and pulls the covers back gently, an inch at a time, exposing Desi's blond hair. Her blond hair that's absolutely perfect, even sort of styled, a kind of flip-turn at the bottom.

What?

Charlotte runs her hand along that hair, and it's . . . it's not right.

She grips her hand into it, pulls gently in case this *is* Desi, and an oversized My Little Pony turns to face her. One with an expensive blond mane.

Charlotte pulls the covers lower and Desi's body is all pillows and ponies, puzzled together into the shape of a six-year-old.

"No," Charlotte says, standing before she remembers her leg isn't into that.

She collapses into the beanbag and it envelops her, is a giant pink slug trying to suffocate her, disappear her. She fights, kicks, finally manages to spill out onto the little rug.

On her hands and knees, her hair in her face, she just breathes, breathes.

When she looks to the side, to check the beanbag, it's just a kid's pink beanbag, one Desi will outgrow in T-minus five or ten minutes, and when Charlotte checks her other side, to be sure the bed is there acting like a wall for her, a coolness presses into the wet of her eyes, a harsh oily tang assaults her nostrils, and then she tracks reluctantly to the source, almost hidden in shadow: Tad, under the bed. Not watching her, he can't—no eyes, and also he's *dead*—but tracking the sounds she's making. Sniffing the air for her.

He draws back, deeper into the dark, and Charlotte pushes away as fast as she can, scrabbles across the floor for the door, and the moment she pulls into the safety of the hall, Desi's bathroom door slaps open, startling Charlotte up onto her bad leg, leaving her grabbing for whatever she can find—the railing again.

She pulls hard to it, is about to trust it to take her weight, to keep her safe, but—

"That's what you want," she says, opening her hand, hovering it above that smooth lacquered blonde wood.

She was supposed to go over a second—no, a *third* time— wasn't she? Or through. Down. Because that's when this house that's not the house has her: when she's falling, when she's between places. That's when it can land her wherever. It can nudge her into this version of itself, into that fear, this memory, into some other ready-made nightmare mined up from Charlotte's own head.

Charlotte pushes her back into the wall, makes her way to the linen closet and stands up beside it, the wall still supporting her. The little vacuum doesn't come out to play. Charlotte taps the linen closet door with her palm, nods thank you, then stops, remembers, pulls the door open slowly.

All the board games are back on their shelves. All the sheets are folded and arranged.

She closes the door, holds it there until she's sure it's not springing open.

Ronald's room, right around the corner.

Charlotte stands in the doorway long enough for her eyes to adjust to the darkness. Long enough to see the headless woman in a nightgown standing by Ronald's bed, her chest black with blood.

"This was her room, wasn't it?" Charlotte says. "Tia's."

Nora Spinell's hand is opening and closing, bubbles sliding down to the fingertips, dripping onto Ronald's blankets.

Charlotte backs out, knows that if she were to creep in, pull Ronald's covers down, it wouldn't be him. Worse, Nora Spinell might look up at her with—with the stump of her neck, and Charlotte would fall into that bloody hole, that open windpipe, or that windpipe would try to whisper some secret to her, something that would scream from side to side of her skull, never stop.

So, the twins *aren't* up here.

That's what you came up here to find out, she reminds herself. Nothing else. *That's how you get lost in here. Don't investigate sounds, don't follow shadows, don't open doors you don't need to open. Have a mission and stick to it.* Charlotte's mission right now, it's the twins. And, if they're not tucked into their beds— lights-out eyes-closed or -shut, whatever—then . . . what would Charley have done with them? Where could she have stashed them?

Also: why? If there's no kids to babysit, if the twins are out of the picture, then there's no coming back next Friday. Really, there's probably just going to jail.

And Charley couldn't have stashed them in a funny place, Charlotte knows. Charley doesn't know where the funny places are anymore. Only Charlotte does, now that she's on this side of things.

But—but Charlotte can't *tell* her, can she? Isn't it only Ronald who can see the shadow people? And anyway, if Charley goes back into a funny place with Charlotte's body . . . Charlotte doesn't know. Are they both stuck here forever?

She wishes her mom were here, to help run all this down. She has that step-by-step way of thinking, doesn't allow any nonsense into it, is all about—

Charlotte stops, feels her eyes narrowing with possibility.

Why not call her, then? It's the obvious solution.

She palms her phone up from her pocket and the screen comes alive from being raised.

She puts her thumb on the home button to let it read her print, but, instead, it kicks up the number pad.

"Huh," Charlotte says, but swipes through the four numbers—her initials plus Murphy's, so cute. The screen goes black before she can finish.

She shakes the phone awake, goes through it all again, entering her code faster this time. The numbers aren't glowing from her touch, though. Because she's not really touching them, even though she brought the phone across with her. It should be made of whatever she is, shouldn't it? Can't a shadow make contact with a shadow, at least?

"Shit," Charlotte says, and shoves the phone back in

her pocket, turns to clock the hall behind her, make sure no headless women are shambling her way, and then the wall beside her explodes into her head.

The doorbell.

She reaches up, touches her ear canal on that side with the pad of her index finger. It comes back powdery white. She snaps by that side of her head, has to look at her fingers to be sure they're snapping.

So, no more sound on that side now.

Wonderful.

With her other ear, though, she can still hear the after-chime of the doorbell. Charlotte reaches up, touches that high-up box with her whole hand, letting it vibrate down her arm, the tone filling her for a moment before she realizes what this sound actually maybe might mean.

Someone's here.

It doesn't matter who it is, who it might be, Charlotte has to be there before Charley. That's the only important thing. Never mind that, like with the garage door, she probably can't haul this one open anymore. Never mind that she can't sneak past whoever it is, *not* run into a hanging vinyl nightscape.

It's not about thinking, it's about getting there. Down the stairs. Which Charlotte takes two at a time, also not thinking about them, or herself.

Her bad leg gives on her second long step and she falls grasping for the handrail, goes head over feet into the second half of the wooden stairway, her mouth filling with dry white when her face slams into a step. She sputters it out in a dull white spout, keeps rolling, and instead of coming down in a jagged pile on the hard tile floor of the entryway, or in some scene still happening in the past, or in what could have been, instead of all that she splashes into *water*.

Because that's what she told the kids the entryway was.

She gulps it in and it's soapy, so when she tries to gag it out the bubbles remain, are still choking her, and it's deep under her feet, and—she's only just registering this—it's *hot*.

Charlotte thrashes, kicks, clamps onto what's supposed to be the hardwood floor of the living room but is a slick bathtub shelf of shampoo and bubble bath bottles, and one squeeze turtle.

She throws herself the other way, just manages to grab the last upright post of the stairway railing. At which point the surface of the water around her gets soupy and thick, starts to get regular lines. It's gridding up, it's—it's turning back into the tile entryway, shit.

Charlotte grabs the railing with her other hand and pulls, fights up onto the hard-enough surface, makes it all the way out except for . . . the last half of her right foot? It's embedded in the tile?

She pulls gently at first, the doorbell ringing above her again, filling her head with sound even though it can only be coming in through one ear, and then, when Charley is hustling up from the couch, Charlotte just jerks with everything she's got.

The front part of her foot breaks off, stays there.

She drags herself up onto the first step, inspects her foot. It's—it's like one of those Fun Dip candy sticks, one you just dipped into the colored sugar, so it's all blue on the outside, but, if you bite it in half, then it's shockingly white and dry on the inside.

She touches this white candy center and feels a nerve twinge in her calf, but otherwise there's nothing. Just the feel of the pad of her finger pushing against that springy tofu.

She looks up from this to Charley, standing by the couch and saying, "Wait, wait," trying to pause *SpongeBob*. She bustles up onto the entryway to answer the door exactly like Charlotte was told not to do, but then at the last moment she stops, turns back to the living room, holding her hand out, fingers spread as if she's checking things one last time, to make sure there's nothing left out to give her away.

When it's clear—just two costumes on the coffee table, folded and packaged away like new, and one jester costume on the arm of the couch—she shakes her head, getting limber for whatever interaction this is going to be, collects her hair behind one shoulder, and shoves her hand into her pocket for the key.

Charlotte touches her own pocket for that same key. It's not there. Not in the other pocket either.

Charley pulls the door back just enough to see out, like you do at night.

"Yes?" she says, her voice neither inviting nor standoffish. Just polite.

Whoever's out there doesn't say anything.

Charlotte leans over to try to see but now the alarm is giving its little reminder chirrup, the keypad blinking some countdown.

"Oh, oh," Charley says, going from foot to foot to remember

the code. "Hold on," she says to whoever's out there, and, choosing each glowing number at the last moment, she gets it right first try. The keypad relaxes back into peaceful green.

"Now," she says, her attention coming back to this caller, her body still blocking the doorway, her nervous left foot digging into the still-tacky tile. Charlotte fixes on that, waits to see if the sock will stick. It's close, she thinks, but it doesn't quite grab onto the tile. Or the other way around, she guesses. Charley doesn't seem to feel the slick of bubbles at the edges of the entryway either. The entryway's just an entryway again.

When Charley's left hand drops to the knob on the house side, like to open the door farther, Charlotte pushes back across the tile, stands fast against the closet door, catching the back of her head on the knob again.

Her hands find this new pain without her having to tell them to and the world spins and tilts, her eyes the shaky center of that ride. She holds on as best she can, one hand flat to the closet door, the other exploring this new injury. If it looks like it feels, then it's shrimp meat puffing up from its thin shell. When she pushes it back in, slower this time to keep from having to scream, it rewinds her back to years ago then fast-forwards her all at once, through playing in the sprinklers on Murphy's lawn in first grade, getting gum stuck in her hair the morning of a sleepover, sitting in the ER waiting for her mom's shift to be over, her legs not long enough to reach the ground, and then before she's even close to ready she's rushing through the PSATs, her heart beating in her throat, only, when everybody in that classroom with her turns around to the disturbance she's being, they all have black diamonds painted over their yellow eyes, and—

Charlotte opens her eyes to a murmured response from the porch, the question already gone.

"Excuse me?" Charley says, her hand still to the door like any girl knows to do, even if she's been shuttered in the ghost-half of a house for more than half her life. Meaning it's a *man* out there, not early trick 'r treaters, not a neighbor-mom informing the babysitter that the parents are going to be later than they meant.

Cop, cop, cop, Charlotte prays, not at all sure how a police officer could make this situation better, then she gets a glimpse.

It's the homeless man. The one Neighborhood Watch was supposed to have already called about. Which is maybe even better than a cop, right? People living on the street aren't fitted with society's blinders, can see what's really happening—who's *really* answering this door.

At least Charlotte wants this to be true.

She reaches across for the round newel at the head of the stairway rail, pulls herself around to see more of her savior.

His clothes are grimy and layered, his face bristly with beard, his eyes dull under the brim of his crooked cap. It's the kind of look you can smell, the kind that stings your eyes.

"Who are you?" he's saying to Charley, like he doesn't understand who knocked on whose door, here.

"Who are you looking for?" Charley asks back.

The man considers this question for an awkwardly long moment, and Charlotte realizes it's not the actual question that's gumming up his thoughts, it's that it's a response at all. Someone's talking to him like a person.

He looks like he might be about to cry.

"My—I'm looking for my daughter," he finally says, trying

to peer around Charley, and when she steps to the side to let him, letting the door swing back all the way, Charlotte can see how she's now *watching* this man. Not like he might be the threat Mrs. Wilbanks was sure he was, but like . . . she recognizes him?

There's wonder on her face. A kind of waiting excitement. Charlotte can feel it radiating off her.

"Tia, you mean?" Charley says to him.

It brings the man's eyes back to her.

"Do you live here now?" he asks, measuring his words, his tone, and maybe—yes—trying to reel his kerosene breath in, too.

"I'm the babysitter," Charley says primly.

"Have you seen her?" the man asks.

Charley turns back to study the living room with him, says, "I don't—do you want to look for yourself, maybe?"

"*No!*" Charlotte screams right over Charley's shoulder, but she can't stop the homeless man from stepping in, and she can't stop the door from closing behind him, the alarm pad on the wall blipping once. Charley twists the deadbolt over, pockets the key.

"You've seen her, haven't you?" the man says.

"You must be . . . *Mr. Spinell*," Charley says, sitting on the couch, patting the cushion beside her for him.

He's just watching her, but a breath or two later he's sitting where she offered, is looking around this living room.

"That wall used to be . . . Nora liked green," he says.

Charlotte turns to a rustling up the stairs and there at the railing, both her hands curled around that smooth wood, is Nora Spinell, bib of dried blood on her nightgown, neck stump still and forever seeping. Maybe you always know the vibration of your husband's voice, though. Maybe you can feel it in the gasping hole of your windpipe, after this many years.

"Why do you think she would still be here?" Charley asks, the cheer in her voice sick to Charlotte's ears—Charlotte's *ear*.

"I told that detective," Mr. Spinell says, blinking away tears, his nervous fingers clamping onto the jug of BBs at his knees, tilting them right then left, the little copper balls avalanching back and forth.

"Murphy's dad . . ." Charlotte hears herself saying, trying to make sense of Mr. Spinell's response.

"You must be starving," Charley says to him, standing in that way that means she's been forgetting her manners.

"No, I—"

She's already making for the kitchen.

Charlotte reaches forward with her half-foot, gives it her timid weight. It doesn't hurt to touch its blunt edge, but it's searing agony to put weight on it. Trying to keep her weight in her arms—like that works—she limps and hitches into the center of the living room, planning to . . . she doesn't know . . . get Mr. Spinell's attention somehow?

Instead, trying to stand on her heel, she loses her balance, tilts backward into the entertainment center, the television.

A book or two spills, a vase tilts over on its shelf without breaking, but not a thing shifts in the real living room.

Charlotte stays leaning against the bright television screen, is slight enough on this side that she can feel its warmth like a space heater. It's not just warmth, though. It's almost like . . . gravity? No: static cling.

Mr. Spinell looks up, grins . . . right at Charlotte? He can *see* her?

She waves wildly, desperately, and his eyes track away.

"What?" she says, and leans back, away from the pain in her foot. Into the pleasant warm television screen.

Mr. Spinell grins again. Or—Charlotte looks down to her hand on the screen—he's not smiling about *her*, but the television. Her hand is distorting the paused picture.

She pulls her fingers away and it's like trying to get free from suction. The light from the screen goes with her for an inch or two, then drips back into *SpongeBob*. At least to her eyes, on this side.

Mr. Spinell can probably only see some version of the ripples, an interruption of the screen or the colors, some pebbly imperfection the picture's finding its way around.

"Yes, yes!" Charlotte says, and touches the screen with her other hand, dragging iridescent swirls down across Patrick's starfish face.

Mr. Spinell looks away, up to Charley, mincing back in with a plate.

"I don't walk like that," Charlotte tells her.

It's the second container of lasagne, dumped out and warmed up, a fork chocked into it at exactly the right angle for that first bite, like Charley's primed this lifesaving meal.

"What are these for?" Mr. Spinell says, setting the jug of BBs down to take the plate.

"They were just there," Charley says, taking her place on the couch and tucking her feet up under her. "Maybe the dad who lives here now . . . maybe he doesn't like squirrels?"

Mr. Spinell looks over to the idea of the backyard, says, as if connecting this word to the concept, to the animal, "Squirrels."

"Tree rats with bushy tails?" Charley says with what Charlotte can tell is a fake smile—is *her* fake smile.

"Squirrels hibernate, don't they?" Mr. Spinell says.

Charley watches him like the holy oracle he isn't, and shrugs, playing along.

"You bitch," Charlotte says.

It falls on no ears.

"*Look, look!*" she screams, and rakes all her fingernails across the screen, nearly dragging sparks.

Patrick wavers and undulates, almost dances, but nobody's watching him.

"I used to live here," Mr. Spinell says around his first bite—*through* the bite, really.

"It's a good house," Charley says, blinking twice like to make it true. "Lots of . . . *room.*"

"I found my daughter in the wall once," he adds, like it's the natural next thing to say, like this is something any father might say about his kid.

"In the . . ." Charley says, ever so politely, then abandons the question, opts for another: "What did you—what did you *do*?"

"I think she's there again," he says. "This house . . . I don't know. I think it's like a Venus flytrap. Do you know what that is?"

"It's for flies?"

"It waits for a fly to stumble in, and then it traps it inside, digests it for . . ."

Charlotte looks high on the wall to whatever Mr. Spinell's tracking.

"For years?" Charley completes for him.

"She was in the master bedroom closet," he goes on,

chinning upstairs. "She was . . . the house was already eating her. But I pulled her back. I think it got a taste for her then, though. I think it found a way to—to get her back inside."

"Or something," Charley adds.

This quiets Mr. Spinell. He studies his lasagne.

"I have to save her," he says at last. "That's what . . . I'm her dad, I mean. I'm supposed to. She's been waiting for me all these years."

"I don't know if the people who live here want a—you know," Charley says. "Like, a hole in their wall?"

"I can pay," Mr. Spinell says, looking upstairs and forking another bite in, chewing contentedly until his eyes find the jack-in-the-box.

He stops chewing, rattles the plate onto the coffee table, his hands jerky and unmedicated all of the sudden.

"Yes?" Charley says, so hopefully.

He looks from the jack-in-the-box to her, then back to the jack-in-the-box.

He's breathing deep now. Like afraid.

"That was my—my son's," he says, taking it into his lap reverently.

"Your son?" Charley says, eyes open wide to drink every last drop of this deliciousness in.

"Shut up," Charlotte tells her.

"Thaddeus. Tad."

"You left it behind when you moved out?" Charley prompts.

Mr. Spinell doesn't answer.

Moving slow and deliberate, Charley reaches across, removes the jack-in-the-box from his hands and places it like a ritual object on the coffee table.

Charlotte studies it, looking for that sheen she could see through the nanny cam.

"Mrs. Wilbanks told me not to let the kids play with that," Charley says. "I think she's trying to restore it or something?"

Mr. Spinell nods but Charlotte can tell this isn't quite registering with him. That finally being back in his old house is overloading him.

"Wilbanks?" he finally asks.

"They live here now."

He keeps nodding. He's looking up at the balcony now, pressing his lips together.

"If I can just," he says, "they won't mind if I just go up there and feel around inside there. She's been there for ten years."

"Ten?"

"Eleven."

"Wouldn't that make her . . . about my age now?" Charley asks.

Mr. Spinell keeps staring at the balcony. Finally, he brings that stare down to Charley.

"What's your name?" he asks. "I mean, not to be—"

"Charley," Charley says. "Short for Charlotte."

"Chucky and Charlemagne," Mr. Spinell says right back.

"Um, what?" Charley asks.

"Charley starts like Chucky, with a hard *ch*, and Charlotte is—"

"Charlemagne," Charley completes. "You're not all there anymore, are you?"

"When are they home, these Wilbankses?"

Charley shrugs, says as if she couldn't be less concerned, "Any minute?"

Mr. Spinell gets his lasagne plate again, slurps a big bite in, some of it hanging up in his matted beard.

"There's more in the fridge," Charley offers.

"I know she's still here," Mr. Spinell says back.

"Why do you want to find her?" Charley asks, boring her eyes into the side of Mr. Spinell's face.

He doesn't look over, just says, "When I walked in that night—when I came home, my wife, Nora, she was, she was . . ."

He points to the balcony fast with his fork, cheese trailing behind, hanging between, and then he buries the tines back in the lasagne like he doesn't want to get caught pointing.

"She was waiting for you, wasn't she?" Charley says.

"Tia too," Mr. Spinell adds.

"What do you mean?" Charley asks, turning her whole body to him, her right arm cushioning her head.

"I only saw her for a—a flash," he says, squinting like looking into the past. "I told the detective, even showed him where and everything."

Charlotte leans in about this.

"But she was dead in the bath upstairs, wasn't she?" Charley says. "That's what we all heard at school, I mean."

"She was . . . just out of the bath, I guess," Mr. Spinell says. "She was running through the living room, right over there. I heard her feet on the kitchen floor, slap slap slap, but when I ran in there . . ."

"No," Charlotte says, steepling her hands over her mouth. "No no no."

The stories were *true*?

"They told me I—that it was wishful thinking," Mr. Spinell says. "But there were, the detective found them before they all went away, there were bubbles on the carpet. They wouldn't be there if she hadn't really ran through just then, would they?"

Charley shakes her head no, they probably wouldn't.

"But her skin was all coming off," Mr. Spinell adds, holding back tears now.

"Was that why she didn't like baths?" Charley asks. "Because of the hot water?"

Charlotte studies her about this leading question.

"Kids don't like bath time until they're in the bath," Mr. Spinell says, the skin around his eyes crinkling with the memory.

"Was it that bathroom she didn't like, maybe?" Charley asks, so earnest. "Was it that it only had one door, and is maybe six feet by eight feet, counting the bathtub?"

He looks over to her.

"She didn't like enclosed spaces," he says, like slow-motion agreeing with Charley. "The—the doctor said she would grow out of it, probably."

"So," Charley says, digging into this, "so as she got bigger and the world around her got comparatively smaller, this feeling of being closed in would somehow go away? Interesting."

"But she didn't like going outside either," Mr. Spinell says.

"Because it felt like she might fall up into the sky?"

"How do you—?"

"I've studied this," Charley says. "Agoraphobia at one end of a fragile, incomplete, still-maturing psyche, claustrophobia at the other end, no real happy place between the two."

"Studied it where?" Charlotte asks.

"We had to take her out of school," Mr. Spinell says, buying Charley's sincere understanding.

"Classrooms are so small for a girl with her . . . *issues*."

"We'd have to sedate her to get from the front door to the—to the car," Mr. Spinell says, his eyes getting a shine to them.

"What are you saying?" Charlotte asks him. And her.

"I wonder what kind of space would have been perfect for a little girl like her, then?" Charley says all dreamily, and Charlotte can't help but flash on Ronald and Desi's injunction to her, stepping into the water heater closet: Don't open your eyes. And that vast feeling in there, that was also pressing on her at the same time. It was a cloying muggy closeness combined with the distinct sense of unlimited space. Perfect for a little girl afraid of the sky *and* of closets.

"You don't want to go through," Charlotte says aloud. "You want to go *back*. You want to *stay* there. You opened your eyes when you were in there, didn't you? There was nobody to warn you not to."

"Maybe she would have liked a, a huge cavern underground or something, I guess," Mr. Spinell is saying. "But, she would have gotten better. The doctors said."

"If your wife hadn't killed her, you mean?" Charley says, and Mr. Spinell looks over to be sure he heard right.

"I don't—" he starts.

"Did your wife's head really pop off?" Charley asks with a thrill. "Like a"—she takes the jack-in-the-box, turns the crank slowly ahead—"like one of these, right?"

She smiles about this, holding her breath for that next vital click.

"They never found it," Mr. Spinell says. "Her head. They thought I, that I had—but I wouldn't."

"*Leave, leave, go!*" Charlotte screams to him, and turns to the television screen, hitting it with her shoulder now.

Mr. Spinell doesn't notice, but Charley does.

"Oh," she says. "You're here, then."

"Don't do this," Charlotte says to Charley, and steps ahead like she can actually stop this from happening.

"Look, Dad, it's your daughter," Charley says, pointing to . . . not *SpongeBob*, Charlotte knows. To her own dim outline in the television. "I think you're right. She is still here. She's trying to talk to you."

Charlotte looks back to the screen, still rippling, and shakes her head no, no.

"There's a reason they never found your wife's head," Charley says then, cranking the jack-in-the-box one more quarter-turn. She stops, looks up to be sure she has all of her dad's attention to say it: "When I ran into the kitchen, I was carrying it."

He looks over to her like to confirm she's really saying what he's hearing.

"I didn't get to go to—to any underground cavern, though," Charley says, shrugging that whole ordeal off. "I was stuck . . . I guess you could say 'between,' right? I was stuck between. All I had for eleven years that was real was—you guessed it—my mother's head. But things don't rot away the same over there, when you're between. And, if you've got enough time, and you really really want to, if your parents taught you to never give up, if they told you that you can do anything if you try, then you can take that hair, those bones, those teeth, that white putty on the inside, and you can lick them all together like a baby pearl, shape them into something new.

Something better. Something you can *use*."

She holds the jack-in-the-box up for show-and-tell, and now Charlotte can see that that sheen the paint has, it's dried blood.

"N-*Nora*?" Mr. Spinell says in mounting awareness—the scrollwork in the kind of armored-up corners of the box are teeth, pushed in root-first—and then, maybe a breath later but still years too late, he straightens his arms against the couch cushion he's sitting on, pushes away from Charley.

"You're—you're not her!" he says. "She's in the walls, I know. I can—I can still save her!"

"Funny thing about walls," Charley says. "Feel along them long enough, say, eleven *years*, and you find a doorway. One you can step through."

She presents herself with a flourish, and some style.

Mr. Spinell shakes his head no, no.

"Your eyes were, they weren't—" he tries.

"They weren't like Taddie's, you got that right," Charley says, and rolls over to straddle him, her hands caressing his rough face. "Remember?" she says, "his were more like—"

She punches her thumbs through his eyeballs, one of them spurting up onto her throat so she has to stretch her chin up and away, straighten her elbows to drive her thumbnails deeper and deeper in.

"No!" Charlotte screams.

Charley drives her thumbs in up to her hand, and she, she—no.

She's pulling to the *side*, and smiling as she does it, not just not looking away, but drinking this in, not wanting to miss a single moment of it.

Her dad's hands come up to wrap around her wrist but he can't stop this.

The skin over the bridge of his nose tightens, stretches white, and then the bone in there, his skull, it fractures down the center of his face. Charlotte can't see it, but she can almost feel Charley's hands suddenly pushing a half-inch over in each direction, like she was trying to work a giant walnut open and it just gave.

Mr. Spinell goes limp, his left hand spasming down, the ring finger and pinky curling up right at the end. Blood wells up in his mouth but doesn't quite spill.

Charley leans down to him, whispers in his ear, "You were right, Daddy. I was in the walls. I never left." She kisses him on the forehead and straightens her arms against his chest. "But I'm getting back, don't worry," she adds, standing away from him. "And this time I'm going all the way in, and you can't save me anymore. It's where I need to be."

Charlotte turns away, throws up into her hand.

It's dry white crumbles, like flash-dried cottage cheese.

"You can't stop me either," Charley says without turning around, her shoulders rising and falling, her hands dark with blood, the fingers opening and closing. "Oh, babysitter?"

"I'm not helping you," Charlotte tells her.

"No, no, you're going to bleed on the rug . . ." Charley says about Mr. Spinell's body. To keep his mouth from spilling red out, she props his head up with a pillow. His head immediately rolls to the side, though. Only Charley's fast reflexes and cupped hand keep his mouthful of blood from the rug. Holding his head on her knee, she looks around for where to wipe her hand, finally thrusts her hand under the end cushion. "There," she says, and props the pillow under his head again. Just like before, his face turns immediately to the side. "Very funny," she says, then to the idea of Charlotte: "Enjoying this, babysitter?" She hauls her father's body up to a sitting position, holding him up from the back, looking around. "Where, where . . ." she's saying, then she shrugs like *whatever*, uses one shoulder to pry up the couch cushion with the bloody underside. With her outstretched foot, she tilts the other two back. Then, having to practically wedge under him, she scooches him up onto the box-spring part of the couch, being sure to jam his face into the rear cushion to keep it from rolling to the side again.

She stands, appreciates her work.

"See, babysitter?" she says. "No blood. And—" she steps forward, arranges the three cushions over him in lumpy, joking fashion—"nobody can even tell he's there, right?"

This is hilarious to her.

"Just temporary," she says to Charlotte, looking around, to the kitchen. No: the garage. "Didn't I have to put a saw back on the wall for you?" she says. "This may be more of a garbage disposal situation, I guess. With trash bags. Unless you want to tell me where any dark light is shining through . . . ?"

"Don't do this," Charlotte tells her.

"You will tell me, don't worry," Charley says, and strides out. Charlotte hears the garage door swing back, the pegboard of tools rattle.

It's just her and dead Mr. Spinell now.

"I'm sorry, sir," she says, and then steps back in wonder, and fear: the couch cushions are sighing down into their place, flattening out.

Charley walks back in right when Mr. Spinell's hand is slipping into the crack between the cushion and the couch. She drops the saw, dives forward, just touches his fingers as they're slipping away.

On her knees now she rips the cushions up and flings them away, jumps up onto the box-spring part but it's too late.

"You could have fucking told me!" she screams all around to Charlotte. "This could all be over right now already! I could already be over there . . ."

She collapses onto the couch, screamcrying with frustration. With loss.

"I know you're still here," Charley says after maybe a minute.

She melts down off the couch and leans back against it, spent, her knees up before her, forearms on her knees, hands hanging.

Looking at her is like looking into a mirror.

Charlotte draws a temporary X on the television screen.

Charley registers it, lets her head fall backward, her eyes watching the ceiling, Charlotte guesses.

"Tad was the one who found the way in, did you know?" she says, just talking out loud. "I guess you wouldn't. He was a cute boy, I'll give him that. But he was a scab picker, too. Mom used to joke that he needed a funnel thing on his head when he had a cut, to keep him from pulling at it."

"Cone of shame," Charlotte says.

"He was—he got in trouble for picking scabs," Charley says, "so he started, like, *hiding* them. That and his eye crust. He was weird, I don't know. Maybe he would have grown out of it too, right?" This is sickly funny to her. "Anyway, he knew about electricity, but he thought it was blue fire, that it would burn up anything he shoved into the light socket. The plugs on the walls."

Charlotte scans the living room wall, finds an electrical outlet right by the front door.

"Some of the plugs he hid his scabs in, though, they'd kick . . . *other* stuff back out, yeah. It was like a kid-secret, the best thing ever. He didn't know what he had. I don't need to tell you that. When I went through up in their closet, though"—she flings her arm at the couch, at the idea of Mr. Spinell—"*he* reached in, pulled me back." She laughs with the memory, adds, "Screaming all the way, believe you me. Screaming and fucking clawing, babysitter."

She brings her head back, is facing the television now.

Charlotte taps the screen twice, two iridescent ripples.

"She kept—" Charley starts, then does it better: "Mom, I mean. She kept asking why I did it, why I . . . Tad. In the bath." Charley shrugs. "He kept saying my eyes looked different, since I'd, well. You know. Since I'd looked around in there. He said he was going to tell Mom that I needed glasses. But it was just because he was scared. Of what I'd seen. That blackness in there, it's . . . I don't know how to explain it. It's not empty. It's like velvet, really big velvet, but it's also like ash pressing in all around you, or really thin smoke, smoke you can breathe so deep and it doesn't hurt, it's cold, like, and alive, it moves around in your chest, and . . . you didn't look, did you? I don't think you did, no."

"He was four years old," Charlotte says, her hand in place on the television screen, ripples wavering out from her touch.

"But now you're him," Charley says, clipping it off like

pulling the two of them into a new chapter. "Now *you* can tell me where they are, the funny places. No, what I mean is, you *will*."

Charlotte knocks twice on the television screen.

Charley nods, gets it immediately, maybe because she has Charlotte's actual brain in her head.

"You *can* see them?" Charley asks.

Charlotte knocks once.

"You'll tell me where they are?"

Charlotte knocks twice.

"That's not just 'yes' two times in a row, is it?" Charley says with a chuckle.

Charlotte flips her middle finger up, presses her hand like that into the screen.

"How about I give you something for free," Charley says. "Took me a while to figure it out. When you're—when you're between like you are, and you're all bleeding white everywhere, leaving powdery tracks like the fucking Easter Bunny, there's something that kind of . . . cauterizes you shut, like."

Charlotte taps once on the screen with the back of her index finger knuckle.

"Brass," Charley says. "When you're between, brass is so cold it's kind of like hot, I guess, I don't know."

"*Brass?*" Charlotte says, incredulous.

She's already looking around the living room.

All the fixtures are brushed aluminum. All the bookends are marble. All the appliances in the kitchen are cast iron or stainless steel.

"The pans hanging above the island are copper," Charley says. "Copper isn't the same. Copper can suck it."

Charlotte knocks once on the screen.

"Somewhere in this house there's a doorstop," Charley says grandly, mysteriously. "It's a dachshund, but kind of like, stretched out long, for a joke. I think it's sentimental. It weighs like five pounds—you can't pick it up. But you can rub what ails ya on it."

Charlotte knocks on the screen again.

"Okay, okay, it's in the *office*," Charley says, pointing up there with her chin. "That's a freebie. A trust builder."

Charley lays her head back on the couch again.

"Hurry," she says. "They're here any minute, I bet."

Charlotte pushes across to the stairs, hangs onto the rail, still not trusting the entryway, and hauls herself up onto the first step.

"But then I *could* be sending you up there so you won't see where I've stashed the kidlings, of course," Charley says with a smile, still staring straight up.

Charlotte stops trying to pull herself to that impossible second step.

"You bitch," she says again.

Charley laughs to herself, her whole body shaking with it.

"I'm not lying about the brass," Charley says, standing now, stretching one shoulder then the other. "And I'm not lying about little Ronnie and oh-so-adorable Desi, either. What does their mother say? 'Lights-out, eyes-closed?' I kind of like that. I mean, it applies not just to going to sleep, doesn't it?"

"Tell me what you did with them," Charlotte says, stepping back down.

"I can tell you right where they are," Charley says, looking for an accidental moment right into Charlotte's soul. "You might even still be able to save them, I don't know. What time is it anyway?"

They both look to the clock on the mantel.

12:12.

"Car wash is getting *steamy* tonight, isn't it?" Charley says, walking around the coffee table, extending the tip of her middle finger to the television screen. It doesn't waver, doesn't ripple, doesn't care that she's touching it. "All these years," she says, shaking her head with wonder, "I never knew I could be jacking with their shows."

Charlotte lunges forward, plants her hand in the middle of the screen. It ripples with color.

Charley nods, likes that.

They're standing right in each other's faces now.

"So I'm going to give you . . . three minutes," Charley says, stepping back, hands held high to show that this is a Charlotte task, not a Charley thing. "You find where that dark light's shining through, and if it's on *this* side of the house"—the kitchen—"you tap on *that* side of the screen. If it's over by the front door, that side of the screen. If it's upstairs, the top. It'll be like . . . what's that game where you tell somebody they're getting hotter or colder? The funny places don't last long, though. Which you should know by now. We do this right, and this is all over right now, I don't ever have to come back to babysit. Believe me, you don't want me to be the new babysitter. I don't just put the kidlings to bed, I put them to *bed*."

Charlotte stares hard at Charley.

"Tap once in the center of Patrick's forehead if you understand."

Charlotte touches where she's supposed to, and it's like a

slow-motion realization is rippling across Patrick's thoughts.

"Three minutes," Charley says then, and turns, falls back into the couch, counting aloud: "One, two, three . . ."

Charlotte stands there until the count of ten—long enough to accept that this is really happening, that this is really what she's about to have to do—and then she grits her teeth and stiff-legs it as best she can across the living room, into the kitchen.

The dryer is just the dryer again, not a major appliance vomiting bright shadow out its stupid round mouth.

How do you even *find* the funny places? Tad Spinell—she knows from being inside his memory—could open his senses, sort of, and "feel" them.

Not Charlotte.

She pulls the door to the water heater closet open, takes a broom from its holder on the wall and reaches in with the plastic bristles, meets resistance right where she expects to.

She doesn't put the broom back. It's her crutch, her cane, what she's using now to pole herself forward. Holding tight to it with both hands, one high, one tight at the middle, the bristles up by her face, feels better than teetering around, always about to fall.

She eyeballs the utility for where else a tunnel could be. That's what they are to her, that's what this stupid house is: a demented game of chutes and ladders. Well, it's that with some haunted carnival ride mixed in. And a whole maze of unwanted trips down every memory lane she has that might hurt. And she's the clown in all of this, just, she's wearing her white paint on the inside. But don't worry, it's leaking out.

She crutches back into the kitchen, forgetting for a moment that this crutch is a broom, meaning she gets an armpit full of sharp bristles stabbing dirty holes into her.

"*Three minutes?*" she groans uselessly.

There's no way.

First, finding a tunnel has got to be like trying to stomp on the head of a firehose someone's turned on, let whoosh around everywhere from the pressure. And all she has to go on are the rules she can back-figure from what she's seen— rule *singular*: it'll be some tight, dark place.

Well, there might be an upstairs-downstairs component to it too. She's seen nothing to prove that you *can't* duck into the linen closet upstairs, come out just down the hall in Ronald's bathroom, or under Desi's rug, but so far it's only been an upstairs-downstairs thing, anyway.

But, that rug, and the couch: it's not always even an actual *place*, is it? Sometimes a tunnel just opens up where there shouldn't be any space at all.

Shit.

And Charlotte's the shadow lady who's supposed to know where that is? Seriously?

Charley—Tia—had eleven years to get all chummy with the tunnels, to plot them out, keep charts in invisible ink on all the walls, to figure out the pattern, the tendencies, *antici-pate* them instead of just luck onto them.

It can even be behind wallpaper, can't it? That's where it was that first time for Tia. For Tad.

"Fuck this," Charlotte says, and crutches into the doorway of the kitchen.

Charley has *SpongeBob* unpaused, is smiling with it—from Squidward's squeaktacular clarinet playing, it looks like.

For eleven years she hasn't had the remote, Charlotte guesses. It must feel good.

"Ninety seconds!" Charley calls out arbitrarily, without looking away from the screen.

Charlotte makes her painful way out into the living room.

Different plan.

Studying for the SATs, Murphy clued Charlotte in that sometimes it's not about getting the *exact* right answer, it's about sketching out what should be the general shape of that right answer. Like, this proposed angle will probably be obtuse, not acute. That polyhedron will have at least this many sides, not below that many sides. Doing it like that, you can usually get down to a couple of likelies, so if you're jammed for time and have to guess, you can do Murphy's trick of looking back to the previous question, seeing if it was A or B or C or D. Chances are this answer won't be the same, just because of odds. According to her. But, even though she's not going to college, she did flat-out ace the SATs, just to show she could, like she wanted to step over to a life she could have had, leave her own little tag.

Charlotte tries to map out what might be the general area of the right answer to her current problem: either the twins, the brass dachshund, or her body. Those are the three things she needs. And hopefully, of course, the right answer can be all of the above, and all at once. Failing that, though, she itemizes what she's got to solve this problem with: ninety seconds.

Probably more like one minute, now. To be specific, one minute to knock on either this or that side of the television screen, right? Which is a little different than actually solving the problem.

What she *can* do is direct Charley back this way, direct her over to the front-door side of the living room, or send her upstairs generally. And . . . if they're all bullshit, then which bullshit gets her closest to the three things she needs?

If babysitter X has no real options, how can she change the question to eke a few more minutes out, maybe get lucky?

Answer: lie, girl. Lie hard. Lie in a way that benefits you.

"I need that brass dog," Charlotte mutters. Meaning, she doesn't need Charley tromping around upstairs, maybe remembering that she told Charlotte where the dachshund is.

Once Charlotte cauterizes her various cuts shut and sears the pain from the blunt front edge of her foot—once she's keeping her insides from crumbling out—then she can get around better, find the twins, can't she? She won't be able to physically save them, but she's hoping Ronald can at least see her, or some version of her. Maybe. Please. And then she'll find a magic wand that'll get her body back from Tia, yeah. This and other impossible fantasies, coming soon to a venue near Charlotte.

But, possible or not, that's the proper order to come at the first two things anyway: dog, then twins. Dog, then twins.

Say it enough times in a row and it's almost like a plan.

Charlotte nods to herself and crutches forward, slams her palm onto the left side of the screen hard enough that all of Bikini Bottom wavers and ripples.

Charley sits forward, dials her eyes over to the kitchen doorway—what the left side of the screen means.

"Okay, o-kaaayy . . ." she says, standing, pausing the show and then dropping the remote. She's breathing deep, not breaking eye contact with the kitchen doorway, like if she does it might stop being real.

This is everything she's wanted, Charlotte knows. Just to get back to that dark limitless closed-in hug of a place. To step into a tunnel and just camp there forever, infinite space all around in the most pressing, wonderful way.

"It's not the garage," Charley says, thinking out loud. "So . . . kitchen, utility?"

Why not *the garage?* Charlotte wonders. She was counting on the time it would take for Charley to comb three big spaces—the kitchen, the utility, the garage—not just two.

Charlotte touches the left side of the screen again, that warmth suffusing her hand, bleeding up her arm.

"It does like the smell of laundry detergent, I think . . ." Charley says, and disappears into the kitchen, stopping on the way, it sounds like, to check the double oven, the refrigerator, the dishwasher, the trash can that pulls out on smooth rollers from the island.

Charlotte is only just to the entryway when Charley's back, scraping the jug of BBs off the coffee table.

"You can do this," Charlotte tells herself out loud, climbing, not looking back. She's halfway up the stairs with her broom-crutch when she hears the first BB ting off either the washer or the dryer. She stops, considers: What if a tunnel *does* open up in there? If it likes out-of-the-way places, then the utility has to be the default setting for downstairs, doesn't it? And, assuming there's always at least one active tunnel—Charlotte has no real reason to think this—and that they are upstairs-downstairs affairs, then Charley's next BB might *not* be tinging back, right?

And . . . if she does find her happy place?

Then she takes babysitter X's body in there with her, and Charlotte's trapped in this between place for however long she can hold herself together.

She tries to go faster, crutching with the broom, pulling on the handrail.

This can all work, she's telling herself. And wasn't the master bedroom's closet light *off*, earlier, when Charlotte had left it on? Could *that* be where Charley stashed the twins?

But first the office. That brass dog.

This is going to work, she knows. It has to.

She gathers herself for the last push—pull, really—crests up the second half of the stairway, her face level with the floorway of the long hall of the second floor, and—

No.

It's the blue lizard again, but it's the size of a Komodo dragon, is big enough to fill the hall from side to side, and almost end to end as well.

It brings its sluggish head over to fix its black eyes on her, and then, moving languorously, it opens its mouth like to lick her taste off the air, but what it's really doing is exposing the huge black camera lens in its throat, shining it on her like a spotlight. Just, one that's drinking her in.

Charlotte sees the fisheye version of her face in there, flinches from the simultaneous crash of the jug of BBs exploding against the wall in the utility, and then, impossibly, stupidly, she's *seeing* the feed from that camera in the lizard's throat, seeing it on a *screen*.

She looks down to her right hand on the mouse, no red glove on that hand anymore, and then she turns up to the computer monitor in front of her.

Mr. Wilbanks's office.

Charlotte stands so fast from the chair that it rattles over on its back like a roach, one of its lifted casters still spinning in its plastic way.

Don't hyperventilate, don't hyperventilate.

But she does have to breathe, too. Somehow.

She spreads her hand over her upper chest, gasps air in through the spasming constriction she used to call her throat. Then she spins around to the office door, for the giant lizard.

The door's closed. No lizard.

Charlotte takes a step back, feels down for the desk, finds it with her fingertips.

"This is such bullshit," she says at last.

She cases the office again, this time looking for any shadow-people lurking, any spiders darting for cover, any jack-in-the-boxes cranking their little clowns up.

It's the same exact office.

Except . . . she turns back to the monitor, like to interrogate it. She could be wrong, but didn't she knock it over when she ran out earlier? Is this house a videogame? Does each room reset after she leaves?

Charlotte crosses to the door but stops midstep, fascinated with her painless right foot. Her *whole* right foot. She waggles her toes in her sock, says with an almost-smile, "Hey, you." She opens her hand for the cut and her palm is just smooth skin again. She guides it to the back of her head, feels gingerly for the shrimp-meat bulges that make her gag, that send her into random images from her life. They're not there either. She presses her fingers all around through her hair, desperate for at least a bump, a knot, but there's no evidence that the last couple of hours have even happened. Even the tights she was wearing are gone, are probably still on their towel rack in the downstairs bathroom, or maybe even further back than that—in the dryer?

When she brings her hand back, her hair is tangled in the fingers, trails into her vision, is as healthy as ever, doesn't show any signs of having been wrapped twenty times around the hungry roller of a small vacuum cleaner. She brings it to her nose to smell for evidence. Just her same usual shampoo.

"What the hell?" she says, looking around in wonder. It wasn't just the computer monitor that reset, was it? She reset too. Is that how Tia made it across all those years? Do you go back to Go every two or three hours, collect your old body, no harm no foul?

That would be one way to make this last, she knows. And last, and last.

"Then use it," she says to herself, and steps forward with resolve, jerks the doorknob hard, to blast out into the house proper.

It nearly pulls her arm from her shoulder. Because the pull has to go somewhere, she stumbles forward, her face almost making contact with the door. She looks down to be sure her hand's on the knob like it feels like. She turns the knob like insisting that this work, only . . . the knob stays still?

"Hey!" Charlotte barks into the door, kicking it once with her left foot, sure Charley's standing on the other side, holding the knob in place.

No answer. She looks down to her socked foot to see if the stinging she feels was enough to push some dry whiteness up through the fabric's tight weave.

Not quite. Or, not yet. But it does smart.

"Watch yourself," she tells herself, like saying it out loud will make it stick, then ducks down to eye level with the crack at the bottom of the door—houses with hardwood don't have doors flush with the floor—presses her sideways head down to see into the hall.

No feet. Nobody holding the knob. Not that she wouldn't have freaked out if there were, but she had to know, right? She stands, tries to twist the doorknob with *both* hands now, then she spreads her feet wide for a solid base, puts her shoulders and weight into it.

Nothing.

Her left foot, though, it's nudging into something, isn't it? Something both cold and hot through her sock.

Charlotte tracks down, leans over to be sure.

The dachshund. The brass dog. The . . . the supposedly "healing" doorstop.

"You're real," Charlotte says down to it, not looking away, like if she keeps eye contact it maybe won't wag its tail and blip away.

She doesn't know how she missed it before. It's right there behind the swing of the door, its brass muzzle long and pointed and somehow polite, its tail a perfect upturned apostrophe.

She falls to her knees before it, shoves her hands under its long stomach, and . . . nothing. Instead of lifting it up to take it with her, to apply it to her open parts, it's like it's curled its little claws into the hardwood, is standing fast, not budging.

And Charley was right: it's the kind of freezing that burns, that would hiss and sting if she had any white showing through, probably.

Charlotte runs her other hand under the dog's belly as well, gets her feet flat on the ground, and pulls and strains.

Nothing, just a pop in her shoulder that doesn't make sense if she's undifferentiated white through and through.

Is it things in general she can't budge, or is this something new with her?

She raps on the wall to be sure she's solid, and both hears it and—in the bones of her hand and wrist and arm—feels it.

She reaches over to nudge a diploma on its nail. It rocks back and forth.

It's not her, then. She's still here. Here enough. Is this part of some trade-off? Does she get a fixed body, just, she can't do certain things with it?

And—stand still, don't breathe—are those *voices* out in the hall, now?

Charlotte steps right up to the door again, turns her head sideways to press her ear to it, only right then remembering that her eardrum is supposed to be ruptured. But sound's coming in just fine, thanks.

"—and up here is where all the kids' stuff probably needs to stay," Mrs. Wilbanks is saying.

Charlotte's stomach surges and churns and her face washes cold then hot then she doesn't know what. Just numb.

This is the big walk 'n talk tour through the house. It's . . . almost eight o'clock again?

"This is Desi's room on the right," Mrs. Wilbanks is saying, half-muted and distant.

"That short for Desiree?" the Charlotte taking this tour asks, trying to show how smart and capable she is, how tuned in to the twins she's going to be.

"She doesn't like the accent mark," Mrs. Wilbanks says, and Charlotte looks down to her forearm, remembering that Mrs. Wilbanks punctuated *accent* by touching Charlotte there, like to get across how silly children can be, and how Charlotte must surely understand.

Moments later, Charlotte holding her breath in the office to hear better, that drawer in Desi's bathroom screeches open and Charlotte screams with it to try to get their attention, bangs on the door with the sides of her fists, too.

Now the sides of her hands split open. Two or three little bursts on each, a swarm of paper cuts yawning open, her insides that sickly dry white that nearly makes her gag again.

She holds her right hand up and rotates it before her face, gauging these cuts. And then she steps back to see this brass dog again.

It just stares straight ahead, ignoring her in a way that feels elite, like this is a class distinction between it and Charlotte.

"Let's see what you can do, then," Charlotte says to it, and lowers herself to her knees, tries again just on instinct to rotate the heavy little dog around to her. When it still won't budge, she reorients herself to *it*.

"Okay, okay," she says, and nods fast, holds the unhurt side of her right hand with her left to be sure it makes contact, and pushes down all at once.

The white hisses and almost steams and her right hand tries to jerk back but the left is cruel, won't let it.

Charlotte keeps her teeth together, angles her head back, and screams, the cold heat from the brass solidifying tendrils of the whiteness inside, like crystalizing them. After maybe five seconds of this she breaks contact, cradles her hand to her chest and curls forward over it, apologizing. Five seconds after *that*, she gets the nerve to look at it.

The cuts are . . . melted shut? The skin the color of—of *ash*?

It's not pretty, but it's functional. She waggles her fingers to be sure the congealed tofu in her doesn't get in the way. She can waggle fine, but now it's like each finger has a sort of stalk or root in her palm that she wasn't aware of before.

"The Grey Mother," Charlotte says, trying to focus in on which twin said that.

Ronald, it was Ronald.

And it was Grey *Mommy*, but it was really Tia. Just, a Tia who'd lived in this house long enough to have to have grown up, and cauterized her whole body with this brass. Leaving her the color of ash, of shadow.

"You're not like her, you're not like her," Charlotte tells herself, and scooches over to the other side of the dog to press her *left* hand into that healing brass.

It cauterizes the two little ruptures shut, leaves the skin mottled and grey, wrinkled and dead, the shrimp meat on the inside somehow fuller, less giving. Charlotte touches it to her lips and the skin is still warm. It leaves her tongue a pleasant sort of numb, that kind of numb with the sting of returning sensation right under it.

More important: this is really the only brass in the whole house? Are the Wilbankses that well-off, that moneyed-up? When the Spinells lived here, every fixture probably would have been a triage center for any ghost girls caught between houses.

Charlotte stands from the dog, studies the office again.

"Brads," she says, excavating the word up from junior-high art class—from final portfolios. They'd all had to hole-punch their art, then bind it together with "brads." It was the first time she's seen them. Bendy, light—she could lift one of *those*, couldn't she? Even halfway not-here like she is? It wouldn't be as freezing hot, as healing, but it would be portable. She wouldn't be having to clump her way up here for each scratch. She wouldn't have to lie down backward on the hardwood to touch the back of her head to the prissy little dog that's so insulted by this contact that it just keeps staring straight ahead, its back ramrod straight.

"Thanks," Charlotte says to it, and pulls open the top middle drawer of Mr. Wilbanks's desk.

Just like there's supposed to be, it's all binder clips and plastic rulers with price tags still on, staples and paper clips, pens and pencils and snap-rings and one cork coaster with some business logo stamped in raised white on it. And way in the back, a box of BRADS, BRASS, #6, which must be the size or gauge or who cares.

She flicks the top of the thin box open, exposing some fifteen or twenty unbent brads. When she reaches down to pluck one out, though, the cold heat from it already warming her fingertips, there's a sudden and huge bark from *right* fucking behind her. She jerks forward, away from it, driving her right thigh hard into the edge of the desk.

She keeps going, climbs up onto the desk, pulls her feet up. The dog is still just standing there. Same place.

She stares at it and stares at it, finally says, "Seriously, dog?"

Without lowering her feet again, and watching the dog close now, she works the drawer back open, feels down for the box.

It doesn't budge when the back of her fingers knock into it. Like it's superglued to the bottom of the drawer. The top is still flapped back, though.

She crawls her index and middle finger up and in, and this time, instead of a bark, there's a sharp snarl and a *bite*. Not from the open space past the desktop, where that brass dog could conceivably *be*, but . . . from inside the box?

Charlotte jerks her hand back and her index finger is a stump with a white core. She pulls it to her mouth to staunch the blood that's not coming and there's not even any taste, just dryness. She pulls her knees up to her and shudders with sobs, her finger stump still in her mouth, her head shaking no, no, that this can't be happening, no way is this real.

Her index finger is definitely half gone, though. Bitten off by a little brass dog that thinks it's a god. Being digested by a house that's worse than a god. Being digested just like Charlotte is.

"Please, please," she says, and moves over to the corner, farther away from the dog, nudging the mouse enough to wake the monitor again, throw her blurry shadow onto the glass fronts of the degrees on the opposite wall.

She works her way around to see what this is going to be.

It's . . . tweed-brown fabric rushing past too fast for the camera to capture.

And then it's the couch in the living room.

Mr. Wilbanks steps into that field of view and leans down to look into the lizard's mouth.

Of course. This must be what he was getting done while Mrs. Wilbanks was walking the new babysitter around.

He steps back almost to the coffee table, calls upstairs, quiet enough that he doesn't want an actual response, is just kind of checking, "Dear? Hun?"

Because this lizard doesn't have ears, Charlotte has to read it from his lips, and from the hopeful, not-hopeful tilt of his face.

He waits, ready for Mrs. Wilbanks to call down over the balcony, ask him what he wants.

She doesn't.

He flicks his eyes to the lizard again then, and, moving somehow fast and casual at the same time—a motion he doesn't have to think to accomplish anymore—he pulls *his* lizard out.

"Oh, no, no," Charlotte says, turning her face away but not her eyes. Not quite. Not enough.

He's already half-hard.

In two, maybe three strokes, he's all the way there, probably just from the thrill of about to maybe get caught.

"Dear?" he says again, his lips so clear, his eyes so puppy-dog, and then, looking right into the camera, right into his office, "*Charlotte?*"

Charlotte pushes back, away from this, and falls off the desk in a pile of limbs, is scrabbling on the plastic mat his chair rolls on.

It was like he was looking right at her. Like he knew she was watching.

Or, like he had her in his head, anyway.

"Don't don't don't, please," Charlotte says, coming up to her knees to see over the edge of the desk, though she doesn't want to.

She's lost count of his strokes, and probably wouldn't have wanted to count them anyway, but either way he's already hunching forward, about to go off, and then he lunges forward, his other hand pulling the camera down to his crotch, the camera shaking out, spinning to the rug.

It spins to a rest with him in the corner of the frame, sideways, tilted.

He's pulling the blue lizard down, is shooting into its throat, his throat bulging with spasms of pleasure, the lizard swallowing it all, plastic eyes open the whole while.

Mr. Wilbanks nearly falls forward, has to lean his head out of frame, into the shelf or something.

After, spent, he's breathing deep, his eyes kind of dull. He's still with it enough to keep the lizard's mouth tilted up, though. Like a champagne flute he doesn't want to slosh anything thick and white out of. Then he comes back by degrees, finally looks around like just settling down into a living room completely alien to him: his own. One with two women upstairs, two kids who could come crashing to the railing at any moment, to spy on their daddy.

He darts his eyes upstairs, and when he's evidently still alone, he collects the camera again and the feed goes smeary, finally settles back on the couch tableau. On Mr. Wilbanks, wiping his hands on his long plaid scarf then looking at his right palm, smelling it, and rubbing it on the scarf again and then working the scarf ends high and low, brushing it across the back of his neck like anchoring himself in the here and now.

Charlotte looks down to herself, can't remember if he's about to touch her on the shoulder, pat her on the hip, shake her hand.

Mr. Wilbanks walks to the left, his right, and is gone upstairs to remind his wife and the babysitter about certain rooms being off-limits for the night, unaware there's still a red indent pressed into his forehead.

Charlotte shakes her head no, can feel herself crying, she can't even say exactly why. She dabs the wetness from her face and the undersides of her fingers come back white, which is the last color she wants to see right now. Or feel. Or think about.

She rubs it onto the thighs of her jeans and keeps rubbing long after it has to be gone, just to be sure.

Charlotte sweeps all of Mr. Wilbanks's shit off the desk, left to right: the stapler, the lamp, the calendar, the mouse, the mouse pad, the coffee cup of pens and pencils.

They explode against the wall, rattle into the corner.

All that's left is the monitor. She leans forward to hoist it up but its power cord jerks it down, out of her arms. She leaves it lying there on its back, pulls the drawers out instead, throws their papers in the air and walks through them to the wall, tears down the degrees, their thin glass faces shattering at her feet. Then she's face-to-face with the family photographs. Desi and Ronald, growing up. Mrs. Wilbanks looking the same ten years ago as she still looks.

Charlotte turns back to inspect the damage.

The office is the same as it was before.

The only difference is . . . Desi, in the recording?

Charlotte leans over, looks down into the screen, flickering unhappily now.

Desi's standing in the right edge of the lizard's field of view, and her mouth—

It's lasagne.

The twins have already tunneled downstairs to sneak into the kitchen, but Desi just heard Charlotte calling for her from the upstairs hall, and can't help drifting out here in response.

"Desi! Desiree!" Charlotte yells into the recording, lifting the monitor and shaking it.

Desi looks back to the kitchen, maybe to Ronald saying something to her, and walks out of the frame.

Charlotte lowers her face in defeat then stands fast, is to the door in two steps, her left hand twisting the knob because she's missing half a finger on her right.

The knob still won't give.

"C'mon, c'mon," she hisses, turning the knob harder even though she knows it's a lost cause. She opens her hand, pushes away like telling the house she's done with this, she's not playing this stupid game anymore. Except that she has to. It's the only way out.

So, she makes herself think, trying to dial down to the *basic* basics. In this room, this office, she A) can't open the door, B) can't lift a box of brads, and C) can't lift the brass doorstop.

She *can* sweep everything off the desk, she guesses. It doesn't matter, it just resets, like erasing how pissed off she was, but she can have that moment of satisfaction all over again, anyway. For whatever that's worth.

This is what it means to be a ghost, she knows. You can see and hear and know, you can drift through and among, but that's pretty much it. All cause, no effect. The only consequences are on herself.

Yeah, if you're Tia, if you're anybody locked in here for ten, eleven years, you're scrabbling at the exit. At any whisper of an exit that presents itself.

That doesn't make Tia a good person, though. She's still stealing a body, a life. She's still dooming someone else to what she endured. She's still holding two little kids hostage to get what she wants. She still killed her little brother in the bathtub one night, and then ran away with her mother's severed head, her little feet leaving bubble footprints that pretty much killed her dad too.

"How do I do it?" Charlotte says, looking up to the backside of the door right at the moment when the her that was in the hall earlier—which is *now*—bangs her open hand on it and lets that settle, like she can echolocate through the wood. Like she can stand still enough, focus every fiber of her being into the office.

"Desi?" the her out there is asking.

Charlotte slaps her hand into the door from *this* side but there's no response, no step back, no immediate "Who's there?" Meaning there was no sound, no actual contact. Just a shadow brushing a shadow. Less than that.

Charlotte leans forward, presses her forehead into the wood of the door, her breath neither hot nor cold in that small space, just there.

"Desi?" the Charlotte in the hall then says again, so close, tuning in to a feminine presence in this office, but not able to register anything more precise than that.

In the office, Charlotte is crying again, snuffling with the hopelessness of it all.

The her in the hall bangs on the door again, losing her patience, and Charlotte jerks back from the feel and the sound, can feel herself standing on the other side of the door, listening with her whole body.

"They're in the kitchen," she tells the her who's about to figure that wrongness out.

A breath or two later, Charlotte's alone upstairs again. She turns around to slide down the door, sit by the stupid dog. Is the office where she lives now? Is this even living?

Charlotte pushes her fingers through her hair, only remembers a moment too late that she's using her injured right hand.

She brings it down, extracts the strands of hair from the blunt white stump of her index finger, blinking away tears.

Where does Charley think she is? Doesn't she need Charlotte to show her the next tunnel?

Charlotte nods yes, yes, it's *Charley* who will come save her, whenever time catches up and puts them in the same house again. The same-*ish* house. Unless Charlotte will now forever be four hours behind Charley, always playing catchup, never able to run the stairs fast enough to be in the same moment.

But if she came here through . . . through the lizard's throat, or recording, whatever . . . then there must be a way *back*, too. When the things you're interacting with are only half-real, the usual rules can't hold, can they? Not if Charlotte wants to have any hope about this situation.

And: you can fast-forward, can't you? You can, can—she *did*. It was after the doorbell rang, from when Murphy got here. Coming down the stairs, the lights had dimmed and . . . and by the time she got to the bottom, it was an hour later. Long enough for the lasagne in the fridge to be thoroughly chilled.

Never mind that, that time, she's pretty sure she'd been not just stopped for a syrupy-long moment on the stairs by Tia, but had her memories or self or whatever sucked out her ear, but still, forget that if you can, what matters is that an hour had slipped by in what at least *felt* like a snap, a blink, a breath.

Meaning she can still catch up to whatever moment the twins are in.

It's not hopeless. Well, not completely.

Think that, anyway.

Charlotte reaches back blindly for the doorknob to pull herself up with it, and, again, only realizes a moment after she's doing it that she's using her right hand, which is the wrong hand.

But maybe not.

The doorknob gives, slightly.

Charlotte looks down to it, up to the door, then grabs the knob again fast, turns hard.

Nothing.

"Just when I'm not looking?" she says, and tries that, making a stupid show of peering behind her while she turns the knob. Same nothing.

Was somebody from the other side trying the door, and she just happened to be touching it? But the other her and the twins, they're both downstairs, aren't they? Soon, maybe now, Ronald will be up here, scurrying around for his and Desi's costumes, but—the costumes aren't in *here*, are they?

Charlotte looks behind with purpose now, studying every place a dad might stash a couple of unopened costumes. Nothing.

She lowers herself to the floor again, the side of her head flat to the hardwood, and looks under.

No feet, no shoes.

She stands, tries the knob one more time—what else is there?—still can't turn it.

"What the hell?" she says, and then, just to test, she goes to the bifold closet door, pulls on the little dummy knob.

The door folds to the side just as it's supposed to, and Charlotte pulls her knee back from whatever's suddenly burning it.

It's a bright shadow, back behind a tower of stacked boxes.

"Found it!" she calls out uselessly behind her.

The thigh and knee of her jeans are smoking or steaming, she can't tell. There's no smell. She pats the heat away, reaches over the dark leakage from the tunnel, pulls the boxes down, still checking for costumes.

Unshuttered now, the bright shadow blasts up like it wants to, so Charlotte has to fall back to keep from getting singed.

This is a big one. The mother of them all, maybe. Is this where the funny places return to? Where they come to hang out when they're not blipping from cabinet to dryer to closet? If so, then why did Tia never find it, all those years she had been here alone, up here rubbing her injuries on the brass dog?

Maybe it's not big. Maybe it's just the angle, or the

aperture. Can you judge a tunnel's size by the shadow it casts, or bleeds, leaks, whatever?

Charlotte tiptoes around, giving the ray of darkness a lot of room, and folds the door shut, the bright shadow only showing through the louvres now but not really coming out to slice her into sections.

Wouldn't that be about perfect.

"No thanks," Charlotte says, and goes back to the door she *can't* open. Coming upstairs was supposed to get her whole enough to find the twins, somehow communicate with them, but all she's accomplished so far is watching Mr. Wilbanks perv out in the living room.

Using her right hand very intentionally, since it sorta kinda worked once, a little, she grasps onto the doorknob again, just squeezing normal-tight. Trying to think successful thoughts, she turns, fully expecting it to roll over.

No such luck.

But there is a . . . click?

Charlotte spins around, one-hundred-percent expects a tiny floppy clown arm to be sneaking out through the lid of the jack-in-the-box, its hand turning its own crank so it can burst up, stop Charlotte's heart.

She's still alone.

And, anyway: she *felt* this click the same as she heard it, didn't she?

She steps to the side, still holding the knob, and sees what she can't feel: the nub of her finger, the white front of it, when her hand turned around the unmoving knob, it jammed into the little button lock.

It *pressed* that lock, made it click.

Charlotte pushes again with her finger stump. The button lock clicks in and then comes back out, unlocking the door. Was that it the whole time? Excited, Charlotte turns the knob again, not hard, not soft, just natural.

Nothing. It wasn't the lock. All she did just now was lock it, then unlock it.

But that's something.

She climbs her fingers onto the knob itself and pushes against it with the white nub of her finger, trying to roll it back to the left, the direction it needs to come.

It doesn't turn, but it does start to. The only reason it doesn't is because a smooth round doorknob doesn't turn from just one finger stump pressing on it.

Charlotte keeps that finger-nub in contact and grabs the knob with her other hand, cranks around.

It starts to turn, it likes and needs that dry white contact, but it needs more.

Charlotte stands there breathing hard, watching this knob.

It needs more.

"Fuck it," she says, and is already back to the top drawer of Mr. Wilbanks's desk. She comes up with his orange-handled scissors.

All she needs is an opposable thumb with some gription, right?

To be sure she goes back to the door, holds the knob with her stump, paying attention to where her thumb naturally falls.

She goes back to the desk, hikes her rear up onto it and hunches over her right hand, the scissors in her left, open wide, the shorter blade pressing to the base of the underside of her thumb.

"For Desi, for Ronald," she says, and, before she can stop herself, she scrapes it hard down and away, has to drop the scissors it hurts so much.

Her right hand trembling, she raises it.

The white isn't completely exposed, but there are scratches there for sure, a rip or two, and the skin around them is raw and inflamed, almost peeled up.

Charlotte slides down, staggers over to the door, grabs the knob in victory, and turns with her whole arm.

It starts to twist but won't go far enough.

"Shit!" she says, banging her left hand into the door, high up by her face.

Why did it sort of work before, but not now?

Because the lock isn't as big as the knob, she hears herself saying.

Because the lock isn't as big as the knob. Because the raw white she dragged open with the ragged blade of the lower jaw of the scissors is, in relation to the size of the doorknob, not as big or intense as the open part of her finger is to the locking button.

"I didn't cut myself enough," she says.

Which means *depth*, she knows. She didn't angle the scissors in painfully enough, was trying to do as little as possible to get the door open, the same as any sane person would.

This house isn't interested in as little as possible, though. It wants it all.

Charlotte looks down to the weak, timid scrape on the underside of her thumb, considers what even more violence there might feel like. But . . . the dog is here, isn't it? She looks down at it, still hates its aloof, thousand-yard stare. If it's here, though, then won't any cuts be temporary? Enough pain to make Charlotte pass out, sure, but, after pressing that pain to the dog's warmcold brass—*after* opening the door, after after after—all she'll have to deal with will be some mottled grey scar tissue. It's the price of passage. And it's worth it.

But that's later, too. That's after. Right now what she needs is more of her tofu white insides making contact with the metal of the doorknob. Simple as that.

"Don't, don't, don't," she says, stepping back to Mr. Wilbanks's desk.

She has to, though.

She pulls the left drawer open, turns around to put the center of her right palm on the edge of the desk such that her thumb wraps *inside* the drawer space, and then she steps forward all at once, slams the drawer shut with her hip, cranking her face up, away from the pain. Her neck won't go far enough to hide how much this hurts, though. There's supposed to just be dry nothing inside her, but she feels the stubby little bone in her thumb splinter all the same, then crack open, then tear away.

She falls to her knees, the side of her face pressing into the desk calendar. Her right hand is still clamped onto the edge of the desk. Just with less grip, now that there's nothing to oppose the fingers' pressure. Or, nothing connected enough to oppose that pressure.

Charlotte guides her left hand alongside a drawer, finds the edge, and works it back a quarter-inch at a time, dreading what she knows is inside: her thumb. It's not lying there like a prize, though, but's still hanging, her skin more elastic than she would have guessed. It kicks up a pencil drawing from one of her mom's Indian books, of the Sun Dance—of those leather pegs in the chest, leather straps tied to them, the skin being pulled out and out.

Charlotte drags her face down toward *her* strip of flesh and tongues it in, closes her eyes and bites down, having to saw her teeth side to side to sever the connection.

It goes with a pop. She pulls back, looks at her thumb curling there in the bottom of the drawer, on a legal pad, nudging Mr. Wilbanks's samurai-sword letter opener over.

"I'm sorry," Charlotte says down to it, and pushes the drawer shut gently, has already stood away from it when it registers: the letter opener.

She eases the drawer back open.

The letter opener is *brass*.

Steeling herself for the dog's sudden all-around bark—or maybe it's in her head?—she lifts the letter opener unmolested, even though it's as heavy as a gallon of milk to her.

She slides it into her back pocket, all one motion. It pulls hard at the waist of her jeans but screw it. The dog doesn't even know, either. It is real brass, though. Charlotte can feel that hot freeze radiating through her pants, and it's heavy like brass is on this side of the house.

"Smart doggy," she says down to the doorstop.

The dog's tail doesn't twitch.

Because it might make a difference how freshly exposed her inner white is, she jams the stumps of her thumb and index finger hard against the metal of the doorknob, presses them tight with her other hand, her left using the right like a rag on a lid, and twists.

It's still not easy, but this time the knob rolls, turns . . . the tongue in the strike plate clicks back just enough.

The door opens a crack.

Charlotte doesn't let it stop, keeps guiding it out with her left hand, and the first place her eyes fall is of course all the way down the hall, to the sound on the stairs.

It's herself, she knows. She remembers being on those stairs and seeing the office door open just this slowly. Before, after this bad moment, she thought it had been Nora Spinell opening this door. And then, by default, it had to have been Tia. But it was Charlotte herself.

She steps back, isn't sure she wants to have to see herself on the stairs. Which will be the real girl, right?

The door stops exactly where it stopped before.

Without looking down, Charlotte kneels, feeling with her left hand for the dachshund's long back. When she finds it, she crosses her body with her right arm, tightens her lips to a line, and presses the nubs of her thumb and index finger to the healing brass.

It hisses and spits, curls a line of that steam or smoke up, but Charlotte doesn't look down, even when the dog's growl rumbles up from the hardwood floor.

She brings her right hand up to inspect.

The white is . . . congealed over. Like pudding that got a skin overnight, over many nights.

She touches it with the tip of her left index finger and it doesn't hurt, is completely numb. She smells it, has to stop that immediately. She looks down what she can see of the hall and the light there falters, which makes the floor feel like it's dropping out from under her. She holds her arms out to balance even though her head's telling her nothing's really shaking, that she's not really falling, that she's just stepping over the threshold, into the hall. The light sputters again, sucking down to black for an instant. At the end of that blink—it can't have been any longer than that—Charlotte's standing in the minutes after midnight, she knows. In Halloween.

"*Three minutes* . . ." Charley calls from downstairs. "Are you here, babysitter?"

"I've caught up again," Charlotte mutters to herself in wonder. She steps all the way into the hall, the lights intensifying now, nothing but brightness all around.

"Three minutes," she says to herself, the fingertips of her left hand skating along the wall.

She doesn't stop for Ronald's bathroom or bedroom door, and only hesitates at the linen closet to be sure she's seeing what she's seeing: three BBs have rolled onto the hardwood. Meaning the tunnel *was* in the utility when Charley flung the jug at the wall.

Charlotte considers the possibility of the Featherweight vacuum waiting in the linen closet—surely it's back in there, right?—but shakes her head no about it.

She passes Desi's room without trying to get a look into the bathroom, to see what might be going on in there.

There's no headless women in the hall, no eyeless boys in the doorways.

She does stop at the master bedroom, though.

The closet's accent lighting is on again, or still.

Charlotte presses her lips together and makes herself cross the bedroom, tries not to track her lack of reflection in the mirror over the sinks. She can't help looking up once, though. At how insubstantial she is. At how not-there she is anymore. Like she's fading with each step.

Stop.

The closet is just Mrs. Wilbanks's clothes and shoes and boots and the little pegs she hangs her necklaces on. None of them moving, meaning nobody's hiding in and among, ready to spring out at her.

But there is something, isn't there? Behind the dresses still in dry cleaner bags, at or on the wall that should be the exterior wall of the house, if Charlotte's understanding the layout right.

It's like . . . a television screen? A big flat panel in the closet, suddenly on? No, it's a *window*.

Charlotte steps in between that thin clingy plastic, holds the dresses to the side.

A window, yes. It's foggy, but that's because it's . . . it's not glass, it's plastic.

On the other side is . . . not just an emergency room, but *the* emergency room, the one Charlotte used to have to do her homework in in elementary. She presses her face closer, so she can see the blurry forms scuttling back and forth in their teal scrubs and running shoes.

Her mom passes right in front of her, moving from the right to the left, and Charlotte reaches for her.

"Mom," she says, "what, what is it?"

Something about the look on her mom's face. The all-business straightness of her arms, her step a bit faster than it needs to be.

A moment later her mom is bustling back, pushing a gurney now, a patient on it.

Charlotte's mom is crying now, her eyes large and wet but staring straight ahead fiercely. Another nurse steps in to take this patient over for her but Charlotte's mom shakes her head no, keeps going, making herself do this.

When the gurney passes before her, Charlotte expects she's going to see some nightmare version of herself, chewed up and spit out by the house, or—or Arthur Lopez, flattened by some other bumper, dragged under the car and driven over, his back breaking backwards on the first roll, his teeth pushing through what's left of his cheek, the rest of his face just meat, one of his shoes still on but that whole leg twisted the wrong way.

Instead, it's Murphy. Her head's shaved, has come back to stubble, which isn't how it is now or how it ever was either, so Charlotte knows this is a look *ahead*. This is tomorrow night, this is next week, next month.

Murphy is just staring, the drool around her mouth crusted with overdose.

Charlotte runs her hand through her own hair, knows where Murphy's went: to grieving. When they first got together she was always asking Charlotte stupid Indian questions, probably dredged up from place mats in restaurants, from ill-advised stumbles around the internet. The result was Murphy saying that when Charlotte broke up with her, which was definitely coming, which had to come, which was already here pretty much, that Murphy was going to cut all her hair off then, because it's what you do when you lose your Indian girlfriend. It's what you do to mark the beginning of the next part of your life. You can't be who you were anymore, that person can't deal with not having the person she loves around, so you have to be somebody else.

Charlotte puts the palm of her right hand to the plastic

window and pushes her face into it as well, screams into it, the window fogging from her breath.

Her mom wipes her tears on the back of her forearm and keeps going.

"Murph," Charlotte says, stepping to the side to try and track the two of them away, to hold on to them just a moment longer.

She crumples into the dry-cleaning bags, bringing some of them down around her, holding them to her mouth because maybe breathing them in would be easier, would be better.

She does once, on accident—breathes one into her throat, a thin wall of bubble reaching for her windpipe—but is coughing and gagging before she can even tell herself not to.

The closet lights go down around her and she's floating in crinkly blackness now, her breath hitching in and out, her nose snuffling. When she looks up, she completely expects the accent lights to come on in response, but she doesn't count that way anymore, does she? Babysitters who aren't really here can't turn on lights that are.

Still: Murphy didn't do that to herself because Charlotte was *gone*, she did it because Charlotte wasn't Charlotte anymore, right? If this was a look into the future, then that's the future it meant: the one where Charley's Charlotte, as far as anybody knows. And, either Charley's hetero, doesn't have any interest in kissing another girl on the porch after a date, or else Murphy was just too dangerous to have close, since she, of all people, would be able to clock the new driver at the mental wheel.

On the one hand this look ahead, if it's a real look ahead, means that Charley doesn't find a tunnel anytime soon.

On the other hand, it means this has to end, *now*.

"*Ronald, Desi* . . ." Charley's calling from the couch, and kind of laughing at the end of it.

"Oh yeah," she adds, speaking to the room, to Charlotte up at the balcony, "they can't hear me anymore, can they? Their babysitter's let something terrible happen to them, hasn't she? That's so, so *funny*, because, I mean—her references were practically radioactive, weren't they? That means 'glowing,' yeah."

She leans farther back into the cushions, her feet propped on the coffee table, and thumbs *SpongeBob* back into motion.

"I don't know where they are, Mr. Wilbanks, Mrs. Wilbanks," she goes on, just watching the screen now. "I put them to bed at nine just like you said. Maybe they're playing a joke? Do they ever do that? You say they hid dolls in their place? Sounds like them. You did warn me about some big trick. Geez, can't believe they got that one over on me. Anyway, can one of you give me a ride, maybe? I don't know if I should be walking to the bus stop this late. Seems kind of like asking for trouble. My mom's always telling me that nothing good happens after midnight . . ."

Charlotte holds tight to the handrail with her bad hand, squeezing hard enough that the melted white at the end of her thumb splits, crumbles down into the open air. It's gone before it hits—snow that evaporates on the way down.

Charlotte tucks her thumb into her fist and turns to head downstairs, finish this one way or the other, and she only stops when a great shape rustles into the hall behind her.

"What now—?" she says, sure that she's ready for, for *whatever*. Nora Spinell, using the jack-in-the-box as her head, her hand to the crank to puppet her mouth open; *Mr.* Spinell, clean-shaven now that he's dead, his eyes just as punched through as his son's; Tad, hustling and bustling down the hall for some ghost-kid reason or another; a funny place opening its dark sucking mouth from the linen closet, its harsh shadow sizzling into the opposite wall, the vacuum cleaner floating in it like a bad special effect.

But—no way could Charlotte have been ready for *this*: the lizard, even more massive than last time. It's metastasizing in this between-house, is becoming more reptile than toy. Charlotte can tell from its dull eyes more than anything.

There are beanbag beads raining down off its blue scales. Meaning either it crawled up from there or it was nosing around in there, after a smell.

"What are you?" Charlotte says to it, too floored to even do anything grand and proper like fall backward down the stairs, away from this.

The lizard turns its great head to her, isn't quite through Desi's doorway yet, is too long now for that to be an easy turn. It's maybe going to have to roll over onto its side then curl up, claw forward with its front and back feet, stretching its chin forward to tighten its yards of belly skin.

The pearly drool stringing down from its harsh line of a mouth isn't drool, Charlotte knows. It's the life Mr. Wilbanks filled it with, spilling over, frothing up.

"Fuck you," Charlotte says to it, hopefully not loud enough it can hear, and watches her feet the whole way down the stairs, coming down all the way onto one before stepping down to the next, even though that great lizard could be about to slide down behind her, slurp her right up on the way, never a care what it's going to crash into right after.

So, now upstairs is more or less off-limits. Along with the outside world.

Charlotte shakes her head at how unacceptable all this is and takes her last step onto the first floor.

If she'd been thinking, she realizes, she'd have pinched those BBs up from beneath the linen closet, to plink one by one onto the coffee table. They've been through a funny place, taken a one-way trip like her, so that probably means they're still transitioning from one house to the next, are still visible and hearable by people in the real house.

That would be a petty victory, though, showing Charley what she missed in the utility, what she nearly had, what she could have had if she'd just been patient, and deliberate.

"I guess they're home any minute now, aren't they?" Charley announces with a dramatic teenage shrug, like she somehow knows Charlotte's with her again. "Maybe one of them knows CPR, you think? Or, will they expect me to administer that?"

"I'm not here," Charlotte says back to her, in the living room again at last, but not touching the television screen like she's supposed to.

She pulls the brass letter opener from her back pocket, inspects it. It's dull where it should be sharp, but the point still has some bite.

Charlotte looks over it to Charley. To Tia in Charlotte's body.

"I'm not letting you hurt her like that," she says about Murphy-on-the-gurney, and steps around the coffee table, plunks down right by Charley on the couch. She flips the heavy little letter opener around in her hand once to get its balance, takes a solid grip on its smooth handle, and stabs it into Charley's left thigh hard enough to drive it nearly all the way through.

Charley doesn't notice—or, she doesn't realize she's been stabbed, anyway. She does let her idle index finger scratch in a disinterested way at her pants leg, though.

Charlotte does it again, higher up, into what should be the hip joint—Charley doesn't scratch this time, just rubs with the heel of her palm—so Charlotte pulls it out to thrust it right into Charley's chest with both hands, but at the last moment she can't. Because it's her heart, too. The letter opener wouldn't do anything, she's pretty sure, but—just the idea. And . . . and she wants to be back *in* there at some point, right?

Charlotte lowers her face, presses her eyes shut, the brass warm against her face, probably sending tendrils of grey out from the contact. She lowers it, studies it again, holds the flat of the blade to where she opened her thumb stump. The brass hisses on the uncongealed spot. Charlotte works the blade over and back, making herself feel this, and flashes on Mrs. Wilbanks letting the eyeliner burn her just the same way.

Charlotte leans back, screams in frustration.

Charley just sits there soaking Bikini Bottom in, the kids dying, maybe already dead, the Wilbankses practically home. *The babysitter isn't the babysitter anymore*, Charlotte wants to write on the wall, but the words would never take, she knows. *This* babysitter, "Charley," she'll be skipping the SATs in the morning, she'll be breaking up with her girlfriend later, and she'll probably be offering to babysit for whoever lives here next, after these grieving parents have gone their separate ways. Because she needs to find a funny place she can burrow down into for eternity.

There's not one single thing Charlotte can do about any of that, either. She can't even hold a letter opener in a real way. All she can do, if she pays the price, if she can take the pain, is turn a doorknob, open a door. Maybe mess up an episode of a cartoon. Sacrifice herself to the giant plastic lizard pulling the long runner in the upstairs hall to it now, as it tries to scrabble its way out of Desi's bedroom.

Charlotte looks up fast to the lamp table in the upstairs hall spilling over from the bunching-up rug, the bulb popping in a blue flash that throws the distinct shadow of the lizard's giant head onto the big wall by the stairway.

Charley's eyes don't even flick at all this. The other house doesn't register for her anymore. Just the television.

Charlotte looks back to the screen with her, to SpongeBob giving the dragon jellyfish the Krabby Patty he's been carrying all along, saving all of their animated medieval lives.

If only, right? Still, she pats her pocket for if she's been carrying a magic Krabby Patty all along. All she finds is her useless phone. On it, a stack of text messages?

"Mom?" Charlotte says, swiping at the lock screen, the texts not moving from her touch.

The phone *Charley* has is buzzing now, though. Her stolen thumbprint unlocks it, no problem.

"Ah," Charley says, and Charlotte reads over her shoulder:

Here.

Here.

Here.

Here.

Here.

Here.

Here.

Charlotte stands fast, frantic, looking around.

As always, for safety, just standard operating procedure, probably even in chapter one of the babysitter manual, she'd given her mom the address of tonight's job. That's . . . she wants to say that's how Murphy found her, but really it's what Tia drank in from her memory: that Charlotte's girlfriend *could* have gotten this address that way. Still, the inescapable fact, the not-another-lie part of this, is that Charlotte's mom definitely does have this address. And now that her shift's over—midnight—here she is, Charlotte's ride, surprise, no thanks necessary, just being an overachieving single mother.

"*No, Mom!*" Charlotte screams, rushing to the door.

The doorbell rings on the way.

Charlotte shakes her head *no, no, please,* but behind her, *SpongeBob* mutes.

"What do you call her?" Charley says, all around. "Moms, maybe? Ma? There some Indian word the two of you use, like, a tribal thing? I don't want her to know right away, I mean. That would spoil the—the *fun.* It's better if she starts to clock small things over a week or two. And then thinks she's seeing me standing in her doorway at night, that kind of stuff—you know, you've seen the movies."

Charlotte bangs on the door and kicks it, opening her thumb and finger back up but who cares. As a last-ditch effort she pulls the closet door open, angles it across to catch on the doorknob of the front door when it swings back.

Charley inserts the key, hauls the door open, the closet door not immaterial, exactly. Just, shut again. Never open in the first place.

"Mom!" Charley says, so chipper, so surprised with this happy coincidence, with not having to walk to the bus stop, now.

It's going to be the Mr. Spinell scene all over again, Charlotte knows.

She falls back in agony, sits on the stairs then stands all at once, swaying away from the distinct noise of claws on wood. She turns fast, stepping ahead at the same time, sure the lizard's already going to be to her.

It is out of Desi's room, anyway. It's in the upstairs hall now. It's taking up the whole *length* of the hall. And—and it has a *tongue* now, long and iridescent and split, flicking in and out, slapping the air for floating molecules of taste, settling finally on the handrail that still has all-but-invisible white flecks of Charlotte on it. The handrail's probably even—to a lizard—still warm from Charlotte's touch.

"Why do you care about me now?" Charlotte says up to it.

The lizard either doesn't hear or doesn't care about sound. Just scent. Taste. The pieces of Charlotte she can't help but be leaving in her wake.

And why do you have a tongue now? she adds, to herself.

The answer is obvious: because it needs it. It's not a nanny cam anymore, it's not a spooge repository. It's becoming an animal. One that can eat. One that *needs* to eat, because it has actual insides, a digestive tract to siphon energy from whatever it swallows, push it out into the muscles so it can eat more. And—no.

Charlotte lifts her right hand to her nose, sniffs it.

Is the *grey* what the lizard's tasting the air for? It makes sense. The grey is like ash, is probably sloughing off at a faster rate than her usual skin cells.

Charlotte holds her hand side-up in front of her mouth and blows past it, sighing a good grey taste up the stairs.

The lizard stills into a statue, which has to be what it does when it gets that good scent reading, and then digs its claws into the hardwood, anchoring itself. If it were a hunting dog, it would be lifting one forepaw up under, to point. Since it's a reptile, it just lowers its face, angling its poor eyesight down the stairs.

Moving slow, Charlotte guides her cauterized hand behind her back.

It wasn't supposed to work *that* well.

She backs away carefully, sure the lizard can surge down the stairway at whatever point it gets its nerve up to try. It's probably never seen stairs, though, has it? Not at this size. Not when they're not giant wooden cliffs it had to jump up to, claw and scrabble over.

Still backing away, Charlotte bumps into her mom, who doesn't register the contact, is all eyes, studying this grand living room.

"How much they paying you?" she asks Charley.

"*That's not me!*" Charlotte screams.

"One year of college," Charley says with a daughterly smile. "Three more Fridays and I'll have a degree."

"Then you better not—" Charlotte's mom starts, playing along, but stops herself, seeing Mr. Spinell's blood on the couch. "What's this?" she asks, sitting down primp and proper on the edge of the couch and touching a dab of that tacky red with the pad of her middle finger.

"Fake blood," Charley says with a shrug, settling in beside her and snuggling in, her socked feet drawn up under her. "Mr. Wilbanks is like *super* into Halloween, right? He Scotchgarded under each spot, he said, I don't know. He promised his wife it would come right up."

Charlotte's mom cases the rest of the living room for decorations that could be in keeping with a random splash of blood on the couch.

She brings the pad of her middle finger up to her nose, gives it a smell.

"*Yes, yes, it's blood, Mom!*" Charlotte says, halfway across the coffee table.

Her mom rubs it away, says, "The kids?"

"Sleepy time," Charley answers, folding her prayer hands under her tilting-sideways head.

Charlotte stands, screams in her closed mouth in frustration, then dives for the television screen, rubs all over it, completely distorting the picture.

"Been like this all night," Charley says about what looks like a corrupt signal, a bad connection, and feels around for the remote, kills *SpongeBob*.

"*This* a decoration?" Charlotte's mom says then, impressed, hauling the jack-in-the-box over to inspect.

"Oh, yeah," Charley says, taking it into her lap. "Mrs. Wilbanks, like, restores them or something? She told me not to let the kids play with it, I don't know."

"Either know or don't know," her mom says back, on automatic. "Don't guess. That leaves room for people to make your decisions for you."

"Check," Charley says with an appreciative grin.

Charlotte rushes forward, over the coffee table, grabs at the jack-in-the-box to, she *doesn't know*, throw it across the room?

Surprising her and Charley both, the crank clicks over once.

Charlotte stops, holds her guilty hand up: the thumb and index finger stumps are both raw, open, new. And her right hand's the side the crank is on.

"Like the doorknob," she says in wonder, and pushes back from the couch breathing hard, trying to figure what this might mean, how this might help her.

The jack-in-the-box, it's—it's what Tia was initially trying to use to come back, isn't it? Didn't she say that? And the reason she could smuggle it across to Ronald from this between place, for him to crank a doorway open, was that Tia had made the jack-in-the-box from Nora Spinell's head in some twisted wrong-side-of-the-house way, so pushing it across, from house to house, was really just bringing it back.

It's special.

And, because it's special, because it came from the top house and slipped into the middle one, Charlotte's white insides can *touch* it. Not her real hands, just her white ones.

"Oops!" her mom says, about the single click. "Maybe we shouldn't, I don't want to get you in trouble on your first night with them."

"I kind of want to see what it does . . ." Charley says, speaking directly to the open air in front of her, a grin ghosting the corners of her mouth.

Charlotte's thinking hard, is making herself think.

If babysitter X can make the magic box move with just the whiteness of her thumb and index finger, then what could she do with a lot more whiteness exposed?

Before she can talk herself out of it, she spins the letter opener up from her rear pocket, fumbles it for a moment but catches it on its heavy way down, and, breathing fast five shallow times and then holding it in, trying to make herself stronger than she is, she stabs the point dead center into her open left palm—it feels exactly as bad as she expected—and then rotates the blade over, to drag the sharp point up over the heel of her hand, slitting the skin as far up the fish-belly part of her forearm as she can reach. Almost to the elbow.

White shrimp meat bulges from the incision.

"Old Indian trick," she says through clenched teeth, her whole left arm spasming with pain, her teeth grinding. "You fuck yourself up before fucking everybody else in the room up."

She hunches forward around the swirling vortex of pain her left arm is now. Her hand automatically starts to clench into a fist but that just amps the pain up even more.

Charlotte gags, the pain trying to find a way out, and the living room greys out before her, mutes itself.

"No, no," she says, and makes herself breathe in, makes herself focus, stay awake, not pass out, not give up.

The letter opener falls with a thunk. Charlotte tracks its soft bounce—it's so *heavy*—waits for it to come to a stop before turning back to her cut-open arm. Shaking her head no, she lowers her teeth to the flap of skin at the inner elbow end of that slit, and she pulls away, extending her hand from her teeth since she can't stretch her neck any more than it already is.

The pain is so deep she can feel her soul huddling up around itself.

Inch by inch, tug by tug, she works the skin of her forearm and wrist and hand down and off like removing a long fancy glove, one she's surprised to find is red on the *in*side. Underneath there's just white, like she's made of Styrofoam, like she's been this secret blank mannequin all along.

And, with the skin gone, it doesn't even hurt so much anymore.

She waggles her fingers before her face, looks past them to Charley. To Tia in a body that's not hers.

With one hand she's holding the base of the jack-in-the-box. With the other she's cranking it slowly, slowly, her head angled slightly away, her mouth ready to burst into laughter, infect Charlotte's mom with it.

Charlotte dives forward just as the flap springs, and—

Instead of that little clown popping up like before, what comes up is Charlotte's bloody arm—*red* muscle, white tendons, thin yellow sheathing it in places, blood all through it.

Her skeletal raw hand grabs Charley by the throat, pulls her head forward through the jack-in-the-box hole, into this hell with her.

Charlotte doesn't stop to think what her mom must be seeing. Really, the moment she pulls Charley through, her Charlotte-skin sloughing off, the lights blink like gulping this new person in, and it's just them on the couch, just them in the living room.

Tia is here now. The real Tia.

On this side she's scarred and torn and grey, seventeen years old, her hair long and matted, her clothes rags, her lips cracked deep, her eyes the eyes of someone who doesn't sleep anymore, who maybe hasn't slept since she looked around inside a funny place and realized it could be a home for someone like her.

She screams a guttural scream to be here again and comes at Charlotte like an animal.

They crash back into the television set, bring it down over them, pulling and tearing, screaming and clawing.

"No!" Tia screams right into Charlotte's face, into her mouth practically. "This isn't fair! I'm not supposed to be here! I got out!"

"You don't get to be me, Tia," Charlotte says, bringing her knee up into Tia's gut hard enough to drive her to the side.

Upstairs the dog is barking alarm, is loud enough to be shaking the foundations of the house, rattling the windows, making the spilled glass from the shattered television screen dance. Charlotte can feel its massive voice in the bone on the underside of her jaw on both sides, close to her ears.

She spins Tia away, scrabbles around behind the coffee table, falls over something that wasn't there before.

Mr. Spinell, lying where the couch spit him up.

He's dead on the floor, and now Charlotte's tangled up in him, trying to extract her right foot from between his arm and his side but trying to do so without touching him even a little.

She falls sideways, into the couch, and tries to roll away but Tia's slamming the coffee table forward, into her, pinning her all over again.

Tia's calmer now, her rage burned off, replaced by something darker, and worse.

She grins, waggles whatever she's holding low down by the

thigh of her ratty nightgown: the pruning saw she'd carried in
to dispose of her dad with.

"This is *my* house," Tia says, drawing the wicked little saw
back, its teeth like shark teeth, going every which way, hungry
for the slightest bite of skin. "You're going to be so sorry,
babysitter."

"I already am," Charlotte says, and surges sideways, under
the slashing blade but not low enough that its grabby teeth
don't latch into her hair, yank her head sharply over, something tearing in her neck—maybe her *skin* tearing. That's what
it feels like.

She's already falling too, though, and her weight is more
than Tia can hold with one arm, meaning Charlotte takes the
pruning saw down with her.

It rips into her shoulder and her left hand comes up on
automatic, grabs the blade the instant before it's to her face,
her palm gouging open. She keeps kicking, no time to hurt,
just have to get enough distance from whatever's next. It gives
her enough space to pull her legs up onto the couch, try to
climb the back. The pruning saw falls away behind the couch
and then the couch itself is tilting back, nothing stopping it
this time, no fake Murphy to take that weight. Charlotte goes
with it, the cushions folding over onto her.

Right now would be a good time for a tunnel, she thinks.
Except she's still in the wrong house—on this side, the bright
shadow from a tunnel mouth will fry her.

Tia hauls the couch back down onto its feet and Charlotte
can feel one of its big wooden feet crunch into Mr. Spinell.

"No, no!" Charlotte's already saying, but Tia's got her by
the hair, is dragging her from the couch, across the valley of

Mr. Spinell, onto the coffee table and then jarringly *off* the coffee table.

Charlotte reaches up to take Tia's wrist and manages to get it, but it doesn't matter even a little, just maybe saves her hair and her scalp some.

"Want to show you something," Tia says, dragging Charlotte to the kitchen.

Charlotte grabs at the doorway but she's not strong enough. She's crying now, and hating herself for it.

"I've been here so long I can *hear* them when I'm on this side," Tia says, throwing Charlotte into the island but not letting go of her hair yet. "It's like—it's like a place where there isn't any sound? Does that make sense, babysitter? It would have after a few years, if you lasted that long."

She drags Charlotte through the kitchen, into the utility, the mat in front of the sink bunching up under Charlotte, then speed-bumping under her when it goes upside down.

"See?" Tia says, jerking Charlotte's hair up so her face is parallel with the washer and dryer.

The dryer is spilling a thick beam of the bright shadow Tia can evidently *hear*, and—and Tia's right: there's not a sound, exactly, but there is a whooshing nothingness, sort of. A blowing absence. How did Charlotte not hear it before?

She tries to kick back, away from it, claws her fingers into this doorway with what she wants to be more strength, desperate strength.

Tia pulls harder, comes away with a handful of hair.

She catches Charlotte fighting back through the kitchen, alongside the island, and slams Charlotte's face into the tile, filling her mouth with powdery white shards.

"Know how hard it is to get your *gums* onto that idiot dog's back?" Tia asks. "You have to take its tail in your mouth, rub it around like a Q-tip. It doesn't bring the teeth back, but it does plug up the holes. And sometimes that's all you can ask for."

She laughs because this is so hilarious.

"You don't deserve anything this quick," she hisses down at Charlotte, dragging again, "but I don't have time for what you do deserve, for making me come back here. And don't worry, I'm pretty sure this'll *feel* like forever."

This time Tia jerks Charlotte hard enough ahead that she slings through the utility room doorway, into the wall that's right there.

"It likes the dryer," Tia says, stepping in, getting a grip closer to Charlotte's scalp, "I don't know why. Maybe it's the spinning, or the holes."

Charlotte pulls and fights and kicks at Tia's legs but she's not strong enough to keep Tia from forcing her into the distinct edge of the bright shadow. The freezing-hot burn starts on the left side of her face, her neck, her shoulder and arm, and it's pushing and pulling at the same time somehow, which is ripping her apart at levels small enough she can't see. But the result is her skin flaying away, flaking up into the air and disintegrating, leaving White Charlotte underneath like a Styrofoam mannequin getting slowly exposed. And the white doesn't burn away, it *melts* away, like pouring gasoline onto packing peanuts, like dripping water onto ash.

Charlotte screams, kicks some more, brings her ravaged right hand up to protect her face but her hand burns just the same, her index finger stump steaming like the barrel of a pistol.

Think like Murph, think like Murph, she tells herself, losing it fast, trying to crawl deeper into herself, away from the pain, away from Tia, away from this house.

What do you do when you can't get away? When your killer's stronger than you are?

You use that against her. Just like with the pruning saw on the couch. That was accidental, though, that was momentum, that was dumb luck. And—and Charlotte doesn't want to do this, can't imagine having to do this, having to *submit* to it, having to *choose* it, but there's nothing left for babysitter X.

Her only option is to move *with* Tia, not against her.

Instead of pulling away from the clean bright shadow the dryer's blasting, she pushes forward, *into* it, across it, the darkness boiling her right side on the way, stripping even more of her down to the white.

Tia screams when the shadow touches her, screams and finally lets go.

Charlotte crashes into the storage bins on the opposite wall and Tia pulls back the other way, holding her burnt arm to her, her eyes flinty mad.

"You bitch," she says.

"You don't get to have my life," Charlotte says back, from the safety of the other side of the bright shadow, her right side trailing vapor.

Tia makes to step forward, can't bring herself to step into that frigid blast of heat again.

"You can't stay over there forever," she says. "Or, you can, I suppose, but *it* won't."

As if on cue, the bright shadow sputters, fails. Five seconds later it's a thready wisp of exhaust, and then it's gone, ashing up into nothingness.

"Well well well," Tia says, stepping into that now-safe space, still holding her arm.

Charlotte reaches up, brings the fold-down ironing board down onto Tia's head hard, crumpling her down and back. In the same motion she's running, is pulling through the doorway, sliding into the kitchen, bouncing off the island with enough force that something in her hip gives in a soft, permanent way. There's no time to slow down, though. There's no time for anything.

"Babysitter!" Tia bellows right behind Charlotte, forcing her to sway her back in, away from whatever sharp thing's got to be coming for her.

It's not enough. She's just into the living room when a hand in her hair jerks her back all at once.

Charlotte goes down flat enough to whoosh the breath from her lungs, but she comes up with the letter opener she dropped.

It's hot enough that it cuts right through her hair, leaves Tia with a big handful of it, Charlotte spinning down, looking back to see which way Tia's going now.

She's just standing there, waiting for all of Charlotte's attention.

Moving like show-and-tell, she pulls the ripped-out hair up into her hand and then stuffs it into her mouth and chews its dry grossness in, staring Charlotte down the whole time, having to guide some of the strands up from what teeth she's got left. She swallows the tangled lump hard enough that it makes her eyes water.

"Watch this, now," she says, and opens her mouth, finds a tendril of unswallowed hair at her throat, judging by how much of her hand she has to force in. She pulls the strand steadily forward, working it out farther and farther, her throat clumping in reverse, like giving birth. She dangles what she's extracted up before her face.

It's . . . maggots? In the wet hairball?

They're wrong, though. They're shuddering too fast, and they're—they're too dry, is that it?

"No, please," Charlotte says, looking down to her mostly white left arm.

Its surface is already writhing.

She's not made of tofu, she's ghost-meat, and ghost-meat is dry, blind maggots.

They're what makes the doorknobs turn, *they're* what drives this place. Scratch the surface of the house on this side, it bleeds rot and ruin, decay and putrescence.

Tia smiles one side of her mouth.

"You think it was all rainbows and unicorns over here?" she says, then nods down to whatever's happening in this maggot hairball. Charlotte, shaking her head no, tracks down, down.

The soft whiteness of the maggots has hardened into roach-brown shells, which are cracking open at one of the tapered ends, and now one—no, two . . . *five* of these maggots are managing to struggle up and out of this transformation chamber, their long grey hairs wet, plastered to their bodies, their iridescent eyes sort of inflating. The maggots are shuddering into flies.

Charlotte falls back gagging.

Tia laughs, snatches a wet new fly from the air, her hand closing around it.

She turns her fist sideways in front of her mouth like to

blow through it, but then sucks instead, taking the fly back in with a clear *pop*. She has to angle her chin up to swallow big enough to get it down, but it's a fighter, must be crawling back up her throat. She thumps her neck hard with her middle finger, making a hollow sound, then swallows deep again, finally bringing her chin down.

The fly's in her now.

It crawls across the backside of the white of her eye and she feels it, blinks it away.

"You don't have digestive enzymes over here," she says to Charlotte. "It's something I could have taught you. You have to . . . to co-opt some helpers, if you want to eat anything. And if you don't eat, well."

Charlotte throws up now, from deeper than she ever has. It's just inert bile.

Tia laughs about this, frees her fingers from the maggot hairball, and says, "You're just dragging this out, babysitter. You can't beat me. I killed my little brother, I killed my dear old dad, and I ran away with my mom's head before I was even in first grade. Nothing you can do even comes close to that."

She's right.

"I can help you find the tunnels," Charlotte tells her, stalling for time, scrabbling backwards across the living room. "We can go back, I can touch the television, show you—"

"Just because I was homeschooled doesn't mean I'm stupid," Tia says, advancing.

Charlotte pushes back with her heels, turns to run and falls immediately into the remains of the television. She fights out of that, her arm on fire, her face half-gone, her scalp crawling with new holes, her white arm just crawling generally, but she can fight her way upstairs to the brass she needs, she knows, to the aloof little dog that'll make everything right. She has to.

Except.

When she plants a hand on the stairway railing to pull herself around, there's a giant blue lizard stepping carefully down at last, its midsection not over the top stair yet, or else it would be sliding down fast.

Shit.

Charlotte shakes her head no.

The only place left to go now, it's outside, isn't it? To suffocate in the fake vinyl sky. And, and she never found the twins, and she doesn't know where her mom is right now, and Murphy's going to overdose when Charley dumps her, and and and—

"*The floor is lava!*" she turns around to scream at Tia, because maybe if she believes it enough, if she needs it enough, and if Tia can buy into it for just a flash, then it can *be* real, it can be true.

Tia stops between the coffee table and the fallen television, cocks her head over to be sure she's hearing Charlotte's last attempt right.

She even looks down, lifts her right foot away from the rug.

It comes up easy. Her bare, rotten foot isn't flickering with flame. It isn't even steaming.

"What if, right?" she says to Charlotte, and grins, her lips never leaving each other.

Charlotte falls back onto the entryway and it's slick with bubbles again, meaning she believed enough for *that* part, just, not the lava she actually wanted. She pushes back, back, and Tia shakes her head in amusement, steps forward but . . . she can't?

She looks back, down, Charlotte looking with her.

It's Mr. Spinell.

He's reaching under the coffee table, is bringing his other hand over now to clamp around Tia's ankle as well, his eye sockets hollowed out like burst from the inside, his lips sputtering, his skull split enough inside the sack of skin his head is that his two front teeth are cocked away from each other now.

"Is that you, T?" he manages to creak out. "Is that my little girl?"

Tia shakes her leg as if insulted, inconvenienced.

Mr. Spinell doesn't let go.

Tia tries to step forward, out of this, but her father's got her. Her chest heaves and her eyes get wild, desperate. She falls forward, still pulling away.

Charlotte latches onto the closet doorknob, pulls herself up unsteadily enough that the closet clicks open, swings her around a bit, which is lucky, since otherwise she might be falling into the bubble bath happening under her feet. From half behind the door, she looks up to the lizard on the stairs, its tongue slapping around in its blind way, lapping the air for the grey taste it's keyed on.

From the living room, Tia is reaching for her, needs Charlotte to pull her away, and the uncertainty and terror on her face is pure first grader, activating the babysitter in Charlotte, activating it enough that Charlotte actually takes a timid step that way, to save the girl who wants her dead. But she's still hanging onto the closet door.

She studies Tia's outstretched hand, looks to the lizard

again, then steps neatly *into* the closet when the entryway under her goes full Jell-O. The lines of grout between the tile are sinking, swirling away.

In the closet, Charlotte moves away from the jacket arms brushing her back, but she's pressed up against the wall now, is suddenly sure the back wall is going to go window, is going to deliver her to a funeral scene, a series of them this time: her mom, Murphy, Arthur somehow. And the twins, shit.

She pushes the door open again and rides it out, giving as much weight as she can to the doorknob, until her reaching left foot can come down on the lip of wood that's the first step of the stairway, her eyes instantly locking on the lizard's to see what it might be about to do.

"I'm nothing, I'm nobody, not even here," she says to the lizard, keeping the grey sides of her hands down by her legs, hidden. She steps across the bubbly top of the water, her right foot landing in the living room, the closet door shutting behind her when she pushes back for the last *oomph* she needs.

The lizard takes another step down in response, keying on her *movement* now, maybe. It lowers its wide nose to the bubbles mounding up from the entryway. The breath from its great nostrils launches tufts of the white up into the air and they hang, drift.

"*Help me!*" Tia is saying to Charlotte.

"Why?" Charlotte says, close enough to take Tia's hand if she wants.

"I can show you how to get back!" Tia says, almost crying now.

"The jack-in-the-box?"

"There's another way, it's—it's upstairs."

"The dog?"

"Fuck the dog, just . . . here, please."

"Where are the twins?" Charlotte asks, stepping closer, her shins just shy of Tia's grasping fingers. At least until Mr. Spinell's fingers dig into Tia's calf. And she has actual blood inside of her now, maybe from visiting topside. It's black and too thin and somehow dry, maybe too floaty too, but still, it's blood. It spurts up. Tia screams in agony, slides back. Mr. Spinell is pulling her calf to his mouth, now.

"He *was* hungry," Charlotte says, impressed.

"Please!" Tia says, reaching.

"Where are they?" Charlotte repeats.

"I put them in the, in the wall!" Tia says, pleading. "In the closet, upstairs! It's the—the first place I went. It's still there, behind the wallpaper. Please! I told you."

Charlotte looks up, over the perfectly scaled back of the lizard on the stairs. It's testing the waters of the entryway with its right forefoot, now.

She considers the closet up there. The one she was just in.

"I'm gonna hate myself for this," she says, and reaches down, takes Tia's hand in her stripped-white left, and she can practically hear her mom over her shoulder, whispering to her to never be a Pocahontas, to never give the enemy a hand, never give them a foothold.

She leans back, jerks Tia away from her father's grasping fingers, from his tearing mouth.

Tia climbs Charlotte's frontside so they're practically hugging, Tia weak and spent and gasping, all her weight on her good leg, Charlotte burned on one side, her left hand mannequin-slick, her hair half pulled out, half cut away, her teeth gravel, her arm sloughing off into maggots.

She leans down into Tia's ear, says, "I was just upstairs *in* that closet? And guess what? No Desi, no Ronald."

Tia pushes away, still in Charlotte's arms, and looks her in the face, sputters a laugh, says, "I told you, babysitter, you can't win, this is where I live, this is where I'm—"

"Shh, shh," Charlotte says, taking Tia by the shoulders, her white left hand screaming from the contact with all that scarred-up grey, "while your mom's gone, the babysitter's in charge, right? And guess what, Tia? It's bath time."

Tia shows confusion in her eyes for maybe the first time and tries to push farther away but Charlotte's already coming around, is stepping into her, driving her back hard.

Her heels catch on the step up to the entryway and she trips backward, arms wheeling, and splashes ass-first into the short, square bathtub the entryway is by now.

It gulps her right in.

Charlotte steps closer to be sure, and, when Tia's hand breaks the surface like she knew it was going to, when it slaps and slaps, finally finds the edge of the step, when she pulls her head out of the water, her mouth open and gasping and screaming air backward into her starving chest, Charlotte leans across for the doorknob of the closet door and twists it, pulls hard, the bottom of the door spatula-ing through the bubbles but stopping hard at the *clunk* Tia's head is.

Blood from her mouth and nose blooms black on the surface of the water and Charlotte looks up at what she thinks at first is a fly buzzing near her face.

It's the split tongue of the lizard.

"All yours," Charlotte says, and steps back.

The lizard lowers its left forefoot delicately into the water, and then it slides in, taking a full fifteen seconds for the bathtub to take all of it. The water surges over the lip of the entryway, washes across the hardwood, past Charlotte's feet.

On the way down the lizard latches onto Tia's body with its wide flat mouth, pulls her into the depths with it.

Charlotte stands there until the entryway hardens back to tile, gets its dusty grey lines back. She tests it gently with her right foot, and when it can hold her, she steps up onto it all the way, to survey the thoroughly trashed living room. The one that should have reset itself, since she can't actually do damage to real things.

Meaning she's all the way over, now. All the way under. All the way gone.

"Desi?" she calls timidly. "Ronald?"

Tia was lying about them being upstairs, of course, but Charlotte has to see.

She takes the steps two at a time, pulling hard with her left hand on the handrail.

The wall in the master bedroom closet is solid, but just to be sure she finds the corner of the wallpaper, peels it up, just finds the drywall she was expecting. Next, Desi's bed and bathroom—nothing. Ronald's is empty too. The office door is still open, though. Charlotte holds on to the doorframe, leans in, says the twins' names to all the corners, to the hidey space under the desk.

She stands in the hall for a long moment afterward, her eyes closed, her chest shuddering with either laughter or crying, she can't exactly tell. She won, but she's still losing.

What else is there to try, then?

She considers the linen closet, even looks in, but it's just games and sheets and that little vacuum cleaner.

Five steps later she's standing in Desi's doorway again. All the My Little Pony eyes stare back at her so hopefully, like they all know the secret answer, are just waiting for her to figure it out.

"What already?" she says, and steps back in to see.

Is Tad under the bed, perched on fingertips and toes, his head cocked to drink her in with his ears? Charlotte stands with her feet right at the skirt, waiting for a decayed little hand to swipe out, grab her ankle, but it doesn't happen.

All that's left, then, is the beanbag.

Charlotte stares and stares at it, finally looks behind her to the hall, for Nora Spinell, to the open door of the bathroom for Mr. Spinell.

She's alone.

All around her, the house is holding its breath.

"I can't believe I'm going to do this again," she says finally, and unzips the beanbag, wades into the spider eggs. Before nestling down into them she looks behind her, to the mirror. It isn't showing the past, but it's not reflecting Charlotte either.

For all she knows, Tia will be in the beanbag once it's zipped up. Or Charlotte will be *in* the lizard, unable to find the zipper tab again, just sloshing back and forth through all Mr. Wilbanks's pearly whiteness. Or she'll be back in the Lopezes' kitchen, Murphy's hands feeling for the button on her pants.

There, she decides. That's a good place to start this all over.

Slowly, like a ritual she's just making up, she settles down into the spider eggs, lies back, and, because this is all that's left, she zips it up over her face like a body bag, closes her eyes, and right when she does, the baby spiders come alive around her, a thousand hatchlings, but it's not hatchling arms that rise up from the depths to embrace her face and chest, her stomach and legs. It's the sharp-legged *mother* of all the spiders. Charlotte's lying with her back to its belly. She arches away, knows she's just being held still like this so the pincers can come down, dig into her skull, or into her inner thigh, her crotch—her *crotch*. She's laying on the spider upside down. She can tell because of the sawing and crunching at her hip, *in* her hip, the . . .

The buzzing in her pocket?

Her phone.

She works her arm down through the cascading beads, digs her phone up with her left hand, which is complicated, and then she brings that glow up to her face to see who's texting her.

Mom.

b2u in 10, love.

Charlotte bursts up from the beanbag holding her phone, looking around the room desperately.

Desi's still not a mound of cuteness in her bed, but, but—

Charlotte falls forward with happiness, with success, with escape.

Her reflection, it's *in the mirror*!

She crawls and falls across the room, flicks the light on to be sure, brings her face close to her reflection, touches the her in the glass.

It's just a normal reflection, like a thousand times before. Like always. No tricks, no weirdness.

She rushes out into the hall, to Ronald's room because sometimes kids really do end up in the same bed. It's empty, but the office door down there, it's closed. Closed closed closed.

Charlotte steps down there, wraps her hand around that knob, and twists.

Locked, even. Or, still. But that's the only reason it's not twisting.

"Yes," Charlotte says, and turns, runs downstairs, is about to race across the living room when she remembers, just normal-walks past the television, only glancing over there once, casually, to be sure there's a lizard with a glass throat positioned there, keeping watch over her.

There is. She's never been so happy for a nanny cam.

She stops in the kitchen doorway, clocks all the clocks on the appliances.

12:28 blinks back at her.

"Okay, okay," she says, looking around fast, with SAT eyes. If—if Tia was trying to mislead her about where the twins were, and she said upstairs, then that means they're actually *down*stairs. And they're not in the living room, unless—

Charlotte walks mechanically back through it, calmly opens the closet door by the entryway, checks the space behind the couch, even opens the cabinet under the television.

No twins.

Okay, good. Think.

If they were in the utility, then Charley, Tia *as* Charley, would have scared them awake when she threw the jug of BBs.

The kitchen, then?

Charlotte goes back to it, her fingertips to the island, her eyes everywhere.

Calmly, methodically, she opens and shuts each cabinet, even looks in the top and bottom ovens, in case this is some ridiculous fairy tale. The refrigerator is side by side but she checks it anyway, imagining one twin in the refrigerator, one in the freezer.

No Desi, no Ronald.

She pats her pocket, has the deadbolt key again—*still*—meaning they didn't go out that way either.

"So?" she asks herself.

So . . . Charley. Tia. She knew about the pruning saw Charlotte left on the floor of the garage, didn't she? She said she'd had to hang it back up? But—*why* hang it back up?

"Because if it's on the ground," Charlotte says, already going there, "then it's the first thing the Wilbankses will see when they pull in. And then they know somebody's been there, in the garage. And they're not supposed to know that, are they? Nobody is."

Now Charlotte's running. She crashes into the garage, slaps for the light, finds the button that grinds the door up but screw it. Where where where.

"No," Charlotte says when she sees it.

The chest freezer.

What if Charley, when she was Murphy, told the kids it was another funny place, that it was the last one before bedtime, that it was the best one of them all, that Charlotte would never find them there?

Charlotte rushes across, flips the heavy white door up, and there's an Indian princess curled up on top of a 1940s nurse, their hair frozen sharp, faces frosted, lips blue, eyelashes ice-welded to their chubby cheeks.

"No no no," Charlotte says, and hauls Desi out first, then Ronald.

Desi writhes but doesn't open her eyes. Can't. Her lashes are frozen to her cheeks.

Ronald, though. He doesn't move, was the bottom of the two, got double the cold, probably.

"Ronald!" Charlotte says, her face right to his tiny one, "Ronnie, Ronbo, Veronica!"

Nothing.

Charlotte stands, doesn't know which way to go, what to do.

"Here, here," she says maybe five desperate seconds later, and collects them both in her arms.

This can work. It's not too late.

She staggers them inside, rests Ronald on the island to rebalance their weight, and then, lizard be damned, she's making her way across the living room, over the entryway, is plodding upstairs.

Desi's bathroom.

She strips the twins down, nestles them into the tub and turns the water on. Not too hot—they're kids—but, compared to how cold they are, even cold water would be warm.

"C'mon, c'mon," she says, a hand to each of their faces, to be sure they don't inhale any of the not-hot, only tepid water, her left hand and arm red from guiding sluices of water down to the twins. Except . . . it's not hot water, right?

The red's like a sunburn, but it stops neatly almost at the elbow.

It's the skin she peeled off. Her arm still remembers.

She'd peel it off again right now with her teeth if the twins would just thaw, though.

Ten agonizing minutes later, Charlotte crying and breathing all the hot breath she has onto them, guiding more and more water over their shoulders, into their hair, Desi gasps awake, splashes her hand down in that panicked way kids have, like they're just waking from a falling-dream.

But then she realizes where she is, who she's with. She smiles maybe the best smile in the whole history of smiles.

"Is he sleeping?" she says about Ronald, her voice creaky enough that she touches her throat to feel that sound.

"Just wait," Charlotte says, crying silently but smiling for Desi.

"Shh," Desi says then, conspiratorially, and snakes her hand up to the bathtub's ledge, dunks the squeeze turtle in, and raises the head just enough to spurt a line of water up at Ronald in a way that takes Charlotte's breath away. The last time she saw this, the result was . . . bad.

Sleeping frozen Ronald takes it for maybe four seconds, and then he sputters, gasps, pushes back from whatever this is.

Charlotte leans in, never mind her flannel shirt, hugs the two of them to her tighter than a babysitter should, longer than they can take, almost.

"Is it tomorrow?" Desi asks.

"Halloween," Charlotte says, bopping her on the nose. "Trick-or-treat, little girl."

"I'm a nurse," Ronald says. It's his first words.

"Listen to my heart," Charlotte says, batting away tears, and hauls them up and out, dries them, pajamas them, and tucks them each into Ronald's bed together, smoothing their hair down at the very end, and not wanting to have to stop doing that.

"You're a couple of great kids," she tells them.

"Are you coming back again?" Desi asks.

Charlotte turns her head to the idea of that and shrugs, says, "If your parents still want me, yeah. Now, new game. Pretend to be asleep, can you do that? For when your mommy and daddy get back?"

Ronald nods, shuts his eyes tight, and Desi giggles, can't even pretend to pretend.

Charlotte squeezes her foot under the blanket like a hug and stands to leave, sits back down fast when something bites her. No: when she stepped on something. One of the tacks from the vinyl poster she pulled off the wall a lifetime ago, that she couldn't find.

Charlotte goes to her knees, finds it and the other three tacks, then wrenches the sole of her foot up to see it, has to smile: there's a single dot of wonderful red blood.

She lowers her lips to it, kisses it away, then leaves the door open a crack, the hall light already on. The hall is just the hall again, is just any hall, every hall.

"Stay good," she says to the upstairs, and follows the handrail down, stops when the garage door grinds . . . not up, but down again, *then* up. Which she has no explanation for, if asked. Maybe the Wilbankses will be tipsy enough or postcoital enough to blame themselves. Premature button-pushing. It's a thing.

Charlotte cases the living room to be sure it's in order— the last chapter in the babysitting manual—and she has to laugh, shake her head.

Not even close. The television is where it always was, but Mr. Spinell's blood is on the couch, on the rug. The house ate him, sure, but it didn't wipe its mouth afterward.

Charlotte breathes in, breathes out, and vaults down the stairs, runs hard for the kitchen, pulls the last container of lasagne out.

At the exact moment the door from the garage into the kitchen opens, the lasagne is arcing through the air in what feels like slow motion, to splash all around the living room.

Charlotte tosses the little storage container behind the couch and stands there as if waiting for them, so she can claim this mess.

"Um," Mrs. Wilbanks says, about it all.

Her hair is mussed at the back, her eyeliner smudged.

Mr. Wilbanks has to suppress the smile that wants to happen.

"There was a, a *food* fight," Charlotte says, chin up. "It's not their fault. I started it, I'm sorry. You don't have to pay me, I understand. And—and I'll come back, clean this up. Or pay for any cleaning, whatever you want, whatever works."

She looks from face to parental face and stands there awaiting her judgment.

After a moment, Mrs. Wilbanks steps forward to touch a smear of the lasagne on the arm of the couch. "Was it—was it good, anyway?" she says, as if considering putting that finger in her mouth.

Charlotte has to look away from this, and in looking away she catches Mr. Wilbanks at the bookshelf, using the back of his index finger to wipe a crusty smear from the lizard's mouth.

It's bubbles, Charlotte doesn't tell him, just letting this pass. But, thinking about the nanny cam, she realizes that there won't be any food fight on the recording, will there? What *will* there be, though? A babysitter smuggling two popsicle children across the living room?

But that's all later, and Mr. Wilbanks can hardly call her on it if he was spy-camming her, can he? Or do babysitters not have privacy either, in his world? In his house?

Charlotte presses her lips together, hiding her smile as well, and says, "I'd never had homemade lasagne, ma'am."

"'*Ma'am*,'" Mrs. Wilbanks says, poo-pooing that away with her hand, like she's holding an imaginary handkerchief. "And the kids? Aside from this disaster, I mean?"

"Little angels," Charlotte says, stepping over to collect her backpack, trying to affect a contrite posture, or step. Something. Mostly? She's just happy to be alive. No, not just alive. *Here.* Back in the real world. On the good side of the house.

"Kids need to have food fights every once in a while," Mr. Wilbanks announces, pushing away from the incriminating evidence at the bookshelf.

"Maybe in the back*yard*," Mrs. Wilbanks corrects with a tone of warning, punctuating it with the playful/not-playful cut of her eyes.

"Thank you for letting me get to know them," Charlotte says, hiking her backpack up onto her shoulder. "Really."

"Did you get some good study time in?" Mrs. Wilbanks asks, holding Charlotte's eyes with hers.

"SATs . . ." Mr. Wilbanks drags out both ominously and with excitement.

"I learned a lot, yes," Charlotte says, in the entryway now. Which is solid, normal, perfect, never mind the toeprint smushed into the grout by the closet door.

"Hey, listen, let me drive you—" Mr. Wilbanks offers, stepping forward like to . . . what? Take her backpack, lead her to the car in the garage?

Charlotte works the key up from her pocket, twists the deadbolt back and shakes her head no, holds her phone up and says, "My mom's almost here already, thanks." She waggles the screen awake like proof.

Mrs. Wilbanks steps brusquely ahead to enter the code into the alarm's keypad, careful to enter the temp one, Charlotte's pretty sure. The one it doesn't matter if the babysitter sees.

"Well," Mr. Wilbanks says, opening his hand to release Charlotte into the big bad night.

"Was it a good time, your date?" Charlotte asks as farewell, standing in the open doorway, and Mr. Wilbanks nods, Mrs. Wilbanks presses her lips into an embarrassed smile, and with that—with no money changing hands, but Emergency Services not called either—Charlotte steps out, closes her eyes and steps off the porch, into the *actual* front yard, not against a child's cartoonish imagining of it.

She breathes the crisp air in deep, holds it as long as she can.

It's over.

She made it.

She wasn't supposed to, she shouldn't have been able to, but she did.

If she can do that, then the SATs will be a snap, won't they? Tonight, this, it was the real test.

Behind her the deadbolt locks, the key retracts, and, presumably, the real code for the alarm's being punched in.

Charlotte can't help but laugh. She hugs her arms to the

wet flannel shirt she shouldn't be wearing in this chill, and shakes her hair out behind her, crosses the Wilbankses' lawn, only twirling around in little-girl celebration once, maybe twice. She steps over the sidewalk and off the curb, the streetlight flicking unsteadily above in such a wonderfully real way. A not-fake way.

She walks the direction her mom will be coming from—the hospital—and her phone buzzes with a stack of texts, the beginning of each new buzz overlapping the end of the last. They're all from Murphy.

She starts with *studybuddy?* and, over the course of nearly thirty messages, graduates to more genuine concern, and finally just a long line of question marks with a stick-figure shoulder-shrug-with-upturned-palms buried in there like Murphy can do without having to even think about it, like her fingertips bleed emoticons.

Charlotte taps a simple red heart in, no punctuation there she can break, and sends it with finality, then looks up into headlights. Not about to hit her, just easing up, lighting the street between her and them, to be sure she doesn't trip coming to the passenger-side door.

"Mom," she says, lifting her right hand to wave her fingertips.

Her mom opens her hand to the passenger-side door but Charlotte doesn't come around yet.

Did she just hear something?

Her mom taps the horn to hurry her—she's from the city, so horns are just another verbalization to her, even at nearly one in the morning, deep in the heart of suburbia—but Charlotte holds her hand up, asking for a moment, a quiet moment, please.

Click.

Charlotte looks around, but this . . . it's not dog claws on concrete, isn't somebody out for a night walk. It's not the car's engine, ticking down, or some loud part of a belt under the hood. It's not a transformer on a utility pole and it's not a late leaf spiraling down from its tree.

Click.

It's not even in the air, really, is more like a sound Charlotte is feeling. In the ground. Through everything.

Click.

Her face goes slack, her eyes heating up instantly.

It's a giant crank turning. A giant jack-in-the-box crank.

Charlotte drops her backpack, looks around fast now, at everything.

"No," she says.

Click.

"*Mom!*" she screams, reaching forward, and her mom leans over the steering wheel like to see better. To understand.

Click.

When the spring pops at last, it's huge and strong and unavoidable, and it's under her mom's seat.

She smushes up into the headliner and windshield, is smashed into chunks and smears, spurts and gouts, some splashing out the window, dripping red down the side of the door, some just sliding down the backside of the windshield, the rest bobbing with the seat as the spring winds down, its job done.

Charlotte falls to her knees, pushes away from this, runs for the safety of the sidewalk, but that whole side of the street—no no no—it's a vinyl *sheet* hanging down, the street-lights just paintings all along it, right at the curb. No, *including* the curb! Charlotte falls back, pulls her buzzing phone up to her face, desperate.

"Mom, Mom, is that you? Listen, don't—"

It's not her mom, though.

"Really, this is too much," Charley is saying not so much into the cell at the other end as in the area *of* that cell.

"No, you were worth it," Mr. Wilbanks says back, his voice different now. More creaky. "They were safe in bed. You can't believe how nervous my—how nervous Regina was all night."

"I only hope the two of you had a good time," Charley says. "Here, you can cut across here."

They're in a car. He's giving her that ride home.

Charlotte stands, switches ears.

"*No!*" she screams into the phone. "That's not me!"

"And they really were little angels," Charley says. "I hope my kids someday are—well. I mean, I wish Ronald and Desi were already mine? But that would mean that you and me would have had to . . . never mind. I'm thinking stupid. It's not like—nothing, sorry. God. Can you make this any more awkward, Charlotte?"

"Here?" Mr. Wilbanks says. "This your bus stop?"

"Your car is so *clean*," Charley says then, like changing away from subjects that don't matter. "How do you keep it like this?"

"You know," Mr. Wilbanks says. "Car wash. It's easy."

"Car wash?" Charley asks, her voice practically blinking its eyes. "Can you show me?"

"The car wash?"

"My mom isn't expecting me home until one," Charley says. "But she'll be asleep anyway."

"The car wash," Mr. Wilbanks says, in a distinctly more

satisfied way. The slimiest purr makes it up to wherever the cell tower is, burrows the tip of its tongue right into Charlotte's ear.

"*That's not me!*" Charlotte screams into the phone again, and then is plunged into darkness when her mom's headlights die down.

She looks up to the painted-on streetlight but now it's flickering and wavering too, sucking its light back into that flat bulb.

Charlotte falls to her knees, hears another sound from her phone so pulls it up and then away again, fast.

There are fast little spider legs reaching out from the speaker, the mic. One of them births up, dives for the ground, Charlotte's open hand dropping the phone right alongside it, since that's what your hands do with things that are full of spiders.

When the phone hits the little lip of concrete where the curb meets the sun-faded blacktop, the screen audibly cracks and it's like the light it had been holding in strobes out, bathing the vinyl wall shimmery silver.

Lit up like that for that slice of an instant, Charlotte sees . . . that little spider's shadow, suddenly large.

But she tracks it back to its tiny self, sees that it's running for the vinyl backdrop not because it thinks it's real, but because its cluster of eyes must see in a way Charlotte's eyes can't. That strobe of escaped light from her phone, though, it sort of showed her: there's the lightest tracing on that vinyl, isn't there?

This desperate spider skitters *into* that tracing, showing it to actually be a crack, a cut.

This is a doorway.

"Oh," Charlotte says, reaching to flap it open.

Real night air breezes through, chilling her wet shirt against her skin even more.

"I don't—I can't—" Charlotte says, as if speaking for an audience, some imagined listener, but this is no time to try to think her way through out loud.

If she waits for this to make sense, it'll stop making sense, won't it? If the funny places don't last, then escape hatches have to be even more fleeting, don't they?

She steps forward, into the doorway, and it's a flap, still, but it's also heavy and stiff, is . . . it's metal on the backside, somehow. And set into the side of one of the stalls at what has to be the car wash.

It has to be because what Charlotte's seeing is Mr. Wilbanks's Audi—of course the Audi: Mrs. Wilbanks's Lexus or whatever *already* smells like sex.

The windows are steamed up, and then a hand slaps into that steam, smears down.

Charlotte's hand. What used to be her hand.

She shakes her head no, no, this isn't right, this isn't something she would do, and is stepping through to stop it, the door still open behind her, when something slaps at the side of her left leg.

She flinches up, sure that that little spider that ran through has swelled up to dog size here in the outer world, to match that big shadow it was throwing, but it's just an old yellowy newspaper.

Charlotte reaches down to dislodge it, step through, let it continue on its nighttime whatever, but, right when she's letting it go, she sees her own name there. Her last name.

But, in front of that last name is . . . her *mom's* name?

Over the top of the newspaper, the Audi is rocking back and forth, either a suspension spring squeaking or a seat in there squealing, and Charlotte watches it for a moment, like daring that passenger-side door to open. When it doesn't, she scans the article like Murphy taught her, sort of speed-reading for details she'll need to answer the inevitable questions and realizes it's no accident that this paper found her. Either this edition is blowing around in every direction she could have stepped, or it had been snagged at the edge of this stall, waiting specifically for her.

Which doesn't matter.

What does is that, according to the article, in this world, this version of the world, her mom, coming to get her from the Lopezes' that babysitting night, *did* run over Arthur.

Charlotte lets the paper go.

It blows across the Audi's roof, is gulped in by the vast night on the other side, its assignment completed.

"She didn't, she wouldn't," Charlotte is saying, shaking her head no.

But she understands, too. Yes, here, now, she can haul the door of this Audi open, stop what's going on inside, either kill Charley and stuff her body back on the other side of the vinyl, or—or climb back *into* it—but what she can't do is go back in time, not be fooling around in the Lopezes' dining room while her babysitting charge sleepwalks out into the street, into a pair of headlights.

That's done. It's the price the house exacts, for letting her step back through, into her life.

"But—" Charlotte says, a bare foot pushing hard against the glass of the car now, a long crack shooting up and down from it, which makes her feel weird inside, and all over.

She has no real objection to what the house is offering, though. Or, she gets it: nothing's free. Or, to look at it in SAT terms, in college terms: how bad do you want it? what are you willing to sacrifice to get it?

Charlotte closes her eyes. A tear slips down her cheek. Her throat is swelling. Her right hand is a fist at her throat.

"Mom?" she says, looking in the direction of the hospital.

Thing is? Her mom, to let her daughter blast off into the future, would willingly take this hit, would go to jail for the rest of her life. Or, if running Arthur over wasn't her fault, she would *make* it her fault, to let Charlotte get away.

Charlotte shakes her head no, though.

"Not like this," she says, her voice cracking, chest shuddering with the finality of this, and reaches back, catches the dull blue door to the office of the car wash right before it would have closed, trapping her here, on what's now the wrong side of things.

She holds her lips together and breathes in this crisp real-world air one last time, looks as far as she can out the bay of the car wash, out at the glow of the suburbs, the pinprick light of real stars way up there, the distant buzz of an airplane. A dog, barking.

But the barking's coming from the doorway behind her, isn't it?

The barks are deep and urgent.

"I'm sorry," Charlotte says to the her in this Audi, to Murphy, to her mom, and then she pivots on her right foot, forces herself to step back through. Not into the car wash office, but back onto the street.

The door shuts behind her, the crack becoming just a

tracing again, then sealing into nothing, like it never even was.

Charlotte can't help but sob, fall to her knees, and lower her forehead to the asphalt. When she looks up to the new silence pressing in, it's like she's on a stage at the end of a play, after the theater has emptied out.

Up and down the street, the lights are all dying down.

Except one.

The Wilbankses' porch light.

Charlotte shakes her head no, please, no.

It's the only place left, though. It's either get swallowed by this encroaching darkness, or, or—

She scrabbles forward, picks her phone up on the way. The screen's still cracked, but not that bad. She can still see the time, just one jagged line bisecting it: 7:59 p.m.

Well then.

Charlotte stands, her posture braver than she feels, and slings her backpack over her shoulder. She looks up into the obviously fake sky—planets with cartoony rings, the same way a kid would draw them—and then, each step shaky and uncertain, she crosses the lawn, uses the railing to pull herself up onto the porch, and holds her index finger a shade away from the lighted doorbell button long enough to reconsider, to do anything else.

But this is all there is.

Hi, I'm your babysitter! she practices in her head, jaunty delivery and all, and wipes her eyes with the sleeve of her shirt, noticing the flannel's dry after just having been wet from the bath, but never mind, she was supposed to be here ten minutes early for the big walk-through, and it's already eight, so she pushes that glowing button in, can just hear the distant chime in this pale giant of a house.

Footsteps hurry down the stairs and then the doorknob turns, that little brass tongue retracting from its brass strike plate with an audible *click* that Charlotte almost remembers, she thinks, but from where?

It doesn't matter. But remember that there's brass in the *door*, the *door*, she tells herself, trying to get it to stick. When this house was updated from the nineties, all the visible hardware went pewter and silver, but this hidden strike plate and tongue are throwbacks, are from the before times. They're how you can make this time through different. They can change everything.

"The door," she says out loud, in private, and then pastes a pleasant, innocent smile on her face, the skin around her eyes crinkling just enough to sell how earnest she is, what a good and perfect babysitter she's going to be.

"Hi, I'm Charlotte!" she says to the opening door, coming up onto her toes, her shoulders rising a bit, the warm air of the house breathing out across her.

I'm Charlotte, and you have something in your door, something I'm going to need later, just give me a moment to remember what it is.

But the night's already starting, isn't it?

Again, Charlotte thinks, wilting inside, but then, once the ball of her right foot touches the tile of the entryway, that's just a leftover word rattling around in her head. One that doesn't touch the smile pasted on her face.

She looks up the stairs, blinks twice.

"Beautiful home," she says, and her back doesn't even straighten when the door slams shut behind her.

ACKNOWLEDGMENTS

Those time-lapse loops of a rose blooming, and blooming, and then blooming some more, like it's got an endless spiral of pedals inside it somehow? That's what writing this novel was, for me: it just kept opening up and opening up. I never have much idea where my stories are going, but this one really kept me guessing, in the best way. Years back, someone explained American Naturalism to me as . . . if, early in the book, the writing veers over here to get some old gnarled tree with a cool and portentous shadow halfway on the page, then you can rest assured that that tree is going to be important later on in the story. I never ran down American Naturalism to see if that's an accurate statement or not, but, all the same, when this person told me that, it kind of struck a Nick Carraway tuning fork in my head, and my heart: that's how I write! I wring twice, I recycle endlessly, and then I sift the ashes of whatever I've burned, in case I missed something. To say it another way: use every last part of the buffalo, Steve. Don't keep moving on and inventing new things until you've drained what's already there. And, it nearly always turns out that what's already there is completely enough.

Which is to say: I was as surprised by that toy lizard as Charlotte is. And the bubble bath. And the dog. Man, that dog; it's based on a series of dachshunds my grandparents had—"wiener dogs" to us. Or: the only dogs that could get hit in the face by a rattlesnake and not crawl into some place dark to die. They just shake those bites off, I have no idea how. Just meanness, I guess? But, really, all this—the lizard, the bubble bath, the dog, the master bedroom closet, the railing, the stairs, the entertainment center, the kitchen island—it all came just from that initial walk-through, which is baked into the genre. Once you know it's there, that the first beat of this story is for us to get a sense of the floor plan, and all the devious possibilities there, it's hard to miss it, isn't it? For figuring that floor plan and the rest of those beats out, though, I have both books and people to thank. First, all the amazing haunted house novels that came before, that got that magical pattern locked in. I can't list them all, but: *The Haunting of Hill House*, *Hell House*, *Burnt Offerings*, *The House Next Door*, *The Shining*, *Solaris* (yes, *Solaris*)—you can learn about all you need to from those six. But I'd never thought about them in the right and helpful way until, first, an independent study with an MFA student, Nick Kimbro, who was writing a legitimately scary witch novel, but was deep-diving into all things haunted housey . . . maybe because he was interested? Maybe because I was? I don't know. But, I do know that, together, we went down all the halls, opened all the closet doors, and listened close for the attic, the basement, the porch, that creaky swing. Next there was a grad seminar I was lucky to lead, with thirteen students along, each of whom got me thinking about the haunted house in a different way. Matthew J. Pridham was the one who first lobbed out the idea that each haunted house has a "hub" of sorts—a central place, the innermost, most dangerous chamber. His story "Renovations" (*Weird Tales* #348, 2008) shows he was there in hub-land long before I was even considering it.

Thanks too to Mike Flanagan, for not doing *The Haunting of Hill House* series until I'd written this. Not sure I would have, had that already been in the world. It's that good, yes. It doesn't leave a lot of shoulder room for other haunted houses, I mean. So cool when a work can be that instantly canonical, that iconic, that formative, never mind if it comes late in the game. The game's always changing anyway. Thanks, obviously probably, to Chutes and Ladders. I don't have the temperament for most board games—okay, Settlers of Catan—but I'll play some Chutes and Ladders. Well, with a kid, I'll play. I love how it makes them smile. Thanks as always to my early readers: Mackenzie Kiera, Michael Somes, Kathryn E. McGee, Reed Underwood. Bree Pye, you read it too, yes? I keep searching my inbox to find out who all helped me with this, but I talk about "The Babysitter Murders" so much that I get too many results. Thanks too to one of my uncles, for haunting my grandmother's house when I was . . . I don't know: four? five? This uncle told me how when the house was being built, a construction worker had lost his arm, then died, so now, if I went out into the hall at night, I might hear that worker walking along in front of me, looking for his lost arm. I was a terrified-of-everything kid (who grew up into a terrified-of-it-all adult), and this was maybe just what I needed to push me over into horror for the rest of my life. Thanks to a porcupine, too. I never knew its name, but one day, miles and miles out in a West Texas pasture, which was my happy place always, I chased this porcupine into a fallen down house I knew my granddad had lived in, probably fifty or sixty years ago. Or maybe I had it wrong, and it was his parents who had lived there? This place was old-old, I mean. The walls had collapsed, so the house was pretty much just a rotting roof in the mesquite, home to snakes and pack rats and maybe even bobcats and badgers, and definitely wasps. Still, I wanted to catch this porcupine—it's hard to have good ideas, isn't it?—so I wormed in right after it dove into the darkness, squirmed through all the rat droppings and grime of decades, finally cornered this porcupine that thought it was safe. Of course by then I'd had to use pliers to get quills out of dogs' faces, and knew I didn't want to have those same pliers used on my face, as one of those quills might come out with my eyeball shish-kebab'd on it, but . . . I really wanted a quill. I had the idea that this was a test, that I would be even more "Indian" if I could do this, and get away. So, squinting, looking away, trying to protect these congealed balls of jelly I call my eyes, I reached ahead and . . . plucked a single quill off the back of that porcupine, then scraped my way out of this ancient place like Indiana Jones, ran away fast with my treasure. To immediately lose it, of course. But at least I have the story of it—I was only two years away from *Mongrels*, yes. More important than the quill or its story, though, what this fallen-down place taught me was that a house can be dangerous, yes, it can be as dangerous as anything, but that doesn't mean it always eats you. Even when it really-really wants to. Sometimes it will—if I'd gotten a face full of quills, or opened my back on a square tenpenny nail, then I maybe bake dead out under that roof—but not always.

There's hope when dealing with a haunted house, I'm saying. There's the thinnest sliver of light waiting up ahead, at the end of this ordeal. Without knowing that, I bet Charlotte comes together differently, and this novel's not even a little bit the same.

Thanks also to a guy I grew up with, Cory Hopper. Cory was older than me, and way bigger and meaner than I'd ever be, and was the kind of white that was reflective, practically. Nowadays he'd be a ginger, but that term wasn't in circulation in 1980-whatever this was, and if you'd tried it on Cory, you'd wake two days later with your face significantly altered. To say nothing of your teeth. That's how Cory dealt with people. He'd smile and laugh and have a good time, but he was quick to come at you, too. Anyway, one Halloween night in Stanton, Texas when we'd sneaked into the abandoned, supposedly haunted convent's cemetery to play around like you do, Cory—who wasn't with us kids—he jumped up from behind a headstone waving his arms and yelling and pretty much glowing in the darkness, and I kind of thought my life might be right-then over, because no way could my heart ever think about beating again. This kind of spiked terror—not dread, just pure, unadulterated, mindless terror—into any haunted-house stuff, for me; I never was brave enough to actually sneak into that convent, no. Very glad I never did. Haunted houses up on the hill are fine to run past, to tell stories about, but if you ever ring that doorbell, then you're asking for it. I try not to ask for it. Anyway, Cory's gone now, but that jumpscare he gifted me with, it remains, and keeps remaining, even when I wish it wouldn't, please.

Thanks as well to a house I lived in for the longest of

any house, from the time it was frame and tar paper until it had stucco on the outside. I had so many nightmares in that house—*The Only Good Indians* comes directly from one of them: four strikes of black lighting at all four directions, and then a deer-person standing up, his antlers rending the sky open—and so many injuries. One morning I woke with wasps all over my neck, biting me. Another time I saw my stepdad run a circular saw across the top of his thigh, and then had to help him try to hold his skin together until the ambulance got there. I did a ceremony there with black widow spiders and candles and Max Headroom—think you can find that on one of my early *Kingcast* visits? My first and most favorite dog of them all, Shasta, she got buried alive there in a plastic bag, breaking my heart forever. The way we can ever only know the emotional contours of a single place, finally? I think we might only ever really know the doors and hallways and rickety staircases of a single house, too. That house, for me, is on County Road 1120, in Greenwood, Texas. I still drive by it about once a year, when I'm back in Texas. Just to remember where I'm from, and where I don't want to have to be again, because I can't handle the dreams. They would break me, I think.

Thanks as well to my agent, BJ Robbins, and thanks to my editor at Saga, Joe Monti, for pushing me (as Michael Somes had) to modulate the ending a little. It was less about changing things, more about changing the feel of those things, if that makes sense. And thanks to Caroline Tew, for dialing up the audio of this and typing it in so I could mess with it for this edition, since of course, like that porcupine quill, I'd long ago lost my file of the acknowledgments. Ralph Berry—who started this whole "writing career"–thing for me by offering to publish my dissertation, *The Fast Red Road*—he opens his amazing story "Metempsychosis" in *Plane Geometry and Other Affairs of the Heart* with the line "Dougherty dreams of second chances. He doesn't feel cheated so much as simply baffled by irreversibility. Things happen. They don't happen again." That's sort of how I feel about files, and porcupine quills, and everything in between: their presence and then sudden and unaccountable absences baffles me. Why, right? I have no answer. But I still find sharp things to poke myself with; please don't ever worry that I'll run out of sharp, poky things, or blood to let out with them. And as long as I'm working with amazing people like Caroline, I may never want for lost files, either. Thanks as well to Christine Calella and Savannah Breckenridge, for getting this flip book on all the shelves, all the lists, in everyone's hands—and me on all the flights, all the Lyfts, all the stages of the world. And of course thanks to Charlotte, for being Laurie Strode here, and watching out for the kids first. It's easy to cut and run, but it's worthwhile to stick around. I like people who stick around. Like . . . my wife, Nancy.

Nan, you and me, we've lived in so, so many houses these last thirty-four years, haven't we? I'm not sure I can even remember them all. But that's a lie. I'll never forget a single place I've lived with you. You're all my best times. And, who cares about houses, anyway? You're my home, and that's so much more important. Wherever you are, that's where I'll be.

THE BUFFALO HUNTER HUNTER

by Stephen Graham Jones

A blood-soaked and unflinching saga of the violence of colonial America, a revenge story like no other, and the chilling reinvention of vampire lore from the master of horror.

Etsy Beaucarne is an academic, who needs to get published. So when a journal, written in 1912 by Arthur Beaucarne, a Lutheran pastor and her grandfather, is discovered within a wall during renovations, she sees her chance. She can uncover the lost secrets of her family, and get tenure.

As she researches, she comes to learn of her grandfather's life, and the life of a Blackfeet called Good Stab, who came to Arthur to share the story of his extraordinary life. She discovers the journals detail a slow massacre, a chain of events charting the history of Montana state as it formed. A cycle of violence that leads all the way back to 217 Blackfeet murdered in the snow.

KILLER ON THE ROAD

by Stephen Graham Jones

Sixteen-year-old Harper has decided to run away from home after she has another blow-out argument with her mother.

Her two best friends, little sister, and ex-boyfriend stage an intervention disguised as a road trip to stop her from hitchhiking her way up Route 80 in Wyoming. What they don't realize is that Harper has been marked by a unique serial killer who's been trolling the highway for the past three years.

Now the killer is after all of them, and they are thrust into an explosive, pulse-pounding, and terrifying race for survival down the interstate. As the body-count rises, Harper will break all the limits to bring the killer down.